T0054335

HIGH SCHOOL DXD

9

PANDEMONIUM ON THE SCHOOL TRIP

"Huh?! You're going to **kiss him** already, Xenovia?!"

Ugh... For some reason, Xenovia's lips seemed particularly sensual today.

"All right...
How about...
we start with
a kiss?"

Maybe that was because I had
been **kissing Asia,** and my
heart was **still racing.**

"I summon you! Breeeeeaaaaasts!"

The magic circle released a huge surge of power! Could I really summon them?!

C-could I really call the person whom I was visualizing...?

PANDEMONIUM ON THE SCHOOL TRIP

9

ICHIEI ISHIBUMI

ILLUSTRATION BY
MIYAMA-ZERO

New York

Volume 9
Ichiei Ishibumi

Translation by Haydn Trowell
Cover art by Miyama-Zero

This book is a work of fiction. Names, characters, places, and incidents are the product of the author's imagination or are used fictitiously. Any resemblance to actual events, locales, or persons, living or dead, is coincidental.

HIGH SCHOOL DXD Vol. 9 SHUGAKU RYOKO HA PANDEMONIUM
©Ichiei Ishibumi, Miyama-Zero 2011
First published in Japan in 2011 by KADOKAWA CORPORATION, Tokyo.
English translation rights arranged with KADOKAWA CORPORATION, Tokyo, through TUTTLE-MORI AGENCY, INC., Tokyo.

English translation © 2022 by Yen Press, LLC

Yen Press, LLC supports the right to free expression and the value of copyright. The purpose of copyright is to encourage writers and artists to produce the creative works that enrich our culture.

The scanning, uploading, and distribution of this book without permission is a theft of the author's intellectual property. If you would like permission to use material from the book (other than for review purposes), please contact the publisher. Thank you for your support of the author's rights.

Yen On
150 West 30th Street, 19th Floor
New York, NY 10001

Visit us at yenpress.com
facebook.com/yenpress
twitter.com/yenpress
yenpress.tumblr.com
instagram.com/yenpress

First Yen On Edition: November 2022
Edited by Yen On Editorial: Jordan Blanco
Designed by Yen Press Design: Andy Swist

Yen On is an imprint of Yen Press, LLC.
The Yen On name and logo are trademarks of Yen Press, LLC.

The publisher is not responsible for websites (or their content) that are not owned by the publisher.

Library of Congress Cataloging-in-Publication Data
Names: Ishibumi, Ichiei, 1981– author. | Miyama-Zero, illustrator. | Trowell, Haydn, translator.
Title: High school DxD / Ichiei Ishibumi ; illustration by Miyama-Zero ; translation by Haydn Trowell.
Other titles: Haisukūru Dī Dī. English
Description: First Yen On edition. | New York, NY : Yen On, 2020.
Identifiers: LCCN 2020032159 | ISBN 9781975312251 (v. 1 ; trade paperback) |
    ISBN 9781975312275 (v. 2 ; trade paperback) | ISBN 9781975312299 (v. 3 ; trade paperback) |
    ISBN 9781975312312 (v. 4 ; trade paperback) | ISBN 9781975312336 (v. 5 ; trade paperback) |
    ISBN 9781975312350 (v. 6 ; trade paperback) | ISBN 9781975312374 (v. 7 ; trade paperback) |
    ISBN 9781975312398 (v. 8 ; trade paperback) | ISBN 9781975343811 (v. 9 ; trade paperback)
Subjects: CYAC: Fantasy. | Demonology—Fiction. | Angels—Fiction. | High schools—Fiction. | Schools—Fiction.
Classification: LCC PZ7.1.I836 Hi 2020 | DDC [Fic]—dc23
LC record available at https://lccn.loc.gov/2020032159

ISBNs: 978-1-9753-4381-1 (paperback)
        978-1-9753-4382-8 (ebook)

10 9 8 7 6 5 4 3 2 1

LSC-C

Printed in the United States of America

CONTENTS

…Demons, fallen angels, dragons—they're the enemies of humankind. And you—you're both a demon and a dragon. You're a threat to all of humanity.

Life.0

"Issei… Give it to me…"

It was the night of the school trip.

Akeno, with her hair hanging loose, had cornered me on my bed!

A thin *yukata* clothed her body, but it had fallen into disarray, revealing the tender white skin of her shoulders. Not only that, th-the area around her breasts hung open invitingly…

Gulp.

I couldn't help but swallow down a mouthful of saliva. My gaze was all but nailed to the glorious pink objects peeking out from behind her drooping *yukata*. Akeno, her expression incredibly seductive, crawled toward me on all fours!

With each careful motion, her wonderful bosom swayed from side to side. The sight was enough to bring tears of joy to my eyes!

"…You're going to leave me behind when you go to Kyoto, aren't you…?" she said mournfully as she wrapped her arms around my neck and pressed her soft, velvety body against mine!

"I-it's only three nights. W-we'll see each other again in four days," I answered in a high-pitched voice.

To be perfectly honest, I could hardly think. My mind was doing somersaults in response to the sensations of her body touching mine!

Her *yukata* had almost slipped right off now. At this rate, she would be completely naked in no time at all!

I was suffering an unstoppable nosebleed...

Akeno's lustrous black hair gave off a wonderfully sweet scent... Her body felt slightly warmer than usual. Maybe she had just gotten out of the bath?

"...That's two full days without you... I might die of loneliness...," she muttered tearfully as she lay against my chest.

What was going on with her? Ever since our battle against Loki, Akeno's habit of fawning over me when we were alone had intensified. Whenever we watched TV in the living room, she would rest her head against my shoulder. On one occasion after she invited me to go shopping with her, I told her I was a little busy, and she puffed her cheeks and pouted angrily. Nonetheless, the second I gave in and agreed to join her, her expression transformed into a cute smile so enthralling that it could have killed me on the spot.

People would've guessed she was younger than me by her voice and attitude.

It wasn't uncommon for her adorableness level to even exceed the prez's. Sure, Akeno maintained her usual elegant sisterlike attitude while we were at school, but whenever we were alone...

The prez and Akeno were becoming masters at killing me with cuteness!

And so she placed her hand on mine, lacing her fingers through my own. "That's why, tonight, I'm going to make up for those lost four days and three nights."

"M-make up for them...?"

All I could do was echo those words. My brain was at a boil! If my adorable Akeno were to have her way with me, I could breathe my last today with no regrets...

"Yes, make up for them. I'll touch you, Issei, caress your skin, embrace your manly body, and experience what it means to be a woman."

Blood continued to gush from my nose at these stimulating words! This was bad! She was supposed to be a respectable demon and my upperclassman! She was so endearing right now that I could have easily mistaken her for a younger girl, but I couldn't afford to forget my place!

"I-if I'm good enough for you...as your underclassman..."

"There's no need to be so formal...," Akeno chided, shaking her head.

Her gleaming eyes were all but asking me why I was speaking like that.

"B-but you're my upperclassman, and—," I began, when she grabbed hold of the bedsheets.

"There are no upper- or underclassmen in bed. Only men and women. That's all that matters."

"M-men and women..."

Gulp...

I swallowed down another mouthful of saliva! M-men! A-and women! Th-those erotic words packed incredible destructive power!

Akeno moved in, her lips about to press against mine... At moments like these, the probability of a certain someone appearing increased dramatically.

"Akeno? Just what are you doing in here...?"

—.

Sensing an indescribable demonic presence, I tilted my head to one side in trepidation, only to lay eyes on my crimson-haired Rias, her aura raging! Yep! I had known this would happen!

Her aura was flaring so much that her hair was fluttering violently behind her! This time, I was dead for sure!

"Hee-hee," Akeno laughed with a seductive voice as she began to stroke her own glossy black hair. "Oh dear. Look at your face. So terrifying. Are you glaring at Issei and me? You must be burning with envy, yes? Hee-hee."

"I step out for a moment to take a bath, only to come back and find you seducing Issei? You've become rather bold, Akeno."

"I've always been daring. Haven't you noticed? Let me show you..."

So saying, Akeno pressed her deliciously soft body against mine, rubbing her flesh back and forth.

Whoooooaaaaa!

Her cheeks! Her breasts! Her arms! Her thighs! Akeno's supple feminine assets were so stimulating that I could all but feel my bodily functions grinding to a halt!

Why was her body so wonderfully soft and squishy?! It was like a perfect fit against mine, wholly drawing me in!

"...Exactly. You're too cunning, Akeno."

A third voice had sounded out of nowhere! When I came to my senses, I realized someone was holding my head in their arms.

"Koneko?! Wh-when did you...?!"

Yep, it was Koneko! How had she managed to get into my room undetected? Her cat ears had popped out on her head, and her tail was snaking out from her thin white robe. My dome was clutched against her petite frame.

Nghhhhh! Her small figure was so smooth and soft, her scent so sweet...

"...*I* don't want to be left behind while you go, either... I'll have to give you several days' worth of treatment with my sage magic..." With a forlorn expression, Koneko pressed her body up tightly against my back!

Whooooaaaaa! How could it feel this amazing, having such a petite girl-like figure hug me from behind?! Her fluffy white tail wrapped itself around my wrist. Ah, her fur was so nice to touch...

Hold on! Koneko! I knew you could be audacious when we're alone, but were you always okay with doing this in front of the others?!

Was she taking after Akeno because I was going away for a few days on the school trip?!

"K-Koneko, too... But Issei is *mine*... He's *my* beloved Issei... You're awful, all of you!"

For some reason, the prez was fidgeting from side to side, her body trembling. There were tears in her eyes, and she puffed up her cheeks. Rias! Yep, that expression of hers was simply adorable!

Click.

That was the sound of the door opening. It was Asia's turn to enter.

When she laid eyes on the sight before her, she cried out at once: "Augh! Th-this... So it isn't just Rias I need to worry about, but Akeno and Koneko, too?! Ugh, why are you all leaving me out...? This won't do, not at all! I need to join in!"

With that, Asia leaped onto the bed! She grabbed my leg, her grip so tight that it felt like she would never let go!

"I won't let you have him! Issei's sleeping with me tonight!"

This situation was getting more intense by the minute! Akeno, Koneko, and even Asia were clinging to me... Was this what happiness was supposed to feel like? It couldn't be. I mean, I was happy, sure, but I had no idea how to react, and everyone was busy bickering!

It may have been the greatest of situations, but the atmosphere was so fraught that I could hardly breathe!

Unable to stand it any longer, the prez cried out, "I've had enough of this! Why don't you all listen to me?! I'm supposed to be your master, and you're all supposed to be my servants!"

Despite Rias's command, the other girls would not relent.

"""He's my Issei!""" they all said as one.

"No! He belongs to *meeeee*!" The prez's tearful cry echoed throughout the house.

With the school trip looming, my bedroom had become a place of joy and tribulation.

Was I going to come out of this all right?

Life.1
Kyoto Calling!

"In the future, I'd like to start my own business. Maybe a school teaching Norse magic in the Gremory territory? A place to train female demons to become a new generation of Valkyries." Rossweisse was laying out her vision for the future.

"As an angel, it's an honor to be able to visit the home of a high-class demon! This must be another of the Lord's blessings…and the Demon King's, too!" Irina seemed rather ecstatic.

The trip to Kyoto was fast approaching, and we members of the Gremory Familia, plus Irina, were attending a tea party with Rias's parents in the dining room of her family's main estate.

The prez had decided to formally introduce us all to her parents again to commemorate her completing her Familia.

Everyone was enjoying small talk while elegantly sipping at their tea. Was this how celebrities lived their lives? I wasn't used to having all these servants wait on me at a social event like this. I was at a total loss.

"Ha-ha-ha, you *do* seem very interested in demon industry, Rossweisse. As the head of the House of Gremory, I can't wait to see your contribution." The prez's father let out a hearty laugh. His refined mannerisms were those of a high-class dandy.

The prez's mother set her cup down as she changed the subject.

"Incidentally, Issei and the other second-year students are going on their school trip soon. To Kyoto, I believe?"

"Y-yes. We'll be there for a few days," I answered.

The prez's mother was so polite that my every interaction with her filled me with anxiety.

"Rias brought back some nice pickled local vegetables from Kyoto last year."

So the prez's mother ate pickled vegetables? The prez ate them all the time back home, so that shouldn't have come as too much of a surprise. Still, I just couldn't associate the image of this elegant upper-class lady of the House of Gremory eating something so common as pickled vegetables.

"I... I'll be sure to bring some back."

"Oh...? That wasn't what I meant... Please don't mind me. There's no need to go out of your way." The prez's mother covered her mouth with her hand, her cheeks turning pink.

That reaction was pretty cute!

The social gathering continued at a leisurely pace until a successful end.

We were getting ready to go home via magic circle after the party when it was announced that Sirzechs had returned to the Gremory estate. As such, we would have to make sure to greet him before leaving.

"I'll come, too!" Millicas, looking forward to seeing his father, decided to accompany us.

There was a special route set aside for Sirzechs whenever he visited. It was there that we found him—along with a certain black-haired guest.

Hold on! That's Sairaorg! And he's dressed in noble raiments!

"Thank you for your hospitality. You look well, Rias, Red Dragon Emperor."

Even when he wasn't fighting, Sairaorg's body positively oozed power and ambition. His violet eyes roared with the flames of his fighting spirit.

"You should have told us you were coming. I hope you're feeling hale as well," Rias replied before turning to Sirzechs. "Ah, my apologies.

Greetings, Brother. We heard you had just come home and so thought we should offer a welcome."

"There's no need to make such a fuss. But thank you." Sirzechs lifted Millicas into his arms, flashing us all a smile.

Why had he returned with Sairaorg? This had to have something to do with our upcoming match...

As I ruminated over the possibilities, the prez asked Sirzechs directly, "Brother, if you're here with Sairaorg..."

"Yes. He's come all this way to deliver some produce from the Bael territory. Fruit, apparently. Our cousin is rather thoughtful, no? We were just saying that you, Rias, should call on the Bael residence to express our gratitude," Sirzechs explained.

To Sirzechs, Sairaorg wasn't an enemy, just his maternal cousin.

"We were also discussing the upcoming match. Sairaorg has no special requests other than to forgo any overly complicated rules. The usual restrictions that govern the field notwithstanding, of course."

"—."

The prez looked startled and narrowed her eyes at Sirzechs's announcement. "Does that mean you'll accept any uncertain variables we might bring, Sairaorg?"

Sairaorg let out a dauntless laugh in the face of this serious question. "Ah, that's right. Whether it's a vampire who can freeze time or a Red Dragon Emperor who can destroy girls' clothes or read their minds, I want to allow every one of your stratagems... How could I claim to be the next heir to the House of Bael if I'm not willing to face you at your strongest?"

"«««««««««« —!»»»»»»»»»»»

Sairaorg's declaration left us all speechless.

...His spirit and determination were incredible. He wanted to face our full might...

Sairaorg's acute gaze focused on the prez for a second before passing to me.

That overpowering aura of his sent a shiver coursing through my flesh. There was no hostility, not a shred of evil intent.

Instead, what I sensed was an unbridled fighting spirit. Like Vali, Sairaorg was obsessed with battle, but there was nothing about his attitude that struck me as malevolent.

"...I'm scared. H-he really wants me to use my powers on him...," Gasper whispered, cowering behind my back.

You can say that again.

This guy was willing to take on that super-powerful time-freezing ability directly.

A-and he's cool with my abilities, too... Thank you! I felt like I owed Sairaorg my gratitude!

As he watched from beside us, Sirzechs commented, "Hmm, excellent. Sairaorg, didn't you say you wanted to spar with the Red Dragon Emperor?"

"Indeed, I did say that. And yet..."

"How about a friendly match? Surely, you're eager to taste the power of a Heavenly Dragon?"

...

That had come so out of the blue that my mind was a total blank. It took my brain a second to register those words.

Wh-wh-whaaaaaaaaaat?!

He wanted *me* to fight Sairaorg?! Seriously?! No, no, this was too sudden...!

Sairaorg paid no heed to my shocked expression, turning to the prez. "What do you say, Rias?"

The prez sank into thought for a moment before settling on her answer. "...If that's what my brother wants... No, if that's what the *Demon King* wants, I can't refuse. You'll do it, won't you, Issei?"

—!

What was she saying?! Seriously?! *I* was going to have to fight *him*...? Ugh, but if that order came from the prez, I couldn't refuse... And I couldn't act like a coward in front of Asia, Akeno, and the others, either.

"...A-all right! I'm fine with it!" I declared, stepping forward!

Now that it had come to this, I couldn't back down!

I'd have to battle Sairaorg, the most powerful up-and-coming demon, sooner or later.

We could use what we learned here to help develop our strategy for the Rating Game match! Surely, the others would be able to learn something of value by watching me fight him.

As Sairaorg and I exchanged measured looks, Sirzechs nodded in approval. "In that case, let's see our number one young demon and the Red Dragon Emperor duke it out."

"This will be a good opportunity. Let me show you the strength of my fists...!" Sairaorg declared, brimming with determination.

There was a vast training hall beneath the Gremory castle, large enough that it could have housed the entirety of the athletic track at Kuou Academy.

We members of the Gremory Familia had made our way there together with Sairaorg, while Grayfia had taken Millicas elsewhere to wait.

Before us, Sairaorg removed his aristocratic clothes until he wore only a set of gray undergarments.

Even through his vest, I could tell how muscular his body was... His biceps were massive, his fists enormous. The physique of his shoulders and back was literally bulging...

On top of that, he just had to be a handsome pretty boy. I should have expected no less from a relative of the prez's mother.

"Let's do this, Ddraig."

"Leave it to me."

I summoned my gauntlet on my hand and began my Balance Breaker countdown.

So long as I didn't go overboard, I could now maintain my armor for a pretty long period, but as soon as I engaged in battle, I would be fighting against the clock.

Sairaorg simply waited while my countdown played out, doing nothing.

Just how confident was he? Undoubtedly, he wanted to see me at my full power and wouldn't jeopardize my reaching it. Everyone assembled seemed to think so, too.

I couldn't afford to put on a bad show in front of the other members of the Familia, especially not with the prez watching. Winning might have been impossible, but I was still resolved to go down having attempted every technique at my disposal.

The countdown reached its end!

"Welsh Dragon: Balance Breaker!"

As that voice sounded from my gauntlet, a flash of red light erupted, enveloping my whole body and solidifying into a set of crimson armor.

It was the Boosted Gear's Scale Mail!

Fwoosh!

I unfurled my dragon wings from my back and readied myself to go on the offensive. Sairaorg, in a precise, flowing motion, adopted a fighting stance of his own.

I had watched a recording of Sairaorg's match against that tough-guy figure from the House of Glasya-Labolas a while back, but it had done little to prepare me for how fast he was. Even Kiba would be in for a tough contest against Sairaorg. I probably wouldn't be able to keep up with him… But now that it had come to this, I had no choice.

I had to prepare for the worst and take the initiative.

Booooooooooom!

I let the propulsion unit on my back roar at its maximum output, and I shot forward!

My plan was to put everything into a hard right punch, but to my astonishment, Sairaorg made no attempt to evade! I was coming straight for him, yet he didn't show the slightest hint that he was trying to dodge!

Dammit! Is he so confident that he thinks he can take my attacks head-on?! Fine! Let's see you take this, then!

Thud!

My fist slammed hard into Sairaorg's face, the strike's impact echoing loudly!

H-he really *hadn't* dodged it! I'd scored a 100 percent clean hit!

Gulp...

Yet the moment I made contact, an indescribable chill swept through my body, forcing me to retreat backward hastily.

Once I had put some distance between us, I reassumed my combat stance. Sairaorg didn't look hurt in the slightest.

Hold on. I put a ton of power into that blow... Sure, I didn't boost it, but he shouldn't have been able to take it without a defensive technique.

Sairaorg pointed to the place where I had struck him, flashing me a smile. "That was a good punch. Direct and imbued with feeling. Any run-of-the-mill demon would have fallen immediately. However..."

Whoosh.

Sairaorg vanished.

"...I'm of another class."

His next words came from behind me!

Wha—?!

Slam!

Sairaorg delivered a strike of his own!

How did he get back there?! Dammit!

I crossed my arms, trying to defend, but the blow was even heavier than I'd imagined!

I had managed to catch the attack, but my gauntlets were shattered! How could a punch manage *that*?!

Having lost my sense of balance, I activated my propulsion unit once more and hurried across the field to escape!

Sairaorg was so quick! My eyes hadn't been able to follow him at all! Seriously, he'd straight-up vanished! And here I thought I was used to swift movements after all my training with Kiba!

Had I been careless? Perhaps. But that couldn't have been the only reason for this. More importantly, my arms were numb! My gauntlets hadn't taken all of the impact...

Fortunately, I could still move my fingers, meaning I could continue fighting. No bones had been broken.

Ddraig, I need you to regenerate my gauntlets, I thought.

"Ah, got it."

That red aura wrapped around my arms, restoring my broken armor. Judging by his smile, Sairaorg looked to be impressed.

"Oh? So that strike didn't send you flying? Well, that was only a greeting."

A greeting?! A warm-up punch had just torn through my armor?! Wh-what was this, some kind of joke?!

This was the first time anyone had ever smashed through my Scale Mail armor with their bare hands!

"I have three weapons—a sturdy body, fast legs, and martial arts. Let's try this again!"

Whoosh!

Again, he outright vanished! Was he coming from my side this time?! Yep, he appeared right next to me in the blink of an eye! I spun, trying to dodge his body blow, but...

Fwoosh!

That was the sound of Sairaorg's fists tearing through the wind! How could they carry that much force?!

Crack...

With that dull sound, fissures erupted across the armor shielding my stomach! A simple graze was enough to fracture it! This was like a bad joke!

"Dammit!" I cursed, lashing out in turn.

Thud! Once again, Sairaorg made no attempt to get away and let my punch connect with his face!

Still, there was no sign of damage!

Sensing an oncoming counter, I activated my booster pack once more in an attempt to move back.

Fwooooooooooosh!

Sairaorg's kick cleaved through the air, missing the mark... Yet the strength of that attack was enough to send a huge crack coursing from the center of the arena to the edge of the training hall!

If that had hit me...

A shiver ran down my spine. My breath was already ragged.

Our fight had only been a few strikes thus far, but that was enough to drive home the point.

My opponent was strong. He was supposed to be of the same generation as the prez and Diodora Astaroth?! This guy was leagues past Diodora!

"Ah, this is a surprise. This man from the House of Bael looks to have increased his power to its maximum level. In terms of your Rating Game types, he's a Power-type fighter who keeps pushing his attack stat to new heights. Interesting. A man pursuing pure destructive potential. Such extreme measures. Yes, very intriguing."

Ddraig was actually displaying an interest in someone other than a Demon King or a dragon. I guess that was a testament to how impressive Sairaorg was.

He was probably several orders stronger than even the prez—maybe more than ten times her strength.

A demon born to a princely House, and yet without demonic abilities of his own. All he had was his body, and so as the next heir to his family, he'd trained it to its absolute limit.

Like me, he was a demon without any inborn talent.

Whatever Sairaorg's training method, he had taken no half measures. And he was part of the same young generation as the prez.

You're going to have a hard time besting this guy, Prez...

Sairaorg was unmistakably a significant obstacle barring the way to the prez's dreams. And to me, that wall was even higher and more distant.

"You're incredible," I confessed. Our brief exchange had been sufficient to fill me with respect and awe. "Is that strength all the result of your training?" I asked.

"...I simply place my faith in my body, that's all," Sairaorg responded.

Yep, he was amazing, all right. Those words were enough to convey all the challenges he'd overcome.

That was why I would have to put everything into this fight, into testing my own limits.

I couldn't afford to lose!

Maybe it was time to try out that piece of advice Beelzebub had given me?

After adjusting the Evil Piece inside me, he'd given me some advice about it.

"I'm Promoting to a Rook!" I declared.

Yep, not a Queen—a Rook.

Power coursed through my body, and my offensive and defensive capabilities skyrocketed!

"A Rook?" Sairaorg repeated dubiously. No doubt he had been expecting me to Promote to a Queen.

The next instant, he disappeared once more! He was coming for me! I concentrated my power into my legs, rooting myself to the floor and entering a defensive stance! Gritting my teeth, I gathered my strength!

"*Boost! Boost! Boost! Boost! Boost! Boost! Boost! Boost! Boost! Boost!*"

I focused my boosted dragon power into guarding—and into my right fist, too!

Thud!

Sairaorg appeared in front of me, forcing a heavy blow to my stomach.

The shock was incredible! The force of that strike pierced all the way through to my spine!

...Gah.

Excruciating pain swept through my body, along with a feeling as though everything inside me had just been blasted out! The blow ricocheted through to my feet, and I couldn't stop my legs from trembling... But having lowered my center of gravity, I managed to keep myself from toppling over. My consciousness flickered in and out for a moment. However, I was able to hold on! If I hadn't clenched my teeth like that, I would have been knocked out then and there!

The armor around my lower body...was damaged but still intact!

Aiming for the exact instant when Sairaorg withdrew his fist, I lashed out with another punch straight for his face!

Thud!

It was like hitting a boulder—but I could sense something breaking.

Blood trickled from Sairaorg's nose.

At that moment—

"Gah!"

Blood also poured from the part of my helmet closest to my mouth. I was similarly bleeding from my body, and I felt as if I'd vomited...

Just how badly had he wounded my abdomen? Were my ribs fractured? Broken? There was a sharp pain with every breath I took.

I could endure it, though...! Me and my armor, too!

Lately, it felt like I was encountering one opponent after another capable of breaking through my Scale Mail, so I had thought to focus my energy on protection. Maybe that was only natural considering how regularly I was pitted against enemies far beyond my level.

Still, this had been an interesting attempt, converting that power to defense. It hurt like hell, but this was proof that using my Sacred Gear's power for guarding could enable me to survive even a super-powered strike.

Just as important as withstanding an attack was knowing how to counter.

Blood was leaking from Sairaorg's nose, proof that I had given decent retaliation.

Part of me had doubted this would even work, but Promoting to a Rook to increase my attack and defense had clearly been worth it!

I could do this! I could fight this guy!

That realization was enough to rouse a second wind within me!

Unfortunately, no matter how you looked at this, I was clearly the more injured one between us. At least I knew it was possible to hurt Sairaorg now, though. Even if I was destined to lose, I might be able to break one of his arms if I got lucky.

Victory might have been beyond me at my current level, but I was going to let this jacked pretty boy have it!

Sairaorg wiped the blood trickling from his nose with a finger—and let out a truly overjoyed laugh. "Promoting to a Rook... Seems like it was a good call. I poured a considerable amount of strength into that punch. As a Rook, your offensive and defensive capabilities are superb. Perhaps the attributes of a Rook are better suited to a Power-type fighter like yourself? The advantages to an all-rounder like a Queen are quite plain. Hmm… What is it? You seem to have a question on your mind. Is there something you want to ask, fighting me?"

"I don't know how to put this… Other high-class demons… Well, they've often looked down on me… But you've treated me seriously from the start. It came as a surprise is all," I replied.

From what I could tell, Sairaorg thought highly of me. Given how Riser Phenex, Diodora Astaroth, and countless other high-class demons had treated me, Sairaorg's demeanor came as a refreshing surprise, enough to leave me feeling awkward.

At this, Sairaorg breathed a sigh. "I see. Have others sold your abilities short? Rest easy. *I* won't underestimate you! Not only have you survived, you have emerged victorious in battle against the leaders of the old demon regime and the evil Norse god Loki. I couldn't possibly underrate you."

Those words…filled me with such joy that my whole body was trembling.

Sairaorg flashed me a dauntless grin. "I enjoy fighting you. You have a strong fist. It's been a while since anyone has given me a bloody nose. Nothing brings me greater joy than fighting an opponent of a similar type to myself. You must have trained your punches well, I assume? I can tell from that last strike. Don't hold back. Hit me as hard as you can. That's why we're here, isn't it?"

I was completely drawn into that valorous smirk of Sairaorg's.

—.

He had acknowledged my strength… Damn. I had to defeat him, and yet…

Once this contest was over, I definitely wanted to speak with him!

I readied myself for the battle to resume. The armor around my lower body had restored!

I take back that plan to break one of his arms! I'm gonna break both!

I would go all out, pour everything that I had into this!

"Come, Issei Hyoudou! Turn your thoughts to defeating me! Show me the power of the Red Dragon Emperor!"

"All right! Here goes!"

"*Boost! Boost! Boost! Boost! Boost!*"

I unleashed a Dragon Shot toward Sairaorg, who was already racing toward me!

Whoosh! Boooooooooom!

With a single horizontal sweep of his fist, he sent the energy speeding into the wall of the training hall.

That was no good! Because I hadn't Promoted into a Bishop, my demonic power skills were too weak!

Right now, I was a Rook! As such, I had no choice but to dedicate myself to physical battle! That meant my best bet was another counterblow!

I raised my fists!

"—! You mean to exchange blows? Interesting! Show me what you've got!" Sairaorg roared.

I prepared to leap forward, when—

"Issei!"

All of a sudden, Asia called out my name. What was going on? I glanced toward her.

"Y-you need a power-up!" she continued. "Y-you get stronger whenever you touch b-b-b-b-breasts!"

…Huh?

Everyone wore looks of pure astonishment at Asia's remark.

Xenovia, however, seemed to hit on an idea. "Right! Issei's the Breast Dragon! Touching someone's chest makes his power skyrocket! Prez! We need you to lend Issei what only the Switch Princess can give him!"

"Rias! I—I don't mind! Please g-give Issei the power of your b-b-breasts! At this rate, he'll definitely lose!" Asia added, voice trembling.

The two girls were both entreating the prez.

Rias, the one on the receiving end of this plea, looked to be at a complete loss.

Asia! Xenovia! I understand how you feel. You don't want me to lose. Still, you shouldn't talk about breasts so openly!

The pair were completely serious. Heck, Asia's eyes were brimming with tears.

"Th-that's right! With the president's breasts, Issei becomes super-powered!"

Now my cute underclassman Gasper was joining in!

"Yes! Sexual desires are what fuels Issei's power!"

Irina, too!

Was everyone *that* worried about me? Maybe they didn't want to see me fail. I was grateful for their support, but I felt a bit conflicted.

"...So it's true? Touching breasts boosts his strength? I thought that was just a rumor."

Oh man, to hear Sairaorg ask that...

"It's true," Koneko replied point-blank!

Sorry for being such a pervert, everyone! I really am the Breast Dragon Emperor!

"Hee-hee. What are you going to do, Rias?" Akeno asked with an amused grin.

"...D-do you want to...touch them? I-if it will make you stronger, I—I..." The prez's face had turned bright red!

Preeeeezzzzz! Is this truly okay?! In front of your own cousin?! If you're sure, I'll touch them to my heart's content and revitalize my strength!

"Does everyone usually get so excited over this? Hmm... This must be another custom foreign to Asgard," Rossweisse said with a look of astonishment.

She'd arrived at a huge misunderstanding!

Kiba was wearing an awkward smile, as though at a loss for how to respond!

"Ha! Ha-ha-ha-ha-ha-ha-ha!" Sairaorg bellowed, obviously amused. "I see, so Rias's breasts make him stronger? Ha-ha-ha! I'll have to remember that. Shall we call it a day, Red Dragon Emperor?" So he suggested.

"I can still fight!"

Yep, with the power of breasts and my perverted nature, I could keep going!

Sairaorg, however, shook his head. "You've proven your spirit. Yes, I'm sure you *can* still fight. And so can I... But at this rate, I won't be able to stop myself. I may battle on till the last blow, and that would be such a waste. After all, you're in the middle of awakening something deep inside you, right?"

—.

He'd noticed during our skirmish that I was probing my own possibilities?

Sairaorg retrieved his aristocratic outfit before approaching me and placing a hand on my shoulder. "Let's continue this after you find what you're looking for. We shall fight each other, both of us in prime condition. *That's* the duel with the Red Dragon Emperor that I want. We can settle things in our Rating Game. When we face each other in front of our superiors and an eager audience, *that's* how we will be measured... You and I both have dreams. I look forward to seeing you there. Rias, and the members of her Familia, let us all carry our dreams to the stage. Come! I shall vanquish you with all my strength." With those parting words, Sairaorg left.

Now that the duel had concluded and the tension was abating, I deactivated my armor.

Sirzechs approached me and asked, "How was he? His attacks?"

"...Similar. I was surprised. He fights just like me."

Sirzechs smiled, nodding. "Yes, he *is* just like you. He has desperately trained himself to make up for what he lacks. That's where his power comes from. Everything's a direct attack with him. That's actually pretty unusual for a demon."

Yep, his style really was like mine: idiotically straightforward. That was undoubtedly why we understood each other so well.

Attack. That was the only thing we knew. How to defeat an opponent.

He had no doubt devoted himself and his training single-mindedly to that purpose.

"By the way, he had placed heavy seals on his arms and legs during that battle to restrain his power."

Sirzechs's words left me both shocked and intrigued.

No matter how much stronger I became, he would always be one step ahead of me.

But it was invigorating to have a goal. Rewarding, too.

"He's already at the level of many a professional King in the Rating Game," Sirzechs continued. "Moreover, he's fended off attacks by the Khaos Brigade several times now, bringing victory to demonkind. Don't sell yourself short, though, Issei. The fact that you didn't lose your determination in the face of his blows is admirable. There are more than a few cases of Sairaorg's opponents losing all will to keep going after only a few rounds with him. Even demons of great power and status have had their spirits broken when they realize their abilities are useless against Sairaorg. The higher one's rank and pride, the harder it is to recover after such a crushing defeat."

"I…just don't want to lose again. I don't want to lose another Rating Game. I've never been able to put up a proper fight in one."

My battle with Diodora didn't count. I'd beaten the living daylights out of him, but it hadn't been a formal match. In the Rating Games against Riser and Chairwoman Sona, I had ended up getting defeated.

"That's why, this time…"

In our match against the House of Bael, I wanted to hold out until the very end, at all costs, and snatch victory.

I'll defeat you, Sairaorg. I'll surpass you. That's a promise. Just hold on until I can catch up.

Burying my frustration with myself, I found a renewed resolve.

"Are you still going to call Rias Prez even after she finishes high school, Issei?"

Just before we headed home, the prez's cute little nephew, Millicas, asked me an unusual question with his head tilted to one side.

Well… Right, once she graduates…

What *should* I call her then? Come to think of it, the Two Great Ladies of the Occult Research Club were both third-year students and would be graduating relatively soon. We'd need a new club president before long.

And it'd be weird to keep referring to Rias as Prez by that point…

What was the best way to address her, then? Lady Rias? Maybe Master would be the most appropriate?

However, the name I wanted to use was…

Rias.

She was family. We already lived together. And she was the person whom I loved most. Even if I could only do it once, I wanted to call her by her name.

-○●○-

And so the day of the school trip was upon us.

I was so excited that I hadn't been able to sleep properly. The prez noticed how I was feeling and wrapped her arms around me in a warm embrace, trying to help me to doze off.

Burying my face in her bosom would normally have been enough to make me forget all about the school trip, but this time, it only worked me up even more, keeping me wide awake! Truly, there was no beating her breast pillow!

And so, after a couple of things, we found ourselves at the bullet train platform at Tokyo Station. We had all gathered at a corner of the platform, trying to keep out of the public eye as much as possible.

Out of all those staying behind, only the prez had come to see us off. Akeno, Koneko, and Gasper had wanted to come, too, but the first- and third-year students still had regular classes. So the prez had come along alone. Because we second-years would be away, our upper- and lowerclassmen had to handle our work for the Academy Festival in our absence. In case you're wondering, the exact plans were top secret.

"Here are your passes," the prez said, handing each of us heading to Kyoto a card.

We each received one, inspecting them.

"Are these what I think they are?" Kiba inquired.

The prez nodded. "Yes. For a demon exploring Kyoto, a free pass is a necessity."

Kyoto was renowned for its temples. On top of that, there were an awful lot of power spots in the city, enough to make it difficult for a demon to move about freely. Sacred sites could be deadly to demons, after all.

That was where the free passes came in. Whoever it was in control of things behind the scenes in Kyoto (maybe a diviner or a monster of some sort) issued these cards for demons like us, so long, of course, as we had a legitimate reason for visiting.

"We used the same type of permits last year. You need to respect the formalities and provide a valid purpose for visiting to receive these. The Gremory Familia, the Sitri Familia, and an emissary of Heaven... I hope you realize how lucky you all are," the prez said with a wink.

"Yep!" I replied joyously. "Long live the House of Gremory! So with these, we can go to all the famous temples? Kiyomizu-dera, Kinkaku-ji, and Ginkaku-ji, too, right?"

"Indeed. Remember to keep it in your skirt or shirt pocket, and you should be fine. Enjoy yourselves!"

""""""Yes!"""""" we responded in unison.

I put the card in my back pocket. I was ready to go!

Suddenly, Asia's cell phone started ringing. "Hello? Kiryuu? Yes. I'm here with Xenovia and Irina." What did Kiryuu want? Asia finished her call and quickly bowed to the prez. "Thank you, Rias. We'll be back soon!"

"We're off!"

"See ya soon!"

"Yes, take care."

Asia, Xenovia, and Irina all bid farewell to Rias before heading off somewhere. Did they have something to check before we boarded the bullet train? For my part, I'd remembered to bring some handkerchiefs, tissues, and a change of underwear. Still, a quick double check to ensure I hadn't forgotten anything wasn't a bad idea.

"In that case, I'll be going, too. I'll bring back a souvenir." Kiba bobbed his head as he went to join the others.

Now it was only the prez and I.

"Fix your collar," she scolded, adjusting my shirt. "You need to present yourself well. You're a student of Kuou Academy, remember?"

"R-right!"

Having straightened my shirt, Rias then leaned her head against my shoulder.

"Prez?"

"...I'm trying to be strong, but I'm no different from Akeno. I'll be lonely without you. Perhaps I've gotten a bit better, though. Last semester, I would have been completely hopeless without you, but now I should be able to hold out for a few days."

Prez...

Maybe it was because she doted on me like a pet cat, but it was clear she didn't want me to go.

Lately, it felt like Rias treated me like a genuine family member. Every now and then, she behaved in a way that she normally wouldn't in front of others or wore a particularly familiar expression.

I gripped the prez's hand in my own, flashing her a smile. "You're exaggerating. Even if I'm not here, you still have Koneko and Gasper."

"I know. But...you don't realize your own charms. Still, I love that part of you." So saying, the prez forced a smile as her face approached mine.

Before I knew it, our lips had connected.

"—."

My brain went haywire, and my face flushed. I was rooted to the spot, unable to move!

I mean...! This was a kiss!

"P-P-Prez..."

Rias fixed me with a cute grin before sticking out her tongue. "That was a good-bye kiss. Why are you acting so surprised? How many times have we kissed now? At this point, *you* should be kissing *me*."

"S-still...! You caught me off guard!"

At this response, the prez's smile turned slightly disappointed. "That's enough for me. I'll be lonely, but I can hold out. Enjoy yourself, Issei."

"Yep! I'll be back soon!"

A kiss from the prez! This was awesome! Ah, she really did spoil me...

This was a good omen! The next few days were going to be a blast!

My school trip was already off with a bang!

Life.2
Our Kyoto Arrival

Almost ten minutes had passed since the bullet train departed Tokyo Station, when...

"This is actually my first time taking the bullet train," Matsuda muttered from his seat in front of me, his expression full of excitement.

I recalled having ridden it once before. Admittedly, I had been pretty young at the time, so my memories weren't particularly clear.

I was sitting at the back of the train car, alone in the final row. The spot beside me was empty. Matsuda and Motohama were just in front of me, and Xenovia and Irina were across the aisle.

The scenery outside the window changed from one minute to the next because the train was moving so incredibly fast. Xenovia and Irina were chattering away as they stared out the window.

Riding the bullet train was refreshing, but after the special locomotive we'd taken to the underworld, it felt a bit underwhelming. I'd watched as we'd entered another dimension during that ride, after all.

Abruptly, Xenovia came over to sit beside me. Then she said, "Issei, I want to tell you something."

"What is it, Xenovia?"

"I don't have Durendal on me right now. I'm unarmed."

Huh. That was an unexpected confession. Seriously?

"You didn't bring it? Why not?" I asked.

"Yeah. So some alchemists over in the Orthodox Church seem to have found a way to suppress its destructive aura. I used some of my connections in Heaven to send it over to them."

The Orthodox Church. If I remembered correctly, that was one of several factions that comprised the Christian Church. From what I remembered, they hadn't helped all that much when the Excaliburs had been stolen…

Xenovia grinned wryly. "I'm sure the seraphim, under Michael's leadership, had something to do with why the Orthodox Church has decided to pitch in. But I thought if these alchemists could reforge Durendal, I couldn't afford to let this opportunity slide."

It sounded like the number of conflicts and disputes among the various Christian sects might have been reduced thanks to the new alliance between the three great powers.

"Suppressing the Holy Sword's destructive aura without diminishing its abilities. I was really intrigued by that idea…," Xenovia continued. "Honestly, it's pretty pathetic that I, as its user, can't even control it properly… I don't deserve to call myself a Knight… Maybe I'd be better off dead…? Ah, Lord…"

And just like that, she started into some self-deprecation. Seriously, she was too quick to lay into herself.

"Got it. How about I lend you the Ascalon if anything happens?"

"Yeah. Sorry about this. I'm always using your sword."

"It's fine. I need it, too, sometimes, but given the situation, it will be more useful in your hands."

"You ought to polish your swordsmanship, Issei. It would be a shame to waste your gifts."

"I am. I've been training with you and Kiba, remember. I've learned a fair bit."

"True."

After that brief exchange, Xenovia returned to her seat.

I peered out the window for a while, watching the scenery, when I heard a chorus of light wails from the front of the carriage. Glancing around—I found Kiba heading my way from his seat up front.

"Huh…? H-he's going to see *Hyoudou*?"

"I-impossible… Kiba's entering that realm of perversion…?"

"So Hyoudou/Kiba is true!"

The girls let out one mournful moan after another! Did they consider me tainted or something?! Dammit! Was it that bad for me to be friends with a pretty boy?!

I'd carried a grudge against Kiba for a while because of how the girls at school treated him, but now I considered him a close friend… That said, I still had reason to hate him! I couldn't forgive him for being a pretty boy!

"Do you mind if I sit next to you?" he asked before doing so without letting me answer.

"…What's up?" I inquired, my eyes half-closed as I rested my cheek against the window.

"I wanted to ask what your plans are once we arrive—in case of any emergencies."

"Ah right. We're in different classes, so we'll probably be split up. What were you doing tomorrow again?"

"We'll be going to Sanjusangen-do Temple. And you?"

"We'll be starting at Kiyomizu-dera Temple, I think. After that, it's Ginkaku-ji and Kinkaku-ji. They're all a bit far from one another, but if we try to see the most famous sights over the first two days, we should be able to spend the third one relaxing and visiting Tenryu-ji."

"Tenryu-ji… The Temple of the Heavenly Dragon? My group will be visiting there on the third day, too. If we have time, maybe we could meet up somewhere near Togetsu-kyo Bridge? What about the final day?"

"We'll just hang around Kyoto Station and buy souvenirs. Irina mentioned she wanted to see the top of Kyoto Tower as well," I said.

Each group had been asked to decide their schedules beforehand to submit to the teachers for approval, so we all had our own itineraries.

Once Kiba and I were clear on our plans, we moved on to another topic.

"I heard you met the Demon Kings, Issei."

"Yeah. I think I've got a new perspective on the underworld now."

Recently, I'd participated in some mysterious Gremory family ritual with the prez in the underworld. There had been a party afterward. Rias's parents had been ecstatic, and they'd lavished me with praise.

On top of that, there had been a huge banner hanging in the banquet hall that read, CONGRATULATIONS, YOUNG MISTRESS, YOUNG MASTER!

Frankly, I didn't quite get it. W-well, whatever it was, it didn't seem like the situation had ended up too bad for me, so I wasn't particularly worried.

"Actually, once it was all finished, Beelzebub gave me some personal advice," I admitted.

"Advice?" Kiba repeated.

"Yeah, about the affinity between my Pawn attributes and my Red Dragon Emperor abilities. I haven't been able to make full use of Queen Promotions when drawing on the Red Dragon Emperor's powers."

While Promoting to a Queen certainly increased my strength, when I did that while using my Red Dragon Emperor abilities, I apparently exceeded my current capacity, which kept me from making good use of my dragon power.

In short, because there was so much more I needed to manage when I Promoted to a Queen, I kind of lost out because I couldn't handle it all. Sairaorg must have realized that after our duel.

There was no denying the truth behind the idea. When I used a Promotion, my power, my speed, and the strength of my Dragon Shot ability all increased. However, it was too much for me to keep track of.

I hadn't mastered the skills of a Knight or Bishop, either, let alone those of a Rook. Even if I bolstered my speed or demonic powers, I still tended to charge forward in the heat of the moment, which could end up leading to tragedy.

Nonetheless, the strongest asset of any Pawn was their Promotion ability, so I had to master it.

"He told me that if I want to bring out the abilities of the Red Dragon Emperor fully, I would first have to perfect the skills of a Knight and a Rook. The best way to learn the unique qualities of the Red Dragon

Emperor is to focus on pouring them into my strength and speed, apparently."

"I see. Is that why you went for Rook when you battled Sairaorg?"

"Yeah. And it was a lot easier to control than Queen. I could feel the difference when I concentrated purely on offense and defense. So I think I'll focus on each of the various pieces and try to master them with my Red Dragon Emperor abilities individually."

Kiba let out a chuckle. "That does sound like you, trying out a new idea in the middle of a fight with Sairaorg. It looks like you're going to get even stronger. You sure are dedicated when it comes to exploring your own strength."

"I might have great power, but I won't be able to win against Sairaorg or Vali unless I know what to do with it. So what were your impressions of the duel?" I asked.

Kiba rested his chin on his hand. "To be honest, I saw him as a considerable threat. He's of the same generation as the president, yet he was able to withstand you in a contest of pure strength. With his bare hands, no less. He's probably the only demon youth—no, the only high-class demon—who could break through your armor with his fists alone. Frankly, my own defenses would be paper-thin against that. And he was also fast on his feet. That clearly wasn't his top speed, either. If I or any of the other members were to take a hit from him head-on, it could be fatal."

Kiba gave me his honest appraisal. That was why I put my trust in him.

"Once we get back from this trip, I'm going to redouble my training to fight him again," I stated.

"That sounds like a good idea. By the way, would you call me when you go souvenir shopping?"

"Why?"

"It'd spoil the fun if I told you."

"Ah. All right. Yeah, I'll give you a heads-up on the last day."

With that settled, Kiba stood and returned to his class in the other train car.

Now that I had finished talking to Xenovia and Kiba, I had some time to myself again. Asia and the others were happily chatting.

As for Matsuda and Motohama…they were both sound asleep.

"Zzzzzzzzzz…"

After a good stretch, I also closed my eyes.

There was still time before we arrived in Kyoto. Maybe I could try delving into my Sacred Gear. How many times had I attempted that now? I'd lost count. It had become part of my routine to try it before going to bed, after finishing my demon work and taking a bath. I gave it a couple of shots on weekends, too.

I had only one goal—to get through to my predecessors, the Red Dragon Emperors of the past!

I closed my eyes, entrusting my consciousness to Ddraig as I delved into my Sacred Gear.

……

…I emerged from the darkness into a vast white space.

My predecessors, the previous vessels of the Red Dragon Emperor, were seated around a table. Their heads were downcast and their expressions vacant.

"Hi. It's me again."

No matter how amicably I tried to greet them, I knew they wouldn't reply…

I called out to one of the figures, a person who looked around my own age, but it proved a worthless gesture.

Ddraig's voice echoed down from above: *"Out of all past Red Dragon Emperors, he was the nearest in years to you. He was gifted, quick to awaken his Juggernaut Drive. Unfortunately, he drowned in his own power, and when he let down his guard, he was slaughtered by another Longinus user."*

"Not the White Dragon Emperor?"

"When drunk on power, he went berserk even without the White Dragon Emperor's intervention. There have been others like him in the

past. A Juggernaut Drive can turn one into a tyrant... But no matter the era, a despot's reign doesn't last long. That's the way of the world."

Ddraig sounded like he was talking about himself there. He'd lost himself to power once, too, long ago.

"Still, he must have had something important to him, right?" I questioned.

My predecessor hadn't spoken a word, but I was sure of it. Everyone had something precious. I'd sought endless power after I thought an important person had been taken from me. That was how I'd activated my Juggernaut Drive.

"As the Heavenly Dragon who usurped God's hegemony..."

"Partner..."

"I'm not going to recite all of it. I'm too scared. There's something I don't understand, though. What's all that about the infinite? And the illusion? Scorning and lamenting them?"

Those words all popped up in the cursed incantation I'd heard upon activating my Juggernaut Drive.

"The infinite is Ophis. The illusion refers to the Great Red. Maybe we scorn Ophis and lament the Great Red? Nobody knows who first came up with it. God Himself, perhaps?"

—! A third voice?!

I spun around and came face-to-face with a young woman. She was a real beauty, with a slender body, long, wavy blond hair, and a dress with a slit down the side!

Most astonishingly of all, she was showing emotion! She was clearly different from my other predecessors!

She stared my way with a smile.

"Elsha?"

"Yes, Ddraig. It's been so long," the woman greeted casually.

"Partner. This is Elsha. Out of all your predecessors, she was one of the two strongest Red Dragon Emperors. Certainly the strongest woman."

The strongest female Red Dragon Emperor?! I had no idea I even had a predecessor like that! But I had never even seen her before! Where had she been?

"You look surprised. Are you wondering about me? There are two exceptions to all these lingering regrets. I'm one of them. Well, I'm buried quite deep within the Sacred Gear, so I don't normally surface."

"...I never expected to see you or Belzard again."

"Don't say that, Ddraig. Belzard and I have both been cheering for you from in here. We used to be partners, after all. Regrettably, Belzard's consciousness is already fading..." The woman wore a forlorn expression. *"He seems to have taken an interest in the current Red Dragon Emperor, so he sent me here in his place."*

"Who's Belzard, by the way?" I asked.

Ddraig was the one who answered. *"He ranks up there with Elsha as the other strongest Red Dragon Emperor of all time. The strongest male Red Dragon Emperor. He really was formidable. He defeated the White Dragon Emperor twice."*

"Twice?! Whoa!"

I had had no idea that was possible. To beat him two times in one life!

"Anyway, I was told to give you this," Elsha stated. She placed a box marked with a keyhole in my hands. *"Beelzebub already gave you the key, yes?"*

"Yeah."

All of a sudden, a flash of light enveloped my hand, a small key appearing in my palm without me even having to consciously summon it. So this was what Beelzebub had given me...

Elsha smiled. *"I didn't mean a literal key. The box and key are really just figures of speech, tools to make this easier to understand. This box contains all the delicate possibilities of the Red Dragon Emperor. Normally, there are parts you wouldn't be able to open or tamper with. But Belzard thinks you might be able to access them. Of course, that's only because of the Evil Piece you've received."*

All of a sudden, Elsha chuckled lightly.

"Belzard and I watched that Breast Dragon show together. That was the first time we've both laughed since finding ourselves here."

She was laughing uncontrollably now.

...This was mortifying! My predecessors had seen all that?!

"There's no need to feel embarrassed, Issei. And don't feel glum, Ddraig. Enjoy yourselves. There's never been a Red Dragon Emperor as fun as you before. Belzard and I were so happy to see you overcome that ominous Juggernaut Drive incantation with your Breast Dragon song. Especially because neither he nor I met with a decent end..." Elsha paused there, placing the box into my hands. *"We're both putting our faith in you."*

I accepted the box and inserted the key into the lock... It was a perfect fit, just as I had known it would be.

"You and the White Dragon Emperor are both different this time. Despite seeking each other out, you have different goals. I wonder what they are, exactly? We were all so thoughtlessly serious... Please open it. But remember that once you do, it will be your responsibility to see it through to the end. Half measures won't do here. Whatever happens, be accepting and keep moving forward."

As per Elsha's instructions, I inserted the key—and the box snapped open with a *click*.

Immediately, a dazzling light enveloped me...

When I opened my eyes, I was back aboard the bullet train.

Was that a dream, Ddraig?

"No. You took the box from Elsha and opened it."

Right. What was inside it, then?

"Beats me."

Hey, hey, hey! H-huh?! I didn't *feel* any different.

Maybe it was the Sacred Gear that had changed?

"Nothing new there, either... But I did notice something pop out of the box."

Wh-wh-whaaaaaaaaaat?!

I glanced around frantically—but couldn't spot anything!

Seriously?! Had all those possibilities just disappeared into the ether?! This wasn't something to joke about! I'd failed Elsha, and I definitely wouldn't be able to show my face to Azazel or Beelzebub again! And they'd all worked to give me such a rare opportunity!

"*Don't panic. It's yours. It'll come back. Fate has a way of seeing to that.*"

That was easy enough to say, but how could I know for sure...?

I breathed a resigned sigh, when—

"Wh-whoooooaaaa! Boobs!"

"Wha—?! Matsuda! What's going on?! It's me! What's so fun about a guy's chest?!"

Matsuda and Motohama were messing around on the seat in front of me.

Ugh! What's so interesting about a guy's breast?! Cut it out, you two!

"Huh?! What am I...? I got this sudden urge for breasts...and then..."

"Matsuda, you've definitely got breast deficiency syndrome... Okay, let's have an erotic DVD night at our hotel later! We've got all the equipment in our luggage!" Motohama said.

"Seriously?!" I exclaimed, leaning forward in my seat!

Awesome! So we could spend the night watching erotic videos!

"That's the spirit, Issei! I bought these especially for this trip! We've got *A View of Massive Rose-Colored Bazongas: Kinkaku-ji* and *A Chance of Skin-Colored Knockers: Ginkaku-ji*!"

""Whoa!"" Matsuda and I both burst out in excitement at Motohama's revelation.

Well, if whatever was in that box would find its way back to me, then there was no harm in enjoying a few tits in the meantime, right?

"Die, Perverted Trio!"

"Gross! We're on a train!"

I turned a deaf ear to the shocked voices of my female classmates.

-O●O-

Right around when I had finished the kombu rice balls Asia had prepared, an announcement came over the loudspeaker.

"*We will soon make a brief stop at Kyoto.*"

It was time! After the bullet train came to a halt before the platform, we picked up our luggage and disembarked.

"Kyoto!"

My first step in the old capital of Japan! How I had waited for this moment! As Kiryuu guided us to the ticket gates, my eyes were captivated by the sights of this unfamiliar train station.

"Whoa! It's huge!"

The ceiling formed a massive atrium! And there were more escalators than I could have possibly imagined!

This station was seriously immense! Tokyo's didn't outshine it at all! That made sense, though. As a major tourist destination, Kyoto needed a grand train station. There were so many people coming and going!

"Look, Asia! That's the Isetan department store!"

"Y-yes, it is, Xenovia! Isetan!"

The two of them were bursting with excitement, pointing from one sight to the next. It was clear they were enjoying themselves.

"I wish we had such a wonderful station in Heaven!" Irina was evidently keenly interested in the building for…slightly different reasons.

"The meeting place is on the ground floor of the hotel. Hey, boys! And you, too, Asia, Xenovia, and Irina! It's all well and good to enjoy the station, but if we don't hurry, we won't have any free time left this afternoon!" Kiryuu, our group leader, was calling out to us all.

Once we were gathered, she pulled out our itinerary and confirmed the locations of all the spots.

"Er, the hotel should be around the station area… We need to leave through the west entrance… Go past the bus stop, turn to the right…"

"Look, let's just find a way outside to start with. We can't hang around the station forever," Matsuda suggested.

Kiryuu stared back at him, a chilling gleam on her glasses. "It won't do to get lost in a strange environment, Matsuda. One person's careless mishap could be the catalyst to innumerable casualties."

"Is this a war zone or something?!"

"She's right, Matsuda. It's important to work as a team. Kiryuu is our boss, so we should follow her lead. Kyoto might conceal hidden dangers."

Faced with Xenovia's persuasive follow-through, Matsuda could do little else but nod in resignation. "I understand…"

"Eek! Groper!" A woman's scream cut through the din of the station. "B-breasts…!"

A man who'd been in the act of trying to touch a woman was being restrained by a group of passersby. His hands still flexed lecherously.

"I guess Kyoto isn't such a peaceful place after all," Motohama remarked.

Indeed. Apparently, there were perverts to be found wherever you went.

"All right, I think I know where we are now! Let's be off!"

With Kiryuu as our vanguard, we departed Kyoto Station and began to stroll the streets of the old capital.

"Oh, it's Kyoto Tower!" Matsuda called.

We all turned our eyes in the direction he pointed. Whoa! It was right across from the station building! So that was Kyoto Tower… Our plan was to go to the observation platform on our last day here.

That bastard Matsuda had already taken out his camera, snapping one photo after another.

Our hotel was only a few minutes away by foot. It had been easy enough to locate—all we had to do was follow the crowd of students all wearing Kuou Academy winter uniforms.

The huge luxury resort was named the Kyoto Sirzechs Hotel!

It sounded like our Demon King was an influential figure even here in the old capital.

Incidentally, the Kyoto Serafall Hotel was situated only a short distance away. Just how much prime real estate did the Demon Kings have around Kyoto Station?!

It turned out that the House of Gremory managed this resort behind the scenes. That was why we had been able to secure accommodation at a bargain price.

We showed our student cards to the bellboy standing by the entrance and were politely ushered inside.

Matsuda, Motohama, and Kiryuu stood in awe of the extravagantly decorated lobby.

"Awesome… Is it really okay for a bunch of high school students to stay here? I mean, it must cost a fortune."

Matsuda's opinion was sensible, but he didn't know the power and reach of the House of Gremory.

Xenovia had a somewhat muted reaction, however. "Hmm. Sure, it's fancy and all, but it's a bit lacking compared to the president's house."

That was certainly true. The prez lived in a bona fide castle. The only reason why the lavish hotel didn't completely floor me was that I'd already stayed at the prez's mansion. High-class demons really were something.

Past the entrance hall was the lobby, where we found many other Kuou Academy students waiting.

When it was time to take attendance, the teachers did a roll call for each group, taking notes on those who hadn't arrived yet.

We all sat on the floor, listening to various announcements from the teachers.

Azazel and Rossweisse looked to be deep in conversation about something, but then Rossweisse stood and faced us students. What was she going to announce?

"There is a hundred-yen shop in the underground shopping mall at Kyoto Station. Please go there if you've forgotten to bring anything. You can't afford to be careless when it comes to how you spend your money. If you begin a life of big spending during your impressionable student days, you'll have no chance of ever becoming a responsible adult. Currency is what makes the world go round, and if you waste everything you have frivolously, you'll soon run out. That's why you should go to hundred-yen stores. They're truly one of Japan's many treasures."

Rossweisse was telling us about hundred-yen shops?! And so passionately, at that! She had even researched their locations ahead of time!

Rossweisse! I get that you found a lot of what you needed at hundred-yen stores, but you're completely addicted to them! It sounded like there were a great many things capable of winning the heart of this former Valkyrie. Still, I had to admit, they were convenient.

Ah, Azazel was holding his head in exasperation. Having to discuss things with Rossweisse couldn't have been easy...

The former Valkyrie, having finished her announcement, passed the baton to another teacher, who started going through all the final announcements.

From her first day at Kuou Academy, Rossweisse had proven to be especially popular among the students. She was beautiful and serious but also possessed a few quirks, which made her an instant hit with everyone. On top of that, she was close and warm with her pupils. Because of how close she was to us in age, we'd taken to addressing her informally by name.

"Please remember everything I just said. Once you've put your luggage away in your rooms, you're free to do whatever you want this afternoon. However, please don't wander too far. Try to stick to the area around Kyoto Station. And remember, be back in your rooms by five thirty." So announced the teacher at the front of the room as he wrapped up the explanation.

""""Okay!"""" the entire group of second-year students answered.

And with that, the roll call, along with all the reminders and precautions about being on our best behavior, was complete.

Carrying my suitcase behind me, I went to receive the key to my room from a staff member by the entrance hall. We were staying in Western-style double rooms, if I remembered correctly. Since I was the odd one out, I had an entire room to myself! Truthfully, I was pretty pleased about that. You see, a teenage guy out exploring a new city tended to accumulate a lot of energy over the course of a day. A space to let off some steam was perfect. With that thought in my mind, I held out my hand to claim my key.

"This one's yours, Issei."

To my surprise, it wasn't a hotel staffer who gave it to me, but Azazel.

I could see something was wrong, as he flashed me a broad grin, and it didn't take long to figure out why.

*　　*　　*

The accommodations reserved for the students were all large Western-style double rooms, each fitted with a pair of sizable beds and a view of the area around Kyoto Station.

"Awesome!" Matsuda cheered loudly.

"I'm so glad I decided to enroll at Kuou," Motohama said in a much more subdued tone.

This was their room. Mine was actually on a different floor. I had a bad feeling about this...

I found my accommodations nestled in the corner of the hall two stories above. It was obviously different from the rest and even had a Japanese-style sliding door.

When I opened it...

"...Th-this is my room...?"

I blinked in disbelief as my eyes beheld a space that was only eight tatami mats in size. It was furnished with an ancient television and a round table, but that was pretty much it. There was no way this met the minimum standards of a hotel! And why was everything so old?!

Matsuda burst into laughter. "Ha-ha-ha-ha-ha-ha-ha-ha! Seriously?! A Japanese-style room? And eight mats in size? Ah, it's perfect for you, Issei!"

"No bed, either—only a futon. Just big enough for one, I see. I guess the organizers had to save money somewhere, huh?" Motohama commented on the situation with calm amusement!

Dammit! Why was I the only one who had to put up with this?!

Was this punishment for thinking this place less extravagant than the prez's home?!

At least it still had a toilet and bathroom. But they were nowhere near as grand as those in the resplendent Western-style accommodations!

Tears were forming in my eyes! At that moment, there came a knock on my door.

"Issei? Are you in here?"

It was Rossweisse. She was wearing a tracksuit. When had she found time to get changed?

Hurrying to her, I whispered in her ear, "Rossweisse! Why was I the only one given a room like this...?"

"Please try to put up with it. Rias selected this one in case we need a space to hold discussions."

"Discussions? Here? Ah, you mean about demon stuff?"

"Yes, that's right. We needed to set aside a place to talk in case anything occurs while we're in Kyoto. Because you were the only one with a room to yourself, we had to take yours."

A place set aside for us demons to chat, if necessary, while we were in Kyoto.

This isolated Japanese-style room had been selected for that purpose. But did it have to be *this* one in particular...? Wouldn't a luxurious Western-style room have been much better?!

With luck, there'd be no reason to hold a meeting anyway. I didn't want something spoiling our trip!

"Please try to put up with it, Issei," Rossweisse quietly repeated, patting me on the shoulder. Then she raised her voice. "I need to attend a meeting with the other teachers, so I'll leave you three to it. You've got the afternoon free, but don't go overboard... We don't want to cause a bother for the people of Kyoto, do we now?"

""""No,"""" my two perverted friends and I replied.

"All right, I'd better find Azazel... That man managed to slip away after all the announcements... I knew I couldn't trust the governor of the Grigori..." Rossweisse departed while muttering about her colleague.

Azazel had managed to disappear, had he? Before we'd come here, I'd overheard him say to himself, "First up is the apprentice geisha! Then I'll have my fill of Kyoto cuisine!" My guess was that he hoped to indulge in some adult pleasures. And as though trying to live up to his reputation, he'd already taken off!

Dammit! *I* wanted to see the apprentice geisha!

My regret and vexation notwithstanding, Motohama pulled out a map of Kyoto, turning to me. "Hey, Issei. Seeing as we've got the afternoon free, why don't we go to Fushimi Inari-taisha Shrine?"

"Fushimi Inari? Ah, you mean the place with the long paths of torii gates?"

I recalled seeing all those red torii gates on TV.

"Right, right. It's only one stop from Kyoto Station. I asked one of the teachers before, and they said it was okay."

"Well, if we've got permission, we might as well," I agreed.

Matsuda wiped his camera lenses as he responded, "If you don't view the sights you wanna see while you can, then you aren't properly touring the city, right?"

"How about we invite Asia and the others to come, too, then?" I suggested.

""Yeah!"" The two of them rejoiced in kind.

Thus, we decided to spend the afternoon exploring Fushimi Inari Shrine, the first main stop on our Kyoto excursion!

-O●O-

After a couple of minutes getting jostled around on the train, we got off at Fushimi Station and set off on the path leading up to the shrine.

"Whoa, see that, Asia and Irina? See all those things on sale in the stores here?"

"Wow, they're filled with cute foxes!"

"Do you think we have enough money to buy a few souvenirs?"

No sooner had we arrived than our Church Maiden Trio immediately partook of the Kyoto atmosphere. When the three chatted like this, they looked no different from regular high school students.

"The Beauty Trio against a backdrop of Kyoto scenery! Let's snap a picture!"

Beside me, Matsuda was taking advantage of this opportunity to take photographs of Asia and the other girls.

"Hold on, why aren't you taking any of *me*?" Kiryuu demanded, eyes narrowed with displeasure.

After passing beneath the first torii, a huge gate appeared before us, framed on either side by a pair of guardian dog–like fox sculptures.

"...Those statues are supposed to ward off evil. Normally, their presence would prevent a demon from entering, but these free passes mean we can move past them without issue," Xenovia explained as she eyed the stone foxes.

"Are we really being watched?" I asked.

I had felt somewhat uneasy since stepping off the train, as though someone was monitoring my every move.

"Of course. We're a group of demons and an angel. As far as the beings who control this shrine are concerned, we're foreign entities. We let them know beforehand that we wanted to visit, but I guess they still feel the need to keep an eye out."

I suppose that made sense. From what I understood, Kyoto was essentially the spiritual capital of Japan's supernatural beings, and to them, we were outsiders.

But in spite of my apprehension, we passed through the gate without issue and proceeded up to the main shrine. Farther along, we arrived at the stairs leading up Mount Inari. Taking pictures along the way, we made the climb up the steps, passing beneath the thousand torii gates that lined the route up the peak.

We had been walking for maybe ten or twenty minutes.

"...Hah... H-hold on... H-how are you all able to keep going...?" Motohama was out of breath.

Matsuda let out a sigh from a few steps ahead. "Hey, hey, that's pathetic, Motohama. Asia and the others aren't tired. See?"

Matsuda hadn't even broken a sweat, thanks to his athletic build.

To be fair, most of us were demons, which meant our physical abilities and stamina were greater than humans'. We had also all engaged in significant amounts of training, so this wasn't difficult for us in the slightest. After the exercises I had gone through last summer in the underworld wilderness, I wasn't even winded.

Guess I've got you to thank that I can climb this mountain so effortlessly, Tannin. I sent some mental gratitude to the former Dragon King.

We paused at a rest stop store partway up the mountain before resuming the trek. Poor Motohama was gasping for air.

"Ah, what a great view!"

"It's amazing!"

"How about we snap some photos, then? By the way, I think people at the local schools use this mountain as a running course. Hmm. It doesn't look like there's anyone here today, though."

Xenovia and Asia were deeply moved by the mountain scenery, while Kiryuu was taking copious shots with her camera as she demonstrated her knowledge of the area.

Seriously, though, no matter how far we kept going, there was no end to the red torii gates. The names of businesses were written on the pillars that supported the arches. Those companies must have donated money to the shrine for the gates.

For some reason, whenever I saw a mountain, I found myself wanting to climb to the summit.

Nothing beat the view from up there!

"Sorry, everyone. I'm going to go on ahead. I want to see the peak," I declared before taking off up the stairs at a dash.

Had I still been human, this hike would've killed me. However, I was a demon who had undergone lots of training, so it was easier than easy!

Doing my best not to disturb the other tourists, I made my way up the mountain until I reached the top.

All that awaited me was an old, worn-out shrine.

Huh? Was this really the mountaintop? Truth be told, the path had branched at a few points along the way, and I hadn't paid much attention to the proper course. Maybe there were other sightseeing spots nearby?

The dense trees kept out most of the sunlight.

Leaves rustled in the wind... I was alone up here. What was I supposed to do now?

I decided to give a prayer before descending. The others were probably still working on climbing the steps.

I clapped my hands in front of the shrine and thought a shameless, yet honest, wish. *Please give me breasts to ogle and touch! Help me get a girlfriend! Help me get up to some erotic fun with the prez and Akeno!*

No sooner had I turned to leave than...

"...You aren't from Kyoto, are you?"

...a voice sounded out of nowhere. I could sense presences gathering around me.

Uh-oh. Was I surrounded? Whoever had spoken, they clearly weren't human.

They didn't seem particularly strong individually, but they were so many in number. Heh, I had no idea that I'd honed my senses this well! Th-then again, I hadn't noticed them until *after* they had surrounded me...

I adopted a defensive stance just as a figure—a girl, short in stature and dressed like a shrine maiden—appeared in front of me.

"...Huh?"

She had glittering blond hair and a pair of radiant golden eyes. Judging by her appearance, she could have been in the earlier years of elementary school.

But the second I laid eyes on the things sticking out from her head, I knew she wasn't a person.

She had animal ears sticking out through her hair just like Koneko did. And was that a fluffy tail jutting out from behind her legs?!

Is she a dog spirit? No, this is Fushimi Inari Shrine, so maybe a fox?

Why would a fox spirit confront me? I had to assume it was because I was a demon, but didn't my pass grant me permission to wander around?

That feeling of being watched... Had it been these creatures? Was this the result of my praying for breasts?!

As these thoughts coursed through my mind, the girl with the fox ears glared furiously my way before angrily crying, "Outsider! How dare you?! Sic him!"

At her command, a swarm of what looked like *yamabushi* mountain hermits with black wings and bird heads and people wearing Shinto robes and fox masks lunged for me!

"Whoa?! What's this?! *Karasu-tengu*...?! And foxes?!"

I had never encountered anything like this before!

The young girl leveled an accusatory finger at me and proclaimed, "Give me my mother back!"

The *tengu* and the fox priests began to attack all at once!

I wasted no time activating my gauntlet as I dodged their strikes. Surely, I could handle this much…right?

"Y-your mother? I don't know what you're talking about!" I shouted back.

I was seriously in the dark here! I mean, I had only just arrived in Kyoto! I didn't know anything about her parents!

The girl wasn't having any of it, though. "Liar! You can't fool me! I know what I saw!"

I wasn't trying to trick her! Seriously, I had only recently arrived in the city! Where was this coming from?!"

Right now, I needed to find an escape route. Unfortunately, a *tengu* lunged toward me with his staff. Was I about to get clobbered?!

I braced myself, when…

Clash!

…something met the *tengu*'s staff before it connected with me.

"What's going on, Issei?"

"What are all these? Spirits?"

Xenovia and Irina were on the scene!

The pair were brandishing wooden swords that they must have purchased from a souvenir stand. Asia rushed over to join them a moment later.

The girl and her spirit companions, startled at the sight of the four of us together, grew even angrier.

"…So you're the ones who… My mother… I won't forgive you! Filthy demons, defiling this holy space! I'll *never* forgive you!"

She wasn't willing to hear us out one little bit! It was pretty unpleasant not being able to get a word in edgewise!

Now that it had devolved into a battle, there was only one thing to do.

"Asia! Do you still have that thing the prez gave you?" I asked.

"Yes!" Asia responded, retrieving a card engraved with the House of Gremory sigil from her jacket.

The prez had given Asia that little item before we left. It allowed Asia to give me permission to use a Promotion in the prez's absence.

Rias had entrusted it to her for the duration of the school trip, her reasoning being that she would be the one most often by my side during our stay. It was certainly true that we were always in each other's company!

"Here goes! E-er…"

Queen! That was what I wanted to go with, but I had to familiarize myself with the other pieces in actual combat! On top of that, Fushimi Inari Shrine was famous. I couldn't go around blowing it up.

The prez had warned me about that before we had left. *"Do you hear me, Issei? Don't destroy Kyoto, all right? It won't do to anger the other factions, and it would cause a major headache for the demon industry, too. And above all, you had better not damage that city, because I like it, okay?"*

I couldn't afford to lay waste to the prez's favorite place!

"All right, I'll Promote to a Knight, then!"

Power coursed through my flesh, leaving my body feeling lighter! If I used this increased speed to evade instead of fighting back, we could keep the damage to a minimum.

Just in case, I had also charged my Boosted Gear for the past thirty seconds, too!

"Explosion!"

I activated my Sacred Gear! *Now* I was ready!

Xenovia and Irina readied their wooden swords. Although their blades weren't metal, those two could still wreak major havoc. I'd have to caution them against it.

"Xenovia, Irina. I don't really know what's going on here, but this is Kyoto. I'm sure it'll be tough, but we can't afford to hurt these guys. Let's just try to drive them away."

""Got it."" The girls nodded in agreement.

Fwoosh!

Then they lashed out together!

Xenovia and Irina used their wooden swords to parry the onslaught of attacking enemies, destroying their weapons with overwhelming force. I stood guard before Asia, blasting away any and all opponents who tried to attack.

All right! Together, Xenovia, Irina, and I were better than this group of assailants! Ha-ha-ha! This was making for a good training session! My movements were clearly swifter than our opponents'!

Plus, this was fantastic practice for moving as a Knight! It made for excellent training!

The attackers, having lost the upper hand, began to fall back.

The fox girl glared balefully at us and raised her fist. "Withdraw. We can't beat them at our current level. Vile demons! You're going to give me my mother back, you hear!"

With those parting words, the girl and her followers disappeared behind a powerful surge of wind.

Seriously, what was that *all about?!*

We relaxed our stances, baffled by this unreasonable turn of events.

Kyoto.

I had an uneasy premonition that something bad was going to happen during our stay here.

–O●O–

""""Thanks for the meal!"""""

We had just finished eating dinner at our hotel on the first night of the school trip. It had been a luxurious feast of Kyoto cuisine. The boiled tofu was seriously delicious! And the *yuba* tofu skin had been so soft and delicate… On top of that, the Kyoto vegetables were unexpectedly flavorful.

After the attack, we had rejoined Matsuda and the others and completed our sightseeing tour of Fushimi Inari Shrine, on guard all the while. Those not in the know had been suspicious of our sudden caution.

Once we returned to the hotel, we made sure to report the incident to Azazel and Rossweisse, who both listened with obvious consternation.

"Why were you attacked here in Kyoto?"

Naturally, the spirits who governed the old capital had been informed of our visit.

Azazel promised to double-check that everything was in order. I pondered whether to report the day's events to the prez, but Azazel urged me to hold off for now. "We still don't know what happened, so we're better off not worrying her unnecessarily," he explained.

It was true that we didn't have enough information to file a proper report.

And there was still a chance this was all my fault for rushing up to that old shrine...

At least I could tell Azazel about my misgivings.

"If they're after you, it'd be best just to wait," he responded. "Just be patient and enjoy your trip. Heck, if you're really worried, I'll ask my subordinates to snoop around and see if they can find anything like what you described."

There was definitely *something* going on, and it seemed to have begun right after we arrived. At the moment, there was nothing to do but leave it to my superiors, though.

After eating dinner and discussing plans for tomorrow with my two perverted friends and the girls, I went to hang out with Matsuda and Motohama in their room.

After that, I returned to my own shabby lodgings and lay down on my futon for maybe ten minutes.

It was time.

I stood up and gently nudged open the door, scanning my surroundings. There was no one to be seen.

Good, good.

I stealthily departed my room and opened the door to the fire escape.

At this time of night, the public baths ought to be full of lovely maidens! Nothing could stop me from catching a peep! All those girls in my class who always looked down on me! Heh-heh-heh! Now it was *my* turn to look down on them—literally—and smack my lips at the sight of their naked flesh!

My mouth twisted into a grin as my raging sexual impulses propelled me down the stairs.

At that moment, a figure stepped out on the platform that linked the fire escape to the women's public bath.

It was Rossweisse. She was standing guard, still dressed in a sports tracksuit.

My lecherous grin turned wry. Yep, she had seen through my plan.

"I knew from the very beginning that you would come here," she said, readying herself. "As a member of the teaching staff, I will defend the privacy of my students!"

"Rossweisse…," I began, my voice calm and composed as I continued slowly down the stairwell. "…I know we're allies, but I can't compromise on this. I'm going to peep on them."

We continued to glare at each other as I entered attack range.

"Hyargh!"

Rossweisse and I began to do battle right there on the fire escape!

Seeing as we were staying at a hotel, we couldn't fire off any flashy attacks. Thus, we struck with constant barrages of small-scale magic blasts and physical blows.

There was no beating Rossweisse without my Balance Breaker, but the former Valkyrie was unable to utilize her strongest magic here, so that helped even things.

I activated my gauntlet and fired a volley of miniature Dragon Shots to overcome her ice spells.

Heh-heh. She couldn't afford to try fire or explosive techniques here! Even when she managed to push past the Dragon Shots, I could use my fire breath to melt her frozen projectiles in a flash! I *was* a dragon, after all, so fiery abilities were right up my alley!

"Gah! Your attacks are even more honed than usual! To think that your libido is capable of increasing your skills to such a degree… This is insane!"

"If it helps me feast my eyes on the naked bodies of my female classmates, I'll gladly take you on!"

"What a lecherous mindset! Isn't it enough for you to worship Rias's and Akeno's bodies, to touch them to your heart's content practically on a daily basis?!"

"That's an entirely separate matter!"

"Ngh! There's no hope for this dragon Lothario!"

Was I really a Lothario? At home, it always felt like the girls were the ones playing around with *me*, not the other way around…

"Just so you know, even if you manage to get by me, the second-year girls from the Sitri Familia are watching you, too. As a last resort, they're even willing to let Saji awaken his Dragon King to stop you. No matter what, we won't let you spy on the students!"

What?! They've already enacted a defensive plan?! The student council had known from the very beginning that I would try to spy on the public baths! Maybe I should have expected no less from Rossweisse and the Sitri Familia?!

Hold on, they were willing to let Saji reawaken the Dragon King that lay dormant inside him to bar my way?! Just how dangerous did they think I was?! Was it really worth calling Vritra?!

"Come on, give me a break! This is why you've never been able to get a boyfriend!" I cried back.

Rossweisse flew into a sudden panic at my remark. "Th-th-th-th-that's got nothing to do with anything! B-b-besides, I was a battle maiden, which meant I *had* to be a virgin! Do you think I *don't* want to get up to all kinds of erotic action with a handsome boyfriend?!"

With a tremendous wail, Rossweisse hurled more magic my way!

Whoa!

Her last attack had been powerful enough to make the emergency stairwell sway from side to side!

This was bad! My thoughtless comment had caused her to stop holding back—at least a little. I must have overstepped my bounds, as Rossweisse's eyes were brimming with tears! At this rate, the whole stairwell would be destroyed, and I would be killed!

If this was what it had come to, I would have to use *that* technique to stop her!

"I'll never forgive you!" she cried while hurling lightning that roared down the emergency stairwell.

I dodged that electric attack, somehow managing to get in close. Rossweisse's bolt made the hairs on my skin stand taut, but I had to endure!

Pouring all of my demonic energy into my brain, I pushed my imagination as far as it would go.

All right! I now had the perfect mental image of my latest delusion! The only thing that remained was to release the power gathered in my Sacred Gear!

"Explosion!"

My preparations were complete! I tore off my tracksuit jacket, throwing it forward! I had to obscure Rossweisse's vision for a brief moment so that she wouldn't see what was coming!

"Is that all you've got?!" she shouted, using her magic to blast away my diversion.

The action wasn't for nothing, however, as it gave me the exact opening I required!

Don't ever mock my lustful nature!

Rossweisse had fallen for my feint, and I pushed past her defenses until I managed to lay a hand on her clothes!

"Take this! Dress Break!"

I sent my demonic energy flowing into her outfit—and blew it apart into countless shreds!

Dress Break, complete! The first obstacle keeping me from peeping had fallen!

Whoa! What wonderful proportions!

This was my first time ever seeing Rossweisse naked! What glorious breasts! Awesome! The prez's were undeniably superb, but Rossweisse's were exhilarating to look at, too. Everything from their overall shape to their plucky tips! Her beautiful legs led up to a narrow waist, making her figure like a work of art!

Rossweisse began to weep. H-had I gone too far…? Yep, I think I did…

"Sniff... Hic..."

"I'm sorry," I tried to apologize. "I wasn't thinking."

"And how does that help me?!" she cried back. "Th-that tracksuit cost me nine hundred eighty yen! I bought it on sale! It's probably more than tripled in price by now! I even waited for price drops before buying my bra and panties!"

Hold on, that's *why she's pissed?!* Her clothes were more important to her than her modesty! This former Valkyrie was really stingy!

"Kyargh! Nooooo! I—I can never get married now!" she screamed, covering herself with her hands as though she'd only just recognized she was naked. That should've come before lamenting your tracksuit, Rossweisse!

Dumbfounded, I said, "You only noticed that *now*?!"

"What's that supposed to mean?! Do you realize how wasteful it is to destroy a good set of clothes?! Your Dress Break is one hundred percent environmentally *un*friendly! And your sex drive knows no bounds! J-just think of all the tissues you must use! As your teacher, I can't forgive this! Where's your respect for the world's natural resources?!"

Undoubtedly, this was the first time I had ever been lectured about respecting the objects impacted by my Dress Break technique!

And she was even cautioning me about my libido and my tissue usage! Look... I couldn't deny that, as a youthful high schooler, I *did* go through tissues kind of quickly...

Rossweisse truly was cheap. Or rather, she genuinely cared about the environment!

Part of me didn't want to disappoint this Valkyrie lady with her addiction to hundred-yen stores.

"No one's ever lectured me about that before! I'm sorry! I apologize!"

After all this hassle, I didn't want to peek in the girls' public bath anymore.

At that moment, a shadow approached.

"Ahem. Sorry to interrupt."

It was Azazel. He was scratching the side of his face as he watched on, his eyes filled with obvious amusement.

"Azazel! Wh-what are you doing here?!" Rossweisse questioned, understandably flustered.

"We've been summoned. We're supposed to go to a restaurant nearby."

Summoned? About what? And why to a restaurant?

"By who?" I asked.

The corners of his lips twisted in mirth. "A Demon King girl."

-O●O-

We members of the Gremory Familia, and Irina, left the hotel in the dark of night and followed Azazel to a Japanese-style eatery on a nearby street corner, a place called Dairaku.

"...Is Leviathan here?"

Evidently, Serafall Leviathan had decided to pay a visit to Kyoto.

She had invited all of us to join her.

We made our way through the traditional Japanese atmosphere of the establishment as we headed for the private room.

Upon opening the door, we found Serafall, dressed in a kimono, waiting for us quietly.

"Hiya! Red Dragon Emperor and other servants of Rias! I haven't seen you all in so long!" Her greeting carried her usual characteristic buoyant personality.

That kimono really looked good on her. And she had done her long hair up to match her outfit.

"Ah, it's Hyoudou and the others."

Saji and the second-year girls of the Sitri Familia were here as well. I guess they'd arrived ahead of us.

"Yo, Saji. How are you finding Kyoto? Where did you go this afternoon, by the way?"

"All the student council's been doing is helping teachers," he responded with a sigh.

That sounded unfortunate, although probably unavoidable, given his position.

However, with the Knight Meguri, the Rook Yura, and the Bishops

Hanakai and Kusaka, there sure were a lot of gorgeous second-year demon girls in the student council. As the only male member, Saji's position was a pretty enviable one.

"The food here is delicious! Especially the chicken! It's exquisite! Eat up, Red Dragon Emperor and Saji!"

We had barely taken our seats before Leviathan ordered dishes one after another. Unfortunately, we'd actually eaten before coming here...

Ah, but the second I lifted the food to my mouth, I was so struck by its exquisite flavor that my appetite suddenly returned. It looked like the same could be said for everyone else as well.

"So what brings you here, Leviathan?" I inquired.

"I'm working with the spirits of Kyoto!" she replied, making a peace sign with her fingers.

Right, she *was* in charge of foreign affairs and diplomacy. That meant she was on duty.

Leviathan abruptly placed her chopsticks down on the table, her face clouding over. "But there's been...a bit of a problem."

"A problem?" I repeated.

"According to the reports I've heard from other spirits here in Kyoto, a nine-tailed fox spirit went missing the other day."

Immediately, that remark called up a scene from earlier.

"Give me my mother back!"

I heard that young girl's words as clearly as if she were standing beside me. A nine-tailed fox? I was familiar with that type of spirit. They popped up in manga every now and then.

"Does that mean...?"

Leviathan nodded, undoubtedly having comprehended what I was getting at. "Yes. I heard what happened from Azazel. This explains it."

Azazel drank down his cup of sake. "So the local spirit boss has been kidnapped. I'm guessing by—"

"The Khaos Brigade, most likely," Leviathan finished in a serious tone of voice.

...

So that terrorist organization had come to Kyoto. And they had abducted the mother of that girl with the fox ears.

She must have mistaken us for the kidnappers, hence her aggression.

"Wh-what have you stuck your noses in this time?" Saji asked, worry written all over his face.

I'm sorry! It seems like my Familia is always getting caught up in these things!

"Damn. Looking after a bunch of kids during this school trip is tiring enough. And now terrorists, too?" Azazel exhaled with clear vexation.

Did a guy who planned on having fun with apprentice geishas really have the right to whine?

Leviathan refilled Azazel's sake cup before continuing. "In any event, we can't disclose this information yet. We have to find a way to settle this ourselves. I'll keep working to convince the local spirits to cooperate."

"Got it. I'll look into this myself. Damn those Khaos Brigade jokers, following us here to Kyoto. Talk about a pain in the ass," Azazel cursed as he downed another cup.

Evidently, there'd be no apprentice geishas for him.

It was still only the first day of the school trip, and so much had occurred... What were we supposed to do? To be honest, this wasn't a holiday anymore. Our high school trip was something to be treasured, an important milestone in our lives. We had to do our best to stick to the sightseeing plan and enjoy ourselves as much as possible.

However, because we were all members of the Gremory Familia, and demons, too, we would probably have to take some sort of action in response to all this.

"U-um, what do you want us to do...?" I questioned nervously.

Azazel breathed out a sigh before flashing us a smile. "For now, have fun."

"Huh? But what about...?"

He stopped me there, patting me on the head. "I'll let you know if anything happens. But this trip is important to you guys, right? Let us adults shoulder the responsibility. Enjoy Kyoto."

Teach… Azazel's words moved my heart.

He was a smooth talker, all right. He liked to act all lazy and carefree, but he still knew what to say in this kind of situation.

"That's right, Red Dragon Emperor, and you members of Sitri's Familia, too! Enjoy your stay in Kyoto! That's what *I'm* going to do!" stated Leviathan.

To my surprise, it looked like out of all of us, she was the most intent on having a good time.

Seeing as we didn't want to cause Azazel and Leviathan any worry, we decided to continue with our tour of Kyoto.

I couldn't relay all this to the prez yet… But if worst came to worst, I *would* take action.

I'd do my best to protect her beloved Kyoto.

Life.3
The Party of Heroes

"All right! Next!"

"Okay!"

The sky was just beginning to lighten with the dawn of the second day of our school trip. Asia and I were busy training on the roof of the hotel.

Basically, we were practicing our movements. Asia would dash toward me, trying to use her magical healing powers at close range to develop her reflexes. Similarly, I was training by evading her.

We would continue with these sessions right up to the day of our Rating Game! This was vital preparation, after all. I needed to find some way to close the gap between myself and strong guys like Sairaorg and Vali.

I had to get stronger!

Even if it was only one step at a time, I wanted to improve. And the only way to do that was practice.

"Sorry for making you help me with this during the school trip, Asia," I said between deep breaths.

She shook her head. "I don't mind. I'm enjoying our morning in Kyoto, Issei." She gave me a radiant smile as though to assure me.

Ah, she really was a wonderful person! I was so proud of her, my precious Asia!

"You can train better with a sparring partner, right?"

That was Kiba's voice. I glanced around, spotting both him and Xenovia.

"I bought these wooden swords, so why don't we use these? Our match against that princely House is coming up soon. We'd better make sure we don't destroy the hotel, though."

Xenovia...

I could see she was enjoying herself, but did she really mean to haul those wooden swords around with her while sightseeing? Then again, that might be the only way to respond to an enemy attack without wreaking absolute havoc...

Just as I thought as much, Kiba created a short sword in one hand.

"Xenovia. Use this to fight if you need to."

"Ah, a short Holy Sword? I should be able to keep this in my schoolbag. Thanks." Xenovia accepted the weapon, twirling it around in her hands.

Kiba's Balance Breaker allowed him to create Demon Swords and Holy ones, of a certain caliber, anyway. They might not have been at the same level as the Holy Swords of legend, but they were still powerful...

Hold on—enemy attacks?

Just thinking about that completely ruined my mood.

A battle could break out here. Was that the power of the dragon within me, drawing potential opponents to my presence...? I didn't want to think about it.

I slapped myself on the face, trying pull myself together.

"Okay! Let's keep practicing until it's time for the roll call!"

And so we resumed our morning training session.

-○●○-

"Come on, you losers! Let's go!" Kiryuu said, her glasses glinting as she pointed to the nearby bus stop.

""""Okay,"""" we boys cried back in unison.

The first day of our trip may have had an unfortunate hiccup, but that wasn't going to keep us from following Azazel's advice and making the most of our time. From what I heard, Saji and his group were doing the same.

Our second day began with a bus ride from Kyoto Station to Kiyomizu-dera. We had each bought bus passes at the station and were lining up with the other students.

Once we were on board, the vehicle began its journey toward the temple, leaving us with time to enjoy the unfamiliar urban scenery.

Upon arriving, we explored the surrounding area before starting the climb up the slope leading to Kiyomizu-dera proper. Elegant Japanese-style houses lined the road on either side.

"They call this place Sannen-zaka, Three-Year Hill. Apparently, if you trip, you'll be dead within three years," Kiryuu explained. "So be careful, got it?"

"Eek! How scary!" Asia seemed genuinely terrified, hugging my arm tightly.

It was only a legend, but seeing how clumsy Asia could be, it was probably best that she took precaution. She was safe in my company!

At that moment, Xenovia grabbed hold of my other arm.

"Wh-what's wrong, Xenovia?" I asked uncertainly.

"...That's a real scary magic technique to cast on a slope!" she responded with a slight waver in her voice. Her expression was stiff.

She actually believed that story?!

Xenovia, you sure have a habit of arriving at massive misunderstandings!

There was no denying that this side of her was cute, however.

And so I climbed the slope with a beauty hanging on from either arm. I could feel the enmity of my two negative influencers watching from behind... Heh-heh-heh. It sure felt good being the object of their envy!

A huge gate stood at the top of the hill! Did it mark the start of Kiyomizu-dera?!

We passed through the gate, flanked on both sides by wrathful guardian statues, and entered the temple grounds!

"See that, Asia? This shrine has only the best of pagan culture!"

"Y-yes! You can *feel* the history!"

"Three cheers to paganism!"

In their excitement, our Church Trio was making some pretty rude comments!

C-come on, you three! There are gods and Buddhas here! Can't you feel them watching? Be mindful of what you say, all right?

The famed side of the temple that jutted over hillside came into sight! I recognized it from TV! One glance over the side was enough to understand how high it was, but in my current state, I thought I might be able to survive the plunge. Hold on, why did my mind keep leaping to combat?!

"Apparently, there are a lot of cases of people surviving a fall to the ground," Kiryuu explained.

Ah, so even regular humans could endure it.

Wait, people seriously fell from here?!

Within the temple grounds, there was also a small separate shrine where people went to pray for health, good grades, and a chance for romance.

I figured that I might as well throw some coins into the offering box and make a wish. Seeing as I was a demon, I had no way of knowing whether the Buddhas would heed my prayer. Still, I *did* hope to enter university one day.

"Hyoudou, why don't you and Asia check your fortunes and see how compatible you two are?"

At Kiryuu's urging, we both drew lots offered at the temple, Kiryuu peeking all the while.

"It says we've got an excellent future ahead. Looks like we're a good match, Asia," I said.

Only then did I realize her cheeks had turned scarlet in clear joy. "Yes! I'm so happy…! Oh, this is wonderful…"

She hugged the piece of paper in her arms, crying happy tears! Seeing her so thrilled was making me feel a bit bashful, too! I'd have to thank the Buddhas for endorsing our relationship.

Thank you! I clapped my hands together in prayer.

"I'm glad."

"Yep, me too."

"This is a bit of a relief, really."

Beside us, Xenovia, Irina, and Kiryuu were nodding their heads in approval.

Cut it out! Now I'm really embarrassed!

"...I guess we've been left out in the cold, huh?"

"Don't cry, Matsuda. We'll just beat Issei to a pulp once we get back to the hotel."

My two lovelorn friends were sulking gloomily in the corner.

We explored the temple area, bought a few souvenirs, and then started back down toward the bus stop.

Kiryuu led the way, checking her watch frequently. "Next up is Ginkaku-ji—the Temple of the Silver Pavilion. We'll run out of time if we don't hurry." Kiryuu, still checking her watch, led the way.

She was right. It was already past ten o'clock. If we were going to visit our other two destinations, we couldn't afford to dawdle.

Ginkaku-ji! As I pictured our next destination, we boarded the bus and left Kiyomizu-dera behind.

"It isn't really silver?!"

Those were Xenovia's first words upon setting eyes on the famed temple.

She wasn't wrong, I guess. It technically wasn't silver. Still, Xenovia's level of shock was incredible. Her mouth was hanging agape.

"...Xenovia was really looking forward to it. I even heard her repeating to herself that Ginkaku-ji is made of silver, while Kinkaku-ji is made of gold. She was expecting them to glimmer in the light. Her eyes were sparkling with excitement," Asia explained as she hugged her friend's trembling shoulders.

I guess I wasn't the only one prone to fantasies, although Xenovia's were quite different.

"There are a lot of theories," Kiryuu stated. "Some claim they gave up on covering it in silver foil when Yoshihisa Ashikaga died because the shogunate's finances ran dry."

Seriously, had this bespectacled girl researched all our destinations ahead of time? She seemed to know a great deal about them.

I was struck by a similar impression to what I'd felt at Fushimi Inari yesterday. The autumn scenery here in Kyoto, the mountains and trees, it was all beautiful. Perhaps it would give off an altogether different impression in winter, too?

After visiting Ginkaku-ji, we purchased more souvenirs and ate lunch at a nearby restaurant. Then it was time to make for Kinkaku-ji.

"It's gold! This one really is gold!" Xenovia was clearly much more pleased this time. "It's gooooold!" she cried out, her face beaming with joy as she stretched her arms to the heavens!

I had seen this building before on TV, but even so, I was overwhelmed by its brilliance.

Here and there, I sighted other students. Everyone was taking photographs. Matsuda in particular was going crazy with his camera. I figured that I would take a few myself as a memento, sending them via my phone to the club members back at Kuou Academy. After looking around, we picked up more souvenirs and decided to take a break at a teahouse.

"Enjoy," said a young lady as she brought us our cups of freshly brewed matcha tea and some Japanese sweets.

I raised the tea to my lips and found that it wasn't as bitter as I had expected. In fact, with the Japanese sweets, its flavor was just right.

"Hmm. Not bad." Irina seemed to like it as well.

"It's a little bitter, though…"

Evidently, Asia was having a bit of difficulty with the flavor. She continued to drink slowly, though, so she couldn't have hated it.

"…That gold was *so* shiny," Xenovia muttered like a person in a dream.

Kinkaku-ji had obviously left a huge impression on her. Her eyes were positively dazzling. She hadn't even touched her tea.

It was interesting to see a side of her today she didn't often show. It occurred to me, with some surprise, that she might actually be the one enjoying our student lives the most.

"Xenovia! Let's pray to commemorate this visit!" Irina suggested.

Nodding in agreement, Xenovia replied, "Good idea."

"I'll pray, too!" Asia chimed in.

""""Oh, Lord,""" the Church Trio began, sending their thoughts up to Heaven.

What kind of commemoration was this...?

Before I knew it, it was two o'clock in the afternoon. We'd been moving from site to site at a rapid pace, but time was still slipping away far too quickly.

Well, technically, we had all lined up to sound the bell at Kinkaku-ji, and that had taken up an unexpectedly long time.

"Kyargh! Groper! Pervert!"

That was a woman's voice. I rushed out of the teahouse to find a man being restrained by the staff.

"B-breasts! Lemme touch 'em!"

Seriously? There were molesters at Kinkaku-ji now? What a way to ruin the mood...

"A groper?" Matsuda said as he returned from the rest area. "Actually, they said something about that on the TV news this morning. There was one in Gion, too, apparently. And the guy we saw at the station. Seems like a lot, huh?"

Motohama pushed his glasses farther up his nose before responding. "What are you talking about, Matsuda? *You're* the one who assaulted *me* on the bullet train yesterday."

Right. That.

"Nah. How do I put this? I was sleeping, so I wasn't really there. But all I could think about was touching boobs. I wonder what came over me?" Matsuda tilted his head to one side, evidently puzzled.

To me, it seemed entirely natural for a guy our age to have urges like that.

"That's youth for you," Motohama concluded.

Matsuda nodded. "The sins of adolescence."

Sure, but you had better quit trying to touch men's chests.

I was about to agree with them, but I was interrupted by my cell phone ringing.

Oh dear. It was Akeno. Why would she be calling now?

"Hello? Is everything all right, Akeno?"

"Hello? Issei? No, it's nothing too important. But, well...something has been bothering Koneko, you see."

"What do you mean?"

"You sent some photographs just now, yes?"

"Yeah, of Kinkaku-ji. Is something wrong?" I asked, perplexed.

"It seems you captured something else in those pictures, too."

"I did?"

"Yes. There seem to be some spirits in the background. Fox spirits. Is something happening over there? Fox spirits aren't uncommon in Kyoto, but even so..." Akeno's voice sounded somewhat worried.

I felt a chill course across my skin.

"No, everything's okay here. Um, it looks like Asia's calling me. We'll have to talk later."

"...Do contact us if anything happens, okay?"

"Sure thing." I hung up.

...That had been a lie about Asia calling me.

I double-checked the photographs I had taken earlier. They all looked like typical images of Kinkaku-ji... I couldn't see anything else. Was this the kind of thing visible only to those who were attuned? There *were* certain phenomena that only *nekomata* like Koneko could detect...

In any event, Asia and the others needed to hear about this.

Looking back inside the teahouse, I found Matsuda, Motohama, and Kiryuu sound asleep! That didn't seem to be the result of typical exhaustion... There was no way they could all have passed out in the short time I'd been on the phone.

Asia and the others were still awake. Xenovia was glaring menacingly at a female employee of the teahouse.

Bewildered, I shifted my gaze to our server.

Ah, so that's what's got Xenovia on guard.

A pair of animal ears were sticking out from the employee's head. She had a tail, too... It was clear she wasn't human. Now that I had time to take a careful look, I realized the figures surrounding us *all* had similarly bestial ears. All the regular tourists were sound asleep right where they had been sitting.

It had been naive of us to assume they wouldn't attack so long as we kept to famous sightseeing spots. Was Kinkaku-ji part of their territory, too?

Xenovia retrieved the short Holy Sword from her bag, urging Asia to move behind her.

I similarly stretched out my left arm and activated my gauntlet.

"Wait!" came a familiar voice. It was Rossweisse!

"What are you doing here?" I asked.

"Azazel told me to come find you," she hurriedly explained between breaths.

"He did? What's going on?" I questioned while keeping an eye on my surroundings.

Come to think of it, these spirits weren't exuding the same hostility that I had felt yesterday.

"It's a cease-fire. Or rather, we've cleared up a misunderstanding... The daughter of their matriarch, the nine-tailed fox who runs things here, wants to apologize to you all," Rossweisse said.

A truce? So that mix-up had been resolved? Did that mean we didn't need to worry about those foxes attacking?

Despite my doubts, a young girl with fox ears approached me and bowed her head. "I am a spirit in the service of our honored leader. We would like to offer our apologies for the incident yesterday. We've asked the princess to make amends as well, so we would greatly appreciate it if you would join us."

She wanted us to follow them? Where?

Before I could ask, the fox woman went on. "Please come to the secret capital where we spirits dwell. The Demon King and the fallen angel governor have already joined us."

Apparently, while we had been sightseeing, Serafall and Azazel had been working to smooth out the incident from yesterday.

-O●O-

We set foot into what I could only describe as another world.

The streets looked like something out of the Edo period, lined with old-style houses, from which the faces of strange creatures loomed from seemingly every door and window.

We'd passed under a secluded torii gate in a corner of Kinkaku-ji and were then instantly transported to this place.

It was a somewhat dim plane of existence with a unique atmosphere. The residents of those old houses emerged to welcome us... A one-eyed spirit with a massive face, another with a plate on its head, probably a kappa, followed by what looked like tanuki standing upright on two legs.

Each of them stared at us with plain curiosity.

We followed the fox lady to what must have been the princess's residence. We moved along the dark path with only a lantern for light.

"Whoo-sha-sha!"

Whoa! I'd been taken aback there! Out of nowhere, the lantern sprouted eyes and a mouth and started laughing! It was a *chouchin-obake*, a lantern monster!

"My apologies. The spirits and creatures here do love to cause mischief... They shouldn't cause you any harm, though...," the fox lady assured us as she led us to our destination.

"Is this your realm?" I asked.

It was clear that whatever this place was, it was connected to Kyoto.

"Yes," the fox lady answered. "This is where most of the spirits of Kyoto choose to reside. I believe demons like yourself make use of spatial fields in your Rating Games. This area was created using similar means. It goes by a number of names. Some of us call it the underside of Kyoto, others, the inner capital. Naturally, just like in your demon society, there are spirits who prefer to live on the main side of the city, too."

The underside of Kyoto? It did seem curiously similar to the fields used for Rating Games.

"...Humans?"

"No, demons, apparently."

"Demons, eh? That's a rare sight."

"Is that pretty foreigner girl a demon, too?"

"There's a dragon as well. I can sense it. Demons and dragons..."

I could hear the voices of many spirits gossiping around us. It seemed that demons were pretty rare around here. Well, that made sense—this was spirit territory.

After passing through a residential area and crossing over a small river, we arrived at a small grove. Inside, there was a red torii gate.

Beyond it stood a huge mansion, its appearance one of ancient dignity.

Azazel and Leviathan were waiting for us beyond the torii gate!

"Good, you're here."

"Yoo-hoo, everyone!"

Even in the world of spirits, those two acted no different from usual.

Standing between them was a blond-haired girl—the one who had led the attack on us yesterday. Maybe I should just call her Nine-Tails?

Rather than her shrine maiden outfit, the girl was dressed now in a gorgeous kimono like something from the Sengoku period.

Trust me when I say she was a genuine petite princess.

"I've brought them, Lady Kunou," the fox woman from the teahouse reported. Then she abruptly vanished with a burst of flame.

Huh? Was that what they called a kitsunebi, *a fox fire?*

The princess stepped forward. "My name is Kunou. I'm the daughter of Yasaka, she who governs the spirits of all Kyoto, both inner and outer."

Having introduced herself, she bowed her head deeply. "I'm sorry about yesterday. I shouldn't have attacked you without knowing the situation. I ask your forgiveness," she said in apology.

I scratched my cheek in embarrassment.

"It's fine, I guess," Xenovia replied. "So long as we've cleared up that misunderstanding. After our long journey, I'd be happy so long as we can enjoy the rest of our trip. We don't wish to cause any trouble."

Yep. She didn't want to get into any unnecessary fights while we were here, either.

"That's right," Irina continued. "An angel needs to have the capacity to forgive. I don't bear you any grudges."

Asia smiled. "Yes. There's nothing more important than peace."

I had no reason to dispute anything the three of them said. However, I felt a touch of shame as a man, being the last to speak up here. "Yeah, I'm fine with things, too. Please, there's no need to keep hanging your head like that."

"B-but…"

Evidently, the incident yesterday was worrying this girl more than it had us.

I knelt down beside the princess and tried to meet her gaze. "Um, can I call you Kunou? You're worried about your mother, aren't you?"

"O-of course."

"I get why you jumped to conclusions yesterday. Things could've gotten out of hand, but we worked it out, and you apologized because you realized you were mistaken, right?"

"Yes… That's right."

I placed my hand on Kunou's shoulder and grinned. "In that case, we won't hold it against you."

Kunou's face turned bright red. "…Thank you," she muttered.

All right. Everything was okay. No more misunderstandings.

As I stood up, Azazel poked me in the back. "That's our Breast Dragon. You sure have a way with kids, eh?"

"D-don't joke about that. I'm doing my best here!"

"No, that was amazing, Breast Dragon!"

"Yes! I'm moved!"

"You really *are* great with kids!"

All I could do was blush in response to Xenovia's, Asia's, and Irina's compliments.

Seriously, you guys, you're embarrassing me here!

"Honestly, you showed a surprising amount of maturity. As your teacher, I'm proud of you," Rossweisse admitted. Had her opinion of me improved?

Just how low did I rank with her right now? Maybe if I tried to start a conversation about hundred-yen shops, I'd go up in her eyes?

"I—I won't lose! The Breast Dragon is out recruiting converts, but my own TV show, *Miracle Levia-tan*, won't come up second-best!"

Why was Leviathan burning with competitive ambition?! Seriously, demon society wasn't at war; there was no need for that dangerous passion!

"...I'm sorry about what I did...," Kunou said, clearly embarrassed. "But please, please! I need your help to save my mother!"

The leader of the spirits who controlled Kyoto—the nine-tailed fox Yasaka—apparently left her mansion residence a few days ago to meet with a messenger of Sakra from Mount Meru.

Unfortunately, Yasaka never arrived at the meeting site. When her fellow spirits investigated, they found one of her *karasu-tengu* bodyguards near death.

Before breathing his last, the *karasu-tengu* revealed that they had been attacked, with their assailants kidnapping Yasaka.

And so the spirits of Kyoto began to investigate any suspicious new arrivals to the city. That was how they had ended up attacking us.

After that, Azazel and Leviathan met with Kunou and the other spirits to clarify that the underworld had no involvement with what had happened and, at the same time, explained that the most likely culprits were the Khaos Brigade.

"...It looks like the situation is getting serious," I stated after hearing all the details.

We had been invited into Yasaka's mansion residence, sitting in the hall, with Kunou occupying the highest seat.

"Ever since the three great powers decided to join hands in an alliance, this kind of thing has been happening nonstop. Last time, it was Loki coming after Odin, right? This time, we're dealing with terrorists," Azazel explained sullenly.

Azazel hoped to live a peaceful life, so there was no way he would forgive the actions of the Khaos Brigade. He was probably simmering with rage.

Kunou was flanked by an older fox lady and a long-nosed elderly mountain ascetic. The old man was the leader of the *tengu* and had enjoyed good relations with the nine-tailed fox clan for a long time. He seemed to be worried about Yasaka's safety, too, just as her daughter was.

"Lord Governor, Lady Demon King, is there nothing you can do to help rescue Princess Yasaka? We shall lend you any assistance you require," he said.

The old *tengu* showed us a painting of a beautiful blond woman in a shrine maiden outfit. And she had animal ears sticking out from her head! I-it couldn't be...

"This is a portrait of our Princess Yasaka."

Seriously?! Her breasts were massive! They were even peeking out from atop her shrine maiden outfit! J-just what were those terrorists planning to do with this big-bosomed fox lady...? I-if it was something indecent, I would never forgive them!

"At least we can be certain that the kidnappers are still in Kyoto," Azazel remarked.

"What makes you say that?" I questioned.

"Because the flow of energy around the city hasn't been disturbed," Azazel replied with a nod of his head. "Nine-tailed foxes play a role in maintaining the balance between different forces of nature in any given territory. If she were to leave Kyoto, or if she had been killed, you can bet there would be some major calamity coming on. Since there's no sign of that, it's most likely that she's all right and that her kidnappers are still nearby."

I—I hadn't realized Kyoto was like that! This trip was full of surprises...

Still, if Yasaka was safe, there was a good chance that we could help rescue her.

Turning to Leviathan, Azazel inquired, "Serafall, how is the investigation going on the demon side?"

"I've ordered our people to look into every detail. I've mobilized all our staff familiar with Kyoto, too."

Next, Azazel's gaze fell upon us. "Looks like we're short on manpower, so we'll likely need your help as well. Given your history fighting super-powered opponents, we might have you pitch in against those wannabe heroes in the Khaos Brigade. Sorry about this, but we'd better plan for the worst. Seeing as they aren't with us, I'll fill in Kiba and the Sitri Familia. Until then, make the most of the trip, but remember that we'll be counting on you in case of an emergency."

""""Okay,""""" we responded in unison.

In the end, our Kyoto holiday was no longer a mere school trip. Maybe getting all the famous sights out of the way quickly had been the right call?

Kunou put her hands together and bowed her head, with the fox lady and the old *tengu* beside her following suit. "I beg you all. Please... please help save my mother... I beg of you..."

—.

The child's voice trembled with evident grief.

She may have had the elegant mannerisms of a princess, but she was still at an age where she was dependent on her mother.

Fury began to rise within me.

I didn't know what they were playing at, but if I saw those Khaos Brigade guys, I would catch every last one of them! Who did they think that they were, kidnapping a lady like that?!

Plus, Yasaka might grant me a special reward for saving her!

Oh-ho-ho. Are you the Red Dragon Emperor? I hear you're the one who rescued me. Just what manner of reward shall I grant you, I wonder...? Oh, I see you're staring at my body... Is that what you desire? Oh-ho-ho, very well. Shall I teach you the pleasures of Kyoto?

Drip... Drop...

That erotic fantasy had just given me a nosebleed. That enthralling, kimono-clad nine-tailed fox lady had possessed my brain! And her breasts! Her breasts!

"…Issei, are you thinking about something dirty?" Asia asked, looking my way with keen displeasure.

She sure had a powerful intuition when it came to my imaginings!

I shook my head, trying to clear my thoughts. This wouldn't do. I had to take the young princess's plea seriously!

With a newfound sense of resolution, I prepared myself for battle as we continued on our school trip.

Where could those new possibilities of mine have disappeared to? I sure could use something like that right about now. There was no sign of them returning, however. Were they even in Kyoto?

There was no explaining how, yet I felt like they weren't too far away…

–O●O–

"Ah, there was so much to choose from!"

Night had fallen, and I was lying on the futon in my room. I had taken a bath after dinner. Yep, there was no beating an all-you-can-eat buffet! And everything had been so exquisite and classy.

After visiting the spirit world, we'd returned to Kinkaku-ji, woke Matsuda and the others, still sound asleep, and continued with our sightseeing. We explored the area around the temple grounds and purchased more souvenirs until it was time to return.

Back at the hotel, we met with Kiba and the Sitri Familia to discuss our next moves.

We would continue to follow our sightseeing plans tomorrow. However, everyone made sure to carry emergency magic transportation circles to jump back to the hotel at a moment's notice. If word came from Azazel, we had to leap into action.

To be honest, all this tension really dampened the fun… We were planning to visit the Arashiyama area tomorrow, where we would meet up with Kunou.

It seemed she hoped to guide us around as an apology. I had tried to turn her down, seeing as no one was upset with her, but she insisted. Actually, it was Azazel who urged us to accept.

He'd said something about this being the first step on the road to greater collaborations between the underworld and spirit society. On top of that, Kunou was basically a VIP, the daughter of one of the biggest names in Kyoto. Was it truly all right to leave someone *that* important to us...? I needed to take care not to make a rude remark.

I wondered what the prez was up to right now. And Akeno, too... And Koneko... Heck, even Gasper. My thoughts drifted to the other club members who'd been left behind at Kuou Academy.

They had no idea what we were embroiled in. After all, this whole affair was still top secret.

Oh, how I missed the prez's breasts. When I got home, I would have to make sure to bury my face in them!

How was I to while away the remaining hours of the day? Matsuda and Motohama had gone to peep in the women's bathing area...but I had decided to pass tonight. Then again, the idea of breaking past Rossweisse and the Sitri Familia's defenses sounded fun... Ah, what was I to do?

I found myself torn over whether to try to sneak a glimpse of the women's bathing area.

Knock-knock came a sound at my door.

"Yes?" I answered.

"Issei? It's me."

That was Asia's voice. Had something happened?

"Come in."

She stepped inside...dressed in her nightgown.

"What's up, Asia?"

"I thought we could have some fun. Xenovia and Irina will be coming later, too. Kiryuu said she's busy discussing Kyoto with some of the other girls from class, so she won't be joining, though."

Seriously?! Three beautiful girls were going to come to my room for a bit of *fun*?! What would we do?!

We could try out that game based on rock-paper-scissors where the loser had to remove a piece of clothing... Heh-heh-heh! That kind of activity was perfect!

While I was formulating my latest perverted scheme...

"Issei!"

"He might have already found it!"

...Matsuda's and Motohama's voices sounded down the corridor! Were they planning on barging into my room?!

"A-Asia! This way!"

"Huh? I-Issei?"

Something inside me didn't want my two buddies stumbling on us together, so I rushed into the closet with a bewildered Asia.

I closed the sliding closet door from within and raised a finger to my lips, urging my hiding partner to remain silent.

Before long, two sets of footsteps entered my room, opening the main door.

"Huh. He isn't here."

"Don't tell me he already knows where the peeking spot into the women's bathing area is?!"

"What?! This is bad! Is he trying to get a head start on us, going to worship the female body alone?!"

"That has to be it! Let's go, Matsuda!"

"Right!"

Their steps faded off, suggesting they'd left.

Hold up! There's a peeping spot into the women's bathing area?! I hadn't known! Dammit! I was majorly intrigued! What was I supposed to do now...?!

As I racked my brain, the words of my comrades in lecherousness echoing in my mind, Asia took hold of my hand.

When I met her gaze, I recognized the determination in it. She looked resolved to do something. "Issei. When you were with Rias, on the platform at Kyoto Station...you kissed her, didn't you?"

H-had she spotted us? Perhaps Asia had come back and happened upon us by accident. Regardless of how it occurred, she had witnessed it.

"I-it was a good-bye kiss..."

"I—I see. You were so intimate... I was right, you and Rias... Issei... But I also want to..." Asia stared straight at me.

Something about her expression was spellbinding.

"Won't you...kiss me, too?" She moved her face near to mine.

A second kiss.

Our lips overlapped so naturally. It didn't feel perverted in any way. There was no sense of lust. It was a joining between two people who treasured each other...

The moment we connected, I nearly jumped at the sense of loving affection that fell over me. I was acutely aware of just how dear this person was to me.

Asia...

My Asia. I would stick by her side for hundreds, thousands, tens of thousands of years.

We would be together forever. That was a promise.

As I immersed myself in that romantic atmosphere...

...the closet door slid open with a *bang*!

"Whoa! H-hey! X-Xenovia, take a look!"

Irina, garbed in her sleepwear and with her hair hanging loose, was staring right at us!

"What is it, Irina? Ah, Asia's precious kiss scene? So this was what you meant when you said you wanted to have some *fun*? I'm impressed, Asia."

Xenovia was similarly dressed in her nighttime attire!

Asia and I had smooched right in front of them!

How could this happen?! Whyyyyyyyyyy?!

What allowed them to sneak in without a sound?! Sure, Asia did say they would be coming by soon, but still!

I had let down my guard! The mood had swept me away, and these two had struck during that opening!

They had seen us! These two had borne witness to Asia and me kissing!

Naturally, we hurriedly pulled our lips apart! Dammit! A string of saliva connected us both! W-we had been about to use our tongues, too!

"Looks to me like this isn't their first time? Ngh... Asia is always getting one up on me..."

"She's so daring and quick to strike!"

Xenovia and Irina were discussing their discovery with obvious interest, so much so that their cheeks had changed color!

Bang!

That sound—it was like an explosion! Asia's face had turned scarlet!

"A-a-aaaaah, ohhhhh…"

Whoa!

Asia was so flustered that her eyes started swirling around! A moment later, she fainted on the spot!

"Asia! Hey, Asia! Hang in there! *I'm* embarrassed, too! I get that there's no enduring this, but don't go passing out on me!"

"Sorry for the intrusion, but I'll be joining."

"Yeah, m-me too."

As I tended to Asia, Xenovia and Irina made the baffling decision to join us in the closet!

Not only that, they slid the door shut behind them quietly!

"Sorry. We came here to enjoy ourselves a little, but it looked like you weren't in, so I opened the closet," Xenovia explained plainly without the slightest hint of remorse.

My room was only supposed to be used in case of emergency. However, this was rapidly becoming an urgent situation in its own way!

Xenovia was approaching me from one side!

"Wh-what is it?" I asked uncertainly.

"It's my turn after Asia," she answered nonchalantly. "You can kiss me or do something sexual. And then Irina can have her turn."

Wh-whaaaaaaaaaaaat?! H-how exactly had it come to this?!

"Huh?! Me?! No way!" Irina's eyes all but popped out of their sockets.

"This is your chance to discover what it's like to be with a guy, Irina."

It looked like the angel had been caught up in a situation that she hadn't anticipated. I knew the feeling.

"Y-you realize I'll become a fallen angel, right?!"

"Just throw yourself all in and go with the flow. Who knows? You might not fall."

"Throw myself all in?! Y-yes, with the right spirit… But if I were to get involved in something like that, as Lord Michael's Ace, I... I...!" Irina continued mumbling to herself, as though in the middle of a mental struggle.

"Issei's a steal." Xenovia pressed her advantage. "He's a good guy. And he's the Red Dragon Emperor. Think about it. If you were to have a kid with the Red Dragon Emperor, wouldn't that be a huge asset as far as Heaven's fighting potential is concerned?"

"...A child... With Issei... The Red Dragon Emperor... Heaven's fighting potential..."

Irina was seriously considering the suggestion! This was swiftly becoming a pretty significant chance for me!

"All right, how about this? We've got three girls and one guy in close quarters. What happens next is only natural."

"H-hey! Xenovia! What about the teachers outside?"

Right, contact between boys and girls was expressly prohibited. After all, there was no telling what might happen if they were to spend the night in the same room together.

The boys' and girls' rooms were on separate floors, and the teachers were keeping a close eye on all comings and goings. Even during the hours we had free before bedtime, they were checking on everyone from room to room. We would be in trouble if someone walked in on us!

"Ah. You mean the male teachers? We've already used our angel and demon powers to construct a barrier. They won't notice anything, so don't worry. We can be as loud as we want, and no one would hear."

"I don't know how it all works, but this room is filled with sacred and demonic magic!"

Xenovia and Irina were both giving me a thumbs-up! How could they be so reckless?! How could this Church Maiden Duo be so insanely strong yet so utterly out of their minds?!

I had no idea what to do, but Xenovia sure did! She crawled right for me!

"All right... How about...we start with a kiss?"

Ugh... For some reason, her lips seemed particularly sensual today.

Maybe that was because I had just been kissing Asia, and my heart was still racing.

"Huh?! You're going to kiss him already, Xenovia?!" Irina looked as though she still hadn't made up her mind about this.

"Yep. This is practice for making a baby with him. Didn't Kiryuu mention something about that? About making the most of the school trip?"

Kiryuuuuuuuuuuu!

That perverted Craftswoman! Didn't I tell her not to fill everyone's heads with weird ideas?! Still, I owed her big-time! If things kept moving along like this, I might actually be able to have some real naughty fun with Xenovia!

"R-r-right! This is an important event! But I'm an angel and a servant of Lord Michael... And a Christian, too! I—I'm not supposed to..."

"Just watch, then. I'll make a baby while an angel watches over me. Heh-heh. It kinda feels like making a kid chosen by Heaven, don't you think? Irina, stand guard while I make an important demon baby. I'd appreciate a holy blessing as well, if you can."

With that, Xenovia began to strip naked! I could see more of her beautiful skin with each piece of clothing removed. Ngh, I couldn't resist those perfectly toned curves! Demons like us could see in the dark, so nothing was left to the imagination.

Irina, for her part, unfurled her angelic wings as a halo appeared above her head. The strength of that light further intensified the heated atmosphere! That heavenly ability of hers sure was convenient!

"Leave it to me! I've always wanted to witness the mystery of life's creation, just as Lord Gabriel did! Ah, this is a crucial moment for the three great powers, for Heaven, and for our faith in the Lord Himself!"

An angel was praying while two demons were about to get it on! What kind of sex scene was this?!

Plop!

Xenovia unhooked her bra!

Bah! Blood gushed from my nose! Damn if they weren't incredible to behold!

Xenovia took no notice of Asia, who was still stunned, as she embraced me in her arms! Ahhhhh, the tactile sensation of those breasts coursed through my body! Their incredible softness paralyzed my brain!

"This is our chance. Once Asia wakes up, hug her like this, too. It will be her first time as well, so she probably won't know what to do. You can learn the ropes with me, okay? Then put that knowledge to use with Asia. That's the best way to look out for her."

"Ah, Xenovia! What a wonderful spirit of self-sacrifice!" Irina remarked.

What fresh madness was this?!

The next thing I knew, Xenovia had begun to remove *my* clothes, her fingers crawling all over my body! An electrifying chill shot through me! B-by its own accord, my hand was approaching her thighs! That even, supple sensation made my thoughts run wild!

A lustrous stream of words soon spilled from Xenovia's lips, "Ah… Yeah, it feels so good, a man's skin. *Your* skin. Just touching it makes me feel like a woman."

Drip. Drop.

My nosebleed wouldn't stop. This girl could kill a guy with comments like that alone!

Now that we'd come this far, I probably had no choice but to let it happen, right? Was I about to get up to something phenomenal in this closet with Xenovia and Asia?!

I swallowed deeply, did my best to calm my breathing, and then stretched out my arms to embrace Xenovia, when…

"A-ah… Huh? What am I…?"

…Asia woke up! She slowly sat upright. Just as Xenovia and I were about to lie in each other's arms, her eyes met mine, shooting wide.

"Oh, Asia, you're awake? I was just about to receive Issei's genes," Xenovia stated far too casually.

M-m-my genes?! Wh-what a way to put it!

"G-g-g-genes… —!"

Asia's voice turned shrill as she came to grips with the predicament.

"I'm just borrowing him for a short while. Don't worry, I won't keep him to myself. I don't think making a baby will require too many attempts."

Xenoviaaaaa! Please, can't you speak more like a girl your age should?! That's a weird way of describing this!

"N-no! Issei's… No, you can't!" Asia puffed up her cheeks, and her eyes were wet.

Xenovia frowned, obviously frustrated. "Hmm. Just a little bit won't hurt, right?"

Then they launched into a full-on argument!

"Th-that isn't the problem! If you want his genes… I-it means doing *that* with him… You can't!"

"Sounds like you already know a lot about it, Asia. I'm guessing you've realized that it isn't storks that deliver babies."

"D-don't make fun of me! I understand how it works! If you're willing to go this far, then I'm going to be honest about what *I* want as well!" Asia wrapped her arms around me and loudly declared, "*I'll* have Issei's child!"

…Xenovia, Irina, and I were left stunned by the dramatic proclamation.

Asia had even begun to take off her nightgown, revealing her snow-white skin!

My nosebleed intensified in response.

And why wouldn't it? Hearing Asia say she wanted to…t-t-to have a child with me… I could feel my face reddening to realms beyond the possible!

"Wow… A contest between two women over a man's genes… Amazing…!" Irina was watching this all unfold with enthusiasm.

Cut it out! You're supposed to be an angel, aren't you?!

"Issei. We're going to be together forever, so isn't it natural to want a child?" Asia asked me.

I didn't know what to think anymore. All I could manage was, "I—I guess so…? I suppose that's…right?"

"Did you hear that, Xenovia? I'm going to have Issei's babies! Lots and lots of babies!"

Xenovia took hold of my arm, hugging it to her breasts. "No, you've gotta give me at least one round of genes. I want a child, too. I'm a woman, and I want to have a baby. I want to raise a child of my own."

Oh man, things were really straying into unexpected territory! Sure, I liked the situation just fine, but it felt curiously suffocating. This closet was stifling, and I could hardly breathe! It was…almost like how the prez, Asia, Akeno, and Koneko had fought over me in my room the night before the school trip…! I couldn't understand these girls!

Xenovia and Asia glared at each other. I managed to wriggle free from their embraces. Unfortunately, I also bashed my head against the shelf above as I made my escape.

Ow…

I tried to adjust my position after bumping my dome. However, the closet was too cramped, and I quickly lost my balance.

Plop.

My hand pressed up against a wonderfully soft sensation…

"…I-Issei…"

I watched as Irina's face turned scarlet!

She had toppled over, and I was leaning right on top of her! To any outside observer, it would've appeared like I'd pushed her down!

What's more, her nightgown had slipped open, revealing her gloriously round white breasts! Th-they were so huge! Incredible! So these were the tits of an angel! And her nipples were so tender and plump! Hold on, my hand was already fondling one of them entirely of its own accord!

This had all been an accident caused by how narrow the closet space was!

Irina's breast was simultaneously supple and firm! My hand seemed to sink naturally into it! It was breathtakingly elastic, like a freshly cooked rice cake!

Damn, this squishy, seductive sensation rivaled even Akeno's! Irinaaaaa!

Her angel wings were flickering between white and dark again! Was she on the verge of falling from Heaven?!

"...Th-this is my first time... I don't know what to do, Issei... Y-you want me to become a fallen angel, right...?"

Irina's expression was one of uncharacteristic feminine charm! This wouldn't do! When the usually innocent and pure Irina looked at me like this, the power raging within me would run rampant! And with her hair hanging loose, the destructive potential of her eroticism soared to new heights!

"S-sorry!"

While removing my hand, I tried to apologize...

Thud!

...and that's when my head struck the shelf above once more. Ouch. The impact sent me falling back down.

Plop.

Naturally, Irina's breasts were waiting for me. My face pressed up against the sublime feeling of elasticity... Ah, they were so large, soft, and spongy... Was this what an angel's embrace was supposed to feel like?

My vision was growing blurry, and I could feel my consciousness slipping...

I must have taken one too many to the skull, or maybe it was the blood loss through my nose...

"Issei! Are you okay?! Issei!"

"Hey, you can't let yourself get knocked out the first time you hold Irina..."

"I'm going to fall... Oh, Lord, please forgive me my sins..."

The voices of the three girls faded into the distance.

When this Church Trio worked as a team, there was no withstanding them.

The next morning, our group left the hotel and made our way to Kyoto Station.

Ah, what a night...

I felt like I was still dreaming. Last night had been one erotic experience after another with the Church Trio in my closet. It had been suffocating, and at the same time, I had been so ecstatic that I could have died...

After passing out from so much blood loss and hitting my head more times than I should have, I awoke on my futon in my room this morning. Apparently, Rossweisse had come to check on us shortly after all that and sent the others back to their rooms while she took care of me. I owed her one...

Man, Asia's sudden declaration last night genuinely astonished me. I was glad to hear her say she wanted a child with me. Honestly, I was totally moved. Yet my feelings remained a bit complicated...

Every time something like that happened, when the crucial moment was at hand, I always found myself lacking. I was fully aware of this problem. Unfortunately, I still couldn't propel myself forward... Maybe the shackles of a broken heart were holding me back. Whenever I considered advancing to the next stage, I grew afraid that the girls might end up hating me, and I faltered.

My life was at an all-time high right now, and I didn't want to do anything that might jeopardize it.

But if things persisted as they were, I would never become a harem king! Truly, this was an incredible dilemma.

At this rate, my relationship with the prez would forever remain out of reach. Maybe that was fine. After all, I was her...

Then again, I wanted the courage to make a move if the chance to embark on the next step presented itself.

And that's when I remembered the upcoming match.

If I could beat Sairaorg, maybe the prez and I could—

"Hey, Issei. What's with the glum face?" Matsuda asked, peering into my eyes.

"I-it's nothing... Anyway, what's with *your* face? And Motohama's, too."

"Ah, well. About that."

"Wounds of honor."

They were both bruised and battered, and covered in bandages to boot.

Apparently, they'd made their way to the fabled peeping spot looking in on the women's bathing area. However, the student council—the Sitri Familia—had been waiting there for them. Matsuda and Motohama had tried to force their way in anyhow, though, hence their injuries.

They didn't stand a chance against the girls of the Sitri Familia... Actually, the student council had been suspicious of me as well. Fortunately, since Rossweisse checked on me in my room, I had a strong alibi.

Still, Rossweisse had summoned the three members of our Church Trio and me this morning for a stern lecturing.

She was like a dependable elder sister to us all. Enough so that I regretted having caused her all this trouble.

Why did *I* have to fall under suspicion because those two idiot friends of mine acted on their own?! Perhaps that was only natural. We were known as the Perverted Trio, after all! Given my usual obsession with all things lewd and obscene, it was understandable that no one trusted me.

Anyway, that's enough of that topic.

Our plan today was to keep sightseeing. Our mission was to conquer Arashiyama. First stop: Tenryu-ji, the Temple of the Heavenly Dragon!

"How far away is Tenryu-ji?" I asked.

Kiryuu looked over our schedule before responding. "Hmm. We'll take the train to Arashiyama and get off at the nearest station. From there, we'll go the rest of the way on foot."

"Got it. So we're heading to Kyoto Station. I guess the prez was right. We really do have to take trains and buses to get everywhere."

"Isn't that what it means to be a tourist?" Matsuda replied.

He had a point.

At Kyoto Station, we boarded the train bound for Arashiyama and began the journey to today's destination.

"This must be it."

Alighting from the train, we continued toward Tenryu-ji on foot. There were plenty of signs, so there was no chance of getting lost.

After a while, we arrived at an elegant traditional gate.

"So this is the Temple of the Heavenly Dragon. Does that name have any special meaning?"

"Beats me. Maybe we did battle in Kyoto in the past? I can't really remember."

Ddraig's memory seemed a little fuzzy on the details. If he *had* fought here, it must have taken place ages ago. The place definitely looked very different, so I couldn't fault him for not recalling perfectly.

Our tour group passed through the towering gate into the temple grounds and paid the entrance fee at the booth.

"Ah, you've arrived," came a familiar young voice.

I glanced around, spotting a blond-haired girl in a shrine maiden outfit.

"Kunou?"

"Yes. I'm here to show you around Arashiyama, as promised."

She had elected to conceal her beast ears and tail today, seeing as we were intermingling with normal people.

Matsuda and Motohama were astonished by the sight of this small blond-haired girl calling out to us. "Whoa, look how cute she is! Hey, Issei, what's the deal? You hitting on kids now?"

Curse that rude bald-headed buddy of mine! He had no idea what we'd gone through yesterday.

Motohama, on the other hand...

"...So petite, so adorable... Ha-ha-ha..."

...was suddenly huffing and puffing! Ah, I forgot! This guy really loved petite figures!

Seriously, Kunou ticked all Motohama's boxes! His glasses were glimmering dangerously.

However, another person threw him to one side, embracing Kunou. It was Kiryuu.

"Wow, she's adorable! Hyoudou, where did you meet this girl?"

Kiryuu was rubbing her cheek against Kunou's! Did she have a special fondness for kids?

"L-let go of me! Stop acting so familiar, you lowly slip!"

Kunou clearly wasn't enjoying this, but that didn't dampen Kiryuu's spirits. "She even talks like an annoyed little princess! How wonderful! What a perfect character act!"

This glasses-wearing high schooler was hopeless...

Letting out a sigh, I pulled Kiryuu away and began to explain. "This is Kunou. We met her the other day."

"Yes, my name is Kunou. It's a pleasure to meet you."

The fox spirit conducted herself with her usual dignity, as befit a real-life princess. Yet at the same time, she came across as standoffish.

"Ah, is she a friend of Rias Gremory? I did hear something about that hotel we're staying at being connected to Rias's parents' business."

"R-right, something like that."

Kiryuu's habit of jumping to hasty conclusions was working in our favor for once. Hopefully, I wouldn't have to try to justify too much.

With Kunou's introduction out of the way, I decided to push on to the next matter.

"Well then, Kunou. If you're going to be our tour guide, where should we go first?" I asked.

Kunou puffed her chest out, answering confidently, "I'll accompany you to *all* the famous sights!"

H-Huh... I suppose I should be grateful...

In a way, it was a kind of cultural exchange, after all.

"Would you show us around Tenryu-ji, then?"

"Of course!" Kunou responded with a buoyant and glowing smile.

And so Kunou led us through the Temple of the Heavenly Dragon, confidently and charmingly relating the stories and knowledge she had been taught.

It was heartwarming to see her working so hard to introduce Kyoto to us.

The Japanese-style garden behind the abbot's quarters was a sight to behold. It was laid out in an enthralling fall pattern and set against the backdrop of the autumn-colored mountains. The carp swimming in the pond were the final touch, perfectly completing the scene.

"The scenery here is beautiful. It's a World Heritage Site, after all," Kunou stated.

A World Heritage Site! Awesome! So that's why it's so inspiring! I have to take some pictures!

After viewing the garden, we headed into the temple hall. I glanced up at the ceiling and saw a painting of an overwhelmingly powerful dragon staring down at me with its formidable gaze! It was an Eastern dragon with a long slender body!

"That painting is called *Unryuu-zu*, the Cloud Dragon. No matter where you stand, it will look like it's staring straight at you."

Kunou was right. We moved here and there, but the dragon's eyes seemed locked on to us!

It really was amazing.

Hey, Ddraig? Are all Eastern dragons like this?

"Indeed, for the most part. It reminds me of Yulong, one of the Dragon Kings."

Ah, so Yulong was similar? Unlike Western dragons, Eastern ones gave off a more sacred vibe than a scary one. The word *ryuujin—dragon god—*was certainly appropriate here, but it seemed like there was more to it than that.

Unfortunately, we weren't allowed to take photos of the painting.

After finishing our exploration of the temple grounds, it was time to move on.

"All right, Kunou. Where to next?" I inquired.

The fox spirit girl looked excited as she pointed in one direction, then another. "Nison-in Temple! The bamboo path! Jojakko-ji Temple! I'll show you around all of them!"

When filled with such zeal, she acted like a typical girl her age.

And so, with this young princess leading the way, we continued to explore the sights Arashiyama had to offer.

"Ah, we've been to so many places," Matsuda said, breathing a deep sigh.

Per Kunou's suggestion, we were enjoying lunch at a boiled tofu restaurant.

After visiting Tenryu-ji, Kunou had taken us all around Arashiyama. We had seen the statues of the Buddhas Shakyamuni and

Amitabha at Nison-in Temple and taken a rickshaw ride through the bamboo groves. The sound of the wind blowing through the groves of bamboo had been nothing short of refreshing.

This had been my first time riding in a rickshaw, and it was fun. The man pulling it explained the various tourist sites as we journeyed through the autumn scenery of Arashiyama. Ah, I was sure glad we had come in fall.

"See? The boiled tofu here is exquisite." Kunou scooped out a piece from the pot in the center of the table and dropped it into her bowl. She was clearly enjoying herself.

This was likely her genuine smile, the sort she showed every day, which made it all the more heartbreaking that she had been reduced to begging us to help save her mother.

I wished there was something we could do to bring Yasaka back sooner...

I tried the boiled tofu Kunou handed me... What a delicious Kyoto specialty! This tofu was even better than what we had eaten at the hotel! I had heard that fresh tofu was the best, so it probably hadn't been long since this had been prepared.

"It's a very Japanese taste. Not bad."

"Yes, it's different to the usual tofu, fresher and more flavorful."

"Tofu is delicious..."

Xenovia, Asia, and Irina looked satisfied, too.

By accident, Irina's gaze met mine.

"..."

She was blushing! Every time I glanced her way today, she ended up like this! I-it must have been because of what had happened last night. That made sense. It must have been a major incident for an angel and a faithful adherent of the Church. She likely felt defiled after I'd touched her pure breasts...

My hands could still feel that lingering sensation. Th-they had been so supple and elastic, all but sticking to my fingers as they sunk in...

The only word that came to mind to describe that chest was *angelic*. Angelic breasts. It sounded like a brand name.

Thank you, Irina, I thought.

"Oh? Hey, Issei," a voice called out to me abruptly.

"Huh? Kiba? Right, you guys planned on coming to Arashiyama today, too."

Kiba and his group were eating lunch at the table beside ours.

"Yeah. Did you go to Tenryu-ji?"

"Sure did. The picture of the dragon there is really something."

"We're headed over there later, after seeing Togetsu-kyo Bridge. I'm looking forward to it."

"Togetsu-kyo Bridge. That's where we're going after lunch."

While I spoke with Kiba, another familiar voice entered the discussion. "Autumn in Arashiyama... It lives up to its idyllic reputation. Have you all been enjoying your fill of the place?"

It was Azazel! And he was sipping sake, even though it was still only noon!

"Teach! I didn't know you were coming here... And should you be drinking in the middle of the day?"

"I was thinking the same thing," replied Rossweisse, sitting across from Azazel. "No matter how many times I tell him, he won't stop drinking. I've explained repeatedly that this kind of behavior isn't appropriate in front of the students..."

Rossweisse was so angry that I could literally see the veins in her forehead throbbing!

"Come on, don't say that. I'm just taking a break after investigating the Arashiyama area."

Did that mean he'd been looking into the Khaos Brigade's activities?

"Honestly, Rossweisse, you've gotta learn to loosen up a bit. This is why you can't get a boyfriend, you know?"

Crash!

In response to Azazel's remark, Rossweisse slammed her face, which was now bright red, onto the table!

"Wh-wh-whether or not I have a boyfriend has nothing to do with this! Stop treating me like a fool! Augh! If *you're* allowed to drink, then *I* will, too!"

Whoa! She snatched away Azazel's cup and began to gulp it down!
Glug-glug-glug...
She drained the whole glass without even pausing...
"*Phew...* Just so you know, you've always got this attitude... You're always so, so, so... Ah..."
I-is she drunk?! That quickly?! She's already slurring her words!
"Y-you're tipsy from one glass?" Azazel questioned, obviously astonished.

Rossweisse poured herself another cup, emptying it in an instant. Then, fixing Azazel within her sights, she began to lay into him. "I'm not drunk, you. Do you know how many times I had to join that, that, that old *dotard* Odin? When *he* went out for drinks...? Huh? Hey, th-that reminds me... I put all that effort into tryin' to take care of him, and what do I have to show for it, huh? He's always talkin' up the ladies or going out for more booze! C-c-completely shameless! And he calls himself a *god*?! Bah! A-a-and all the other Valkyries in Valhalla kept calling *me* his nursemaid! Wh-wh-why did *I* have to take care of him like that? Why? And for *that* salary? Gimme a break! It's all *his* fault! It's *his* fault I don't have a boyfriend! His! Auuuuugggggghhhhh!"

...

She broke down into tears... Not even Azazel knew how to respond...
Azazel scratched his cheek before eventually saying, "I get it, I get it. Just let it all out, all right? I'll listen."
At this, Rossweisse's face lit up. "Really? I had no idea... Maybe there *is* somethin' good in you! Hey! We need another bottle of sake over here!"
She could still drink?! Th-this wasn't good... I had no idea that Rossweisse had such a bad drinking habit...
"Hey, you guys. Get outta here as soon as you're finished. I'll take care of this," Azazel instructed with a resigned exhale.
I exchanged glances with the other second-year students, and we all agreed to do as he advised. We rushed to finish our meals and filed out of the restaurant.

"Yep! There ain't no beatin' hundred-yen shops! Bwa-ha-ha-ha-ha-ha!" Rossweisse's drunken cackle sounded at our backs as we left.

The shop let out right in front of Togetsu-kyo Bridge.

"I wasn't expecting that from Rossweisse."

"Yeah. Who would have guessed she would end up like that after having a bit to drink?"

Matsuda and Motohama were clearly taken aback. Given Rossweisse's popularity with her students, boys and girls alike, it must have been astonishing for them to see her like that. Heck, I was shocked, too.

"Rossweisse might be young, but I'm guessing she's had a hard life. I'm not surprised she'd want to vent, considering she's stuck with *him*," Kiryuu said, nodding with obvious sympathy.

Azazel wasn't the only person stressing poor Rossweisse, though. Her former employer had been a perverted old lecher. Plus, it sounded as though she'd been treated poorly since becoming Odin's attendant. That woman had endured quite a bit.

"Is life always so difficult in your master's Familia?" Kunou asked me.

"…A-a little" was all I could manage in response.

There were a lot of good people in Rias Gremory's Familia, but we all had strong quirks and peculiarities.

That was enough worrying about Rossweisse. Our next stop was Togetsu-kyo Bridge! Having left the restaurant, we strolled through the tourist area for a few minutes until reaching Katsura River.

So that long, traditional wooden bridge that exudes historical significance is Togetsu-kyo? The mountain scenery behind it was superb! The slopes were covered in reds, yellows, and greens—a perfect autumn display!

"People say you shouldn't glance over your shoulder while crossing the Togetsu-kyo," Kiryuu commented.

"Why is that?" Asia asked.

"Well, Asia, if you do, Heaven will reclaim all the wisdom and intelligence it bestowed on you. If that were to happen to our Perverted

Trio, everything would be over for them. They would be nothing but a bunch of genuine idiots."

""""Shut up!"""" Matsuda, Motohama, and I responded in unison.

Kiryuu went on, unbothered by our interjection. "Oh, and one more thing. Another legend claims that you'll be separated from your lover if you turn around. It sounds like some childish jinx, though, so—"

"I won't look back! I won't!" Asia exclaimed, tearfully grabbing hold of my arm.

"I-it's all right, Asia. It's only a story," I assured her.

My words had little effect, however, as Asia shook her head and gripped me tight. "I *won't* look back!"

She's so cute! My adorable Asia! Ah, this is bliss!

And so we stepped foot on Togetsu-kyo. I spotted Kiba's group up ahead.

All the while, Asia stubbornly kept her gaze fixed straight forward.

"Damn, would you look at that? Issei and Asia are like a pair of lovers…!"

"It's a real shame, but look at them. They've turned into blind lovey-dovey fools."

Matsuda and Motohama were gossiping about us behind our backs! And calling us lovey-dovey fools! I wanted to punch the two, but I restrained myself. If I turned around, I would make Asia cry!

"I don't think you have to worry about it… That story about breaking up with a lover is just a rumor," Kunou said.

Be that as it may, Asia tended to take these things to heart.

We safely made it to the other side, and Asia let out a deep sigh, obviously relieved. Hadn't she realized we would have to cross it again to go back? Her ordeal wasn't over yet!

Now then, how were we going to tackle this side of the river? Just as I began to take in the scenery around me…

…a warm, slithery sensation washed over my body from seemingly nowhere.

......

Huh? What was that just now...?

I glanced around, suspicious, and realized that the only people standing around me were Asia, Xenovia, Irina, and Kunou. Kiba was there, too, a short distance away.

Matsuda, Motohama, Kiryuu, and all the other tourists had vanished! What was going on here?!

The others were just as shocked as me at this bizarre development, and they readied themselves. We surveyed our surroundings with wary gazes, yet there was no sign of any suspicious entities.

After a while, a fog-like substance began to rise around our feet.

"This mist..." Asia tensed when she saw the vapor. "There's no mistaking this feeling. When Diodora kidnapped me, that device he chained me to in that temple gave off a fog like this..."

"Dimension Lost," Kiba said as he approached. "One of the god-killing Longinuses. Azazel and Diodora mentioned it, right? This is likely Dimension Lost's doing again..." So saying, he knelt down, reaching out to touch the mist with one hand.

A Longinus... A Sacred Gear like mine or Vali's. Was that the cause of this weirdness?

"Are you all okay?" came a voice from up in the sky. Glancing upward, I spied Azazel soaring above, retracting his black wings as he stepped onto the ground. "Everything's vanished save for us. We've probably been transported to an alternate dimension of some sort and sealed inside... Judging by all this, it's probably a replica of the area around Togetsu-kyo Bridge."

Seriously? There had been no indication that we'd transported anywhere. Although I *had* felt a strange, slightly warm sensation. That must have been it.

"Is this like the kind of places used in Rating Games?" I questioned.

Azazel had just suggested as much, but this definitely didn't resemble the kinds of alternate dimensions I was accustomed to.

"Yeah. Someone must have leaked the special techniques used by the three great powers. This all looks like it was made the same way as your battlegrounds... So the power of that mist is capable of transferring people into a Trace Field, is it? Hmm. I guess Dimension Lost *can* move anything its fog touches... Bringing me and Rias's Familia here all in one go... Longinuses are scary stuff, eh?" Azazel remarked.

This was beginning to make sense. What we saw here was an application of the same technique employed to construct Rating Game arenas. The quality of this reproduction was certainly on par with what demons produced...

Kunou's voice trembled as she spoke from beside me. "I—I told you that we found my mother's bodyguard on the verge of death. He was surrounded by mist, too..."

In that case, this phenomenon and the individuals responsible for creating it were undoubtedly...

Evidently, my hunch was right on the mark.

I detected several presences approaching from the direction of Togetsu-kyo Bridge, slowly emerging from the vapor.

"Greetings, Governor Azazel and the Red Dragon Emperor, too, I see." The one addressing us was a black-haired youth dressed in a piece of traditional Chinese clothing draped over a school uniform.

It was a Chinese robe, right? I'd learned a little about Chinese clothing from my knowledgeable history teacher in middle school. It looked like some kind of national folk attire.

The guy held a spear in one hand, and that weapon gave off an uncanny aura. It was clearly no ordinary polearm.

He looked young—maybe a year or two older than me? But then, it was impossible to really tell from his appearance alone.

His companions were similarly garbed in school uniforms. They were all young men and women, likely around the same age as us.

An odd sense of pressure radiated from them, an atmosphere different from the sort that demons and dragons gave off.

Azazel stepped forward. "You're the guy in charge of the so-called Hero Faction, I take it?"

The guy at the center of the group looked over his shoulder before

answering, "I'm known as Cao Cao. I'm descended from the famed Cao Cao of the Three Kingdoms period...more or less."

Cao Cao...? Hold on, the Three Kingdoms period*?!*

Completely taken aback by this, I turned to Azazel. "Teach, is he...?"

The governor of the fallen angels allowed his gaze to drift from our enemies. "Listen up, everyone. Watch out for that guy's spear. That's the True Longinus, the strongest of them all. It's supposedly powerful enough to slay a god. It's been a long time since I last saw it... And in the intervening time, it's apparently fallen into the hands of a terrorist."

"""""—?!"""""

Azazel's words threw us into a panic. We were shocked more by Cao Cao's weapon than by the man himself.

"So that's the Holy Spear, feared by the seraphim of Heaven...!" Irina was trembling tremendously.

"I learned about it as a kid," Xenovia remarked in a low voice. "The spear that pierced Jesus, drenched in His blood... The most absolute of weapons, used to kill God!"

I-it was *that* powerful?! The prez might have mentioned something about a fabled spear used to stab Christ once before. C-come to think of it, that thing was intricately tied to the roots of Irina and Xenovia's religion. From the point of view of the Church, it probably wasn't an exaggeration to consider that thing a top-tier item.

"That's the Holy Spear...?" Asia stared at the weapon from behind me, mesmerized, as though it was somehow drawing her consciousness into it—

Azazel hurried to cover her face with his hands. "Asia. That thing's dangerous to true believers. It may rob you of your sanity if you gaze at it. After all, it's a holy relic, just like the True Cross, the Holy Grail, the Shroud of Turin, and the Holy Nails."

"You! I have something to say to you!" Kunou screamed at Cao Cao.

"Is that right, Your Highness? Please don't hold back. I'll answer your questions." Cao Cao's voice might have been calm, but it was clear from his tone that he knew something.

"Are you the ones who kidnapped my mother?!"

"Indeed," he admitted plainly.

So I was right, it *was* him!

"What are you doing to her?!"

"We require her cooperation for a little experiment of ours."

"An experiment? What are you plotting?!"

"It's all to fulfill our benefactor's wishes. At least, that's the official stance."

Kunou bared her teeth in evident rage. There were tears in her eyes. She was clearly furious, yet at the same time, at a total loss. Not only had her mother been abducted, but the perpetrators were also planning to use her in some kind of test.

"Your sponsor... You mean Ophis? What brought you to Kyoto?" Azazel demanded.

"There's no need for us to keep to the shadows anymore, so I thought we might meet in person for a little game. I've waited a long time to meet you, Governor Azazel. I've heard a lot about you, too, Red Dragon Emperor."

This bastard sure was getting on my nerves.

Hold on, am I really that famous? I guess I *had* defeated a leader of the old demon regime after triggering my Juggernaut Drive. Admittedly, I didn't *remember* doing it, though.

Azazel conjured a spear of light in his hands. "Let's keep this simple. Return the nine-tailed fox matriarch. We're trying to forge an alliance with the spirits here."

Seeing Azazel brace himself, we all similarly readied ourselves for combat. I activated my gauntlet and started the countdown for my Balance Breaker.

"Xenovia!" I called out, passing her Ascalon.

"Thanks!" she replied, accepting the weapon and taking a battle stance.

It was only then that I noticed Rossweisse wasn't with us.

"T-Teach. Where's Rossweisse?" I asked.

Azazel sighed. "She was transferred into this plane, too, but she's still sleeping all that booze off in the restaurant. I placed a pretty sturdy barrier around her, so she should be safe."

W-well, she probably wouldn't be able to fight in that state, so perhaps that was for the best. Fortunately, it sounded like Azazel had been thorough when it came to looking out for her.

Despite our side preparing for a fight, our opponents didn't do anything.

...Were they that confident? Did they have a secret weapon at their disposal? The Hero Faction was supposed to be composed of humans armed with Sacred Gears, right? To tell the truth, I wasn't looking forward to facing them. Sacred Gears possessed all sorts of peculiar and unpredictable abilities. Anyone in their right mind would've been apprehensive.

I had no intention of giving them an opening to attack, however!

Cao Cao turned to a short-statured boy standing beside him. "I'll let you handle these demons with your anti-monsters, Leonardo."

The boy remained expressionless, only nodding. Following Cao Cao's command, an eerie shadow began to spread beneath Leonardo's feet.

A cold, unsettling sensation ran down my back. Somehow, I felt as though some unspeakable horror was contained within that shadow.

The darkness stretched out, covering the entirety of Togetsu-kyo Bridge. Then it rose from the ground, gradually acquiring shape!

Arms, legs, heads, even eyeballs and gaping jaws all materialized—and there wasn't only one creature! There were tens...no, hundreds of them!

"*Waugh!*"

"*Gyargh!*"

"*Grrrrr!*"

The monsters emerged from the shadow with a chorus of ear-rending sounds. Or rather, maybe they had been created from it? The creatures were pitch-black and stood upright on two legs, with burly, muscular bodies. Worse yet, they all possessed razor-sharp claws and bared ferocious fangs. A group of them formed a line, marching toward us.

J-just what kind of power does that kid have...?

I gulped in spite of myself, astonished at what I was beholding.

"The Annihilation Maker," Azazel muttered.

Annihilation...? Maker...?

Cao Cao broke into laughter at Azazel's comment. "Very good. Yes, my friend here possesses another Longinus. Dangerous in a different way from my True Longinus, but incredibly deadly nonetheless."

A Longinus... So that kid possessed a god-destroying Sacred Gear, too? Come on, this wasn't fair! Since when did this become a Longinus smorgasbord?! All I really knew about those weapons was that Vali and I each possessed one, but now they were popping up one after another. It was enough to make my head spin!

At that moment, my countdown reached its end, and I activated my Balance Breaker! A red aura enveloped me, solidifying into a set of amor.

Now I would be able to put up a fight. And yet...

"T-Teach. I'm finding this a little difficult to follow...," I whispered.

"That boy has a Longinus like you. We've confirmed the existence of thirteen of them so far. We're working with a few of them in the Grigori. Anyway, out of all of them, the properties of those the Hero Faction has are head and shoulders more fatal than the Boosted Gear or the Divine Dividing."

"Y-you mean they're stronger than me?"

"In terms of raw power, you and Vali are leagues beyond. However, in terms of ability... You know how Kiba's Sword Birth can create all those Demon Swords, right?"

"Y-yeah..."

"The Annihilation Maker is similar. It manufactures all sorts of monsters. For example, it could form those massive fire-breathing creatures you see in movies, the ones more than a hundred meters tall. The power to birth monsters through pure imagination. Can't think of much worse than that, eh? That's what it's capable of. Depending on the user, it could be used to construct those things en masse. I'm talking dozens, even hundreds, at a time. It's one of the worst bugs imaginable in the Sacred Gear system, right up there with Dimension Lost. Just so you know, Dimension Lost can also be extremely hazardous depending on the skills of its wielder. Were its mist to extend across an entire country, it could hurl the nation and all its people into the void."

That was… Well, frankly, I didn't know *what* to think!

"Those Sacred Gears sound like world-class trouble!" I exclaimed.

"Luckily, none of them have reached that level yet. There have been a few close calls, though. Still, the True Longinus, the Dimension Lost, and the Annihilation Maker… It's unprecedented for three of the four top-tier Longinuses to be assembled in one place. The vessels of those Sacred Gears should have been under surveillance by either Heaven or the underworld from birth. Guess we've let our guard down these past few decades. Or perhaps…someone deliberately hid them. Locating Longinus users used to be a heck of a lot easier. As you can imagine, they tend to stand out." Azazel's eyes flitted to me during that last sentence.

Right, I was another of those cases. Initially, my Sacred Gear had been branded dangerous, and I'd been marked for death. After that, the belief was that my power had been misjudged, but then that was proven wrong when I displayed that I did possess massive strength.

Was there a connection here?

"…There must be some kind of causal relationship behind all this," Azazel said quietly. "The first Longinuses were said to be errors in the Sacred Gear system… Yet they've all undergone incredible developments that far exceeded our expectations. This is more a hope than anything else, but…watching you grow, Issei, it makes me think all the Longinuses have begun new transformations… It's inexplicable. Are these genuinely bugs, or are they evolutions? Maybe those of us who have been researching and maintaining the system have been too naive. That goes for me just as much as Michael and Sirzechs…"

Azazel was practically monologuing to himself now…

Still, wasn't a Sacred Gear capable of producing that many monsters on a whim a little unfair?!

And it was said to be even more dangerous than my own Sacred Gear?! Plus, if that Leonardo kid was good enough, he could create something on the level of a Dragon King like Tannin or that monstrous wolf Fenrir! That Sacred Gear was annihilation, all right! It sounded like it could destroy the entire world!

"What are their weaknesses, Teach?" I inquired.

If the Boosted Gear and the Divine Dividing had shortcomings, these Longinuses had to have them, too, right?

"Aim for the vessel's body. The user might be strong, too, but they won't be as bad as the Sacred Gear. The Annihilation Maker's vessel is still developing. The Khaos Brigade would have sent legions of monsters against the three great powers if he was capable of it, so now's our chance to defeat him before he reaches that level."

Right. Aim for the user. Leonardo didn't look particularly strong, so perhaps he was still in the midst of honing his Sacred Gear abilities.

Cao Cao, having overheard all that, scoffed. "Dear me. So you've worked the Annihilation Maker out, have you? Right on all counts, Governor. My young friend has yet to completely develop his imagination and potential. However, he *does* excel in one area—creating anti-monsters. These creatures here are all specially designed to fight demons." He waved a hand toward the horde of creatures, and...

...one of them opened its mouth wide!

Stzssssssssss!

It fired a beam of light!

The next instant—

Boooooooooom!

A nearby store was engulfed in a tremendous explosion!

"That light attack... It can't be!" Azazel cried out. "Cao Cao, you bastard! You sent all those infiltrators and assassins against us just to collect data to complete these anti-monsters?!"

"Well, you're half right. There were shadowy combatants among those Sacred Gear users, no?"

So that was it! Those fighters that had collapsed into mist when injured!

"My young friend created those monsters. We sent them against angels, fallen angels, demons, dragons, and the gods of various religious pantheons to gather valuable information for my friend's Sacred Gear. We learned a lot."

"It really *was* all about collecting data?!"

"Our goal was twofold—to increase our stock of Balance Breaker users and to develop these anti-monsters. Our efforts produced soldiers specialized in fighting demons, angels, and dragons. The ones designed to fight demons can wield light comparable to that used by a mid-ranking angel."

Then that attack a while ago had been intended to push more Sacred Gear users to unlock their Balance Breakers while also gathering intelligence required to make these anti-monsters...

Was Cao Cao trying to show off how well prepared the Khaos Brigade was? This guy was a real pain!

Azazel glared at our enemies in contempt but snorted in laughter. "Cao Cao, what you're saying is that you've yet to create any *god-killing* monsters?"

"..."

Cao Cao said nothing to refute this accusation.

"How did you figure that out?" I asked.

"If they could slay a god, they would have," Azazel responded with a grin. "And then they'd deploy those creatures against us. There's no reason why someone capable of attacking multiple other powers simultaneously wouldn't do so at the first opportunity. There's no telling what effect it would have on the world if they slew the deities of every religion. I guess it's fortunate they haven't manufactured a monster capable of doing that yet. It might only be a small detail, but it's valuable info."

Oh, I get it! They don't have any anti-god monsters! Ah, but that reminds me of something!

An image of a massive wolf flashed in the back of my mind.

Cao Cao pointed his spear our way. "Any gods I want to slay, I can do so with this... Now then, let the battle begin."

That was a declaration of war!

"""*Grrrrrrrrrr!*"""

A horde of those anti-monsters charged toward us, letting out terrible growls!

Kiba and Xenovia quickly readied themselves to meet them as our first line of defense!

"Kiba, sorry, but I need you to make me a Holy Sword."

"Got it. You're better off fighting with two blades, after all."

Kiba quickly forged a fresh blade, tossing it to Xenovia, who snatched it from the air, readied herself in a dual-bladed stance with Ascalon, and dived straight into the enemy ranks!

She vanquished a swath of those anti-monsters all at once! As expected of one of our powerful Knights! The force of her offensive strike was unbelievable!

Uh-oh.

Another of those anti-monsters opened its mouth, releasing a beam of light Xenovia's way...

Stzssssssssss!

The radiant bolt surged toward her, until Kiba intercepted it with his Holy Demon Sword, reflecting it into a nearby building, which promptly collapsed into a pile of rubble.

"Against this level of light, we'll be fine so long as we don't suffer a direct hit," our pretty boy Knight explained.

Right on! With his breakneck speed, Kiba wouldn't have any problem dodging!

"We'll just have to take them all down before they can hit us," Xenovia responded as she carved through the horde of anti-monsters with her two Holy Swords.

They were both Knights, but they fought with distinct fighting styles!

"I guess I'll take you down, then, Cao Cao!" Azazel said as he pulled out a gemstone—the one that contained the soul of the dragon Fafnir—and used the artificial Sacred Gear to produce a set of golden armor! Twelve black wings unfurled from Azazel's back as he charged straight for Cao Cao!

"I'm honored! To think that I'm fighting the biblical governor of the fallen angels!"

Cao Cao alighted on the shore of the Katsura River, readying his spear with a fearless grin. At that moment, the tip of the spear spread open, releasing a scintillating golden aura solidifying into the form of a blade!

The moment the tip of that spear bloomed, the very air around us began to vibrate!

What divine power! I thought. Just laying eyes on it was enough to make me recoil at the immense, suffocating pressure! To think that it could possess such a strong effect on someone with as little faith as me!

Booooooooooom!

Violent shock waves erupted all around as Azazel's spear of light clashed against Cao Cao's Holy Spear! The impact of the two weapons' collision caused the Katsura River to swell, with water rising up over Togetsu-kyo Bridge and crashing like a violent rainfall.

The two combatants exchanged blows while moving downstream.

We could leave Cao Cao to Azazel, but that meant we would have to handle the rest!

Our first priority was to assemble a defensive wall around Asia! As our healer, she was essential to our team! Normally, the prez would be in command, with Akeno offering support and suppressive fire. Koneko would engage in a mix of offense and support, while Gasper would scout ahead and back us all up. Unfortunately, we would have to make do without them. Even Rossweisse, who specialized in magic offense, wasn't here to provide assistance.

Azazel and Irina were super-powerful offensive fighters, but we were still five core members short, leaving our team wholly unbalanced. We would need to think of a new battle plan.

On top of that, we had to protect Kunou, too. Here in Kyoto, her safety was more important than ours. We would definitely have to keep her close to Asia.

Xenovia lunged forward into the vanguard—

Think! Think, dammit! This is no time to say I don't know or I can't. I need to act like a King! What would the prez do? How would she respond to this situation?! Think!

I racked my brain trying to come up with an idea, and thankfully, I hit upon something!

"Xenovia! Stick close to Asia and Kunou! Protect them! Use your holy aura to take care of any enemies that try to get close!"

Like that, I started handing out instructions!

I know I'm not the prez, Xenovia, but please hear me out!

"—. Got it!"

Yes! She was quick to respond, retreating to defend Asia!

Come on, think! What would the prez do if she were here? We had fallen victim to a surprise attack and were embroiled in real-life combat! It was up to us second-year students to find a way out of this!

I pushed my insufficient smarts to the limit once more!

Bah! Blood spurted from my nose from pondering so hard...! Heh-heh. Evidently, erotic thoughts weren't the only thing that could trigger a nosebleed!

Our opponents were sending an army of anti-monsters designed to fight demons after us. We could try to deflect their attacks, but if one managed to connect, it would surely cause tremendous damage.

Suddenly, I recalled Kiba's unique abilities.

"Kiba! You can make light-absorbing Demon Swords, right?" I called.

"Huh? Yes... Right!"

He understood what I was hinting at almost immediately! Way to go, Kiba!

Several of the darkness-infused blades he'd wielded against Freed in our battle against Raynare appeared at his feet! He didn't waste a second before passing them around to the rest of us!

"In their inactive state, these swords are just hilts! You'll need to channel your demon powers into them to activate the blades!" he instructed.

"Xenovia! If you're in trouble, use that as a shield to absorb any light attacks! Asia! I know you aren't used to fighting this way, but hold on to one of Kiba's swords! It's better than nothing!" I hurriedly added.

"Got it, Issei!" Xenovia responded.

"O-okay!" Asia added.

Xenovia placed the inactive hilt in her pocket, ready in case of an emergency.

I, too, received one of those weapons from Kiba.

"Hey, Ddraig. Can my gauntlet absorb this thing's powers?"

"There's a high chance it will reduce your life force if you try something excessive like that... But in this case, you might be able to pull it off. So long as you keep it brief. Don't overdo it."

"That's fine. I'll plug it into the gauntlet where the Ascalon is normally kept!"

So saying, I inserted the handle of that light-absorbing darkness blade into my gauntlet!

Immediately, a dark shield emerged from it. Success!

This should help me defend. Next up is...

Our angel, Irina!

"Irina!" I called out, glancing her way. "Sorry about this, but I need you to take Xenovia's place in the vanguard with Kiba! Being an angel, you aren't weak against light, are you?"

"I-it might not be a *weakness*, but it can still hurt me! However, I suppose I *am* stronger than a demon here... All right! I'll do it! I'm Lord Michael's Ace, after all!"

With a flap of her white wings, she leaped forward to take Xenovia's position!

Summoning a sword of light, Irina plunged through the air, tearing into the line of anti-monsters until she found a gap in their formation, and began to lay waste to them.

My strategy might have been somewhat crude, but at least I'd given orders to everyone! I hadn't spent all that time by the prez's side during battle for nothing! I was the only one left, and my place was in the center, between Kiba up front and Asia in the back!

"Asia! I need to Promote to a Bishop!" I shouted.

"Okay!"

With Asia's permission, I took on the properties of a Bishop, and my small reservoir of demonic magic swelled to new heights. I did this to concentrate my powers into a volley of Dragon Shots.

I knew full well what my demonic powers were capable of, and it was time to put them to use! My attacks might have been clumsy and born from pure demonic energy, but in terms of raw power, they were nothing to sneeze at!

"Take this! Dragon Shot!"

Boom! Boom! Booooom!

Bracing myself with my darkness shield, I hurled a barrage of medium-sized spheres of demonic power straight into the swarm of heroes and anti-monsters!

The heroes were able to dodge, but I succeeded in annihilating a huge swath of anti-monsters! At the same time, my darkness shield absorbed all the enemy attacks coming my way! So far, so good!

I similarly deflected a beam of light arcing for Kunou with another Dragon Shot!

"Kunou! Fall back a little!"

"S-sorry..."

We would have a major issue on our hands if this Kyoto princess got injured, and it was wrong to expect a child to join in the battle.

Xenovia loosed attacks from behind, using her Holy Sword to launch destructive waves aimed for the anti-monsters!

The shadowy creatures soon began to succumb to the assault coming from me and Xenovia.

Nonetheless, that huge shadow stretching beneath that hero kid continued to birth more and more of those things! Dammit! There was no end in sight! Still, we couldn't give up! Producing those creatures en masse must have required considerable concentration and physical strength! He would tire out sooner or later! After all, he was just a kid!

Those anti-monsters managed to score a blow every now and then, but Asia was quick to heal any wounded, so we weren't taking major casualties.

She was, quite literally, our lifeline. Asia was the best!

The heroes made no attempt to attack us themselves, merely evading our strikes and sending the anti-monsters in. It was unsettling to watch. Were they just planning to observe from the sidelines as their minions did all the dirty work?

But at that moment, as I unleashed another Dragon Shot, several figures rushed toward me! They were all uniform-clad girls! Did the Hero Faction have its own uniform or something?

"We'll handle the Red Dragon Emperor!"

They were brandishing spears and swords as they closed in!

"Stop! Women can't hope to win against the Red Dragon Emperor!"

cautioned a slender white-haired guy with several swords sheathed at his waist.

Heh-heh. It was true. No girl could defeat me! I quickly concentrated my demonic energy, focusing it into my brain. This was one of the few techniques I had mastered!

"Breasts! Unburden yourselves! Boob-Lingual!" I released my demonic energy toward the group of girls, and a mysterious space unfurled around me. I had activated the ability perfectly! "Come, ye breasts! Tell me your secret intentions!"

The boobs began to respond in voices only Ddraig and I could hear!

"We're gonna confuse him with a feint, then attack together!"

Ah, so they were planning a coordinated attack?

"I'll take him from the right."

So that one would attack from that direction!

"I'll charge from the front."

And that one was planning to approach me head-on!

Ha-ha-ha! Having heard their thoughts, I opened my eyes! *Bwa-ha-ha! Thank you for letting me read your breasts!*

"Yargh! Augh!"

I evaded every incoming blow.

"Impossible! Did he foresee our movements?!" one of the girls cried out, clearly bewildered.

"As if! Our joint attack is supposed to be perfect!"

I flashed the flustered girls a dauntless grin. "Oh, I foresaw them, all right! Or rather, I spoke to them! Your breasts! Now take this! Dress Break!" I shouted.

Yes, while dodging their attacks, I had made sure to brush my fingers against each of their outfits!

Bwa-ha-ha! I rejoiced at the glorious sound of their garments being torn to shreds!

"E-eeeeeeek!"

"He cursed our clothes... And now they're gone!"

The girls shrieked in alarm as they tried to conceal their naked bodies. Hmm! They must have all been working out, as they all had wonderful proportions! I could feel another nosebleed coming on!

They were so embarrassed that they quickly fled to a nearby building.

Heh-heh-heh. Against women, there was no stopping my fantasies! Ah, it felt wonderful to execute my perverted combo so effectively! Used together, my Boob-Lingual and Dress Break techniques were unstoppable!

"Wh-what a foul technique. I've never seen something so terrible..." Kunou was completely taken aback by my fighting style.

Hearing a remark like that from the mouth of a child wounded my spirit a little...

"I thought as much," commented the slender man who had given the warning earlier. "It is nearly unthinkable for a woman to defeat the Red Dragon Emperor. She would need an iron will and the strength to fight without shame... A challenge indeed for any young lady. You are true to your name, Breast Dragon. Now I, too, have borne witness to your famed techniques. However, they are useless against a man."

H-his calm analysis of what I had just done was kind of embarrassing...

"Who would want to use them on a guy?!" I responded.

Seriously, where was the fun in that?!

The man's lips curled in a smile, and he turned to his fellow heroes. "Be careful, everyone. This is the Red Dragon Emperor. He may be the least talented individual to ever bear that title, but he's dangerous nonetheless. Unlike the others, he hasn't succumbed to his immense power. Rather, he's working to conquer it. There's nothing so terrifying as someone graced with power and yet who doesn't fall to arrogance. Watch yourselves around him."

...

Having to shoulder a compliment like that was pretty awkward.

"...I've never heard that from an enemy before."

This was truly a first. I suppose it wasn't praise exactly. More of a warning, perhaps...

The man tilted his head slightly to one side. "Is that so? From our perspective, you're more dangerous than you realize, Red Dragon Emperor. As are your companions...and Vali, too."

Man, this was so weird! Just what was going on here? Sairaorg had expressed a high opinion of me as well, but hearing the same thing from *terrorists*...

Facing opponents who didn't look down on me was surprisingly difficult!

"Now then, I suppose it's my turn," the man remarked as he stepped forward, unsheathing a blade at his waist. "It's a pleasure to meet you all, members of the Gremory Familia. I'm Sieg, a descendant of the hero Sigurd. My friends call me Siegfried, but you can address me however you please."

Xenovia must have seen something in Siegfried's face, for she looked surprised. "...I thought I recognized you. I guess I was right?"

Irina also nodded. "Yes, it must be. Looking at all those Demon Swords he's carrying, there can be no doubt."

What were they talking about? The only person he reminded me of was Freed because of the white hair.

Looking to Xenovia and Irina, I asked, "What's wrong, you two? Do you know this white-haired bad-guy version of Kiba?"

"'White-haired bad-guy version of Kiba'...? That wasn't called for, Issei," responded the real Kiba.

It was only an analogy...

Xenovia was the one to answer. "He's an exorcist, a former colleague of Irina's and mine, and one of the strongest warriors out of all branches of the Church—Catholic, Protestant, and Orthodox included. Chaos Edge Sieg. He was trained by the same organization as Freed. That's why they've both got white hair. It's probably a side effect from an experiment..."

An exorcist! And related to the Church?! In other words, he was just like Freed? Ugh, even thinking about that guy made me ill.

"Sieg! Have you turned your back on the Church?! Have you betrayed Heaven?!" Irina cried out.

Siegfried's lips curled in a grin. "You could think of it that way, I guess. I belong to the Khaos Brigade now."

At this, Irina's temper visibly flared. "How could you?! Forsaking the Church and joining hands with an evil organization means eternal damnation!"

"...That stings," Xenovia grumbled, scratching at her cheek.

Although she was capable of wielding Durendal, she *had* decided to become a demon out of desperation.

Siegfried chuckled softly. "I don't see the problem. With or without me, the Church still possesses the strongest of warriors. *He* alone can make up for my absence and Xenovia's. Still, who would have expected him to be in the running to become a Joker in that Brave Saints system...? All right, now that we've introduced ourselves, how about we go at it? I'm eager to test myself against the famed Durendal-wielding Xenovia; Archangel Michael's Ace, Irina Shidou; and Yuuto Kiba's Holy Demon Swords." Siegfried issued his challenge to our three sword fighters—all with connections to the Church—while the blade in his hand emanated a powerful aura.

That weapon was pulsating with an intimidating quantity of energy. Was it a Demon Sword? Something about it reminded me of the ones Kiba created.

—!

Suddenly, Kiba lashed out with a Holy Demon Sword at breakneck speed!

Claaannnng!

Kiba's strike had little effect, however, for it was caught by Siegfried's blade, its ominous aura unwavering.

"A strike from your Holy Demon Sword is nothing to Gram, the Demonic Emperor Sword. It's the most powerful of all Demon Swords," Siegfried boasted.

Kiba and Siegfried pushed their locked weapons against each other. I couldn't remember when I had ever seen Kiba work to push back an opponent's sword!

Both of the men broke their clash, adjusting their stances before engaging in a violent duel, each strike producing sparks.

"...Is he equal with Kiba...? No..."

Kiba was gradually losing ground. His expression was growing more tense by the second! His opponent was matching his incredible speed! Siegfried could keep pace with movements that were too swift for my eyes to follow. It was unbelievable!

Even Kiba's feints to draw his opponent out and create an opening were ineffective!

Siegfried met every cut with the minimum movement necessary, countering with his own weapon.

Kiba seemed to have his hands full evading, leaving him incapable of countering!

Despite possessing a Balance Breaker, he was being pushed back by this opponent...! I was dumbfounded!

One of the enemy heroes began to explain. "They might belong to different groups, but in our organization, Arthur with his Holy King Sword and Siegfried with his Demonic Emperor Sword are practically identical in ability. Yuuto Kiba's Holy Demon Swords are no contest."

So that Arthur guy was this strong, too? I suppose he *had* been toying with Fenrir during our climactic battle! B-but in that case, could Kiba...?

I glanced his way in alarm, only to find another combatant entering the fray—Xenovia.

She charged at Siegfried from his side, trying to assist Kiba.

"Xenovia!"

"Kiba! You can't do this by yourself! You might not like it, but I'm gonna help!"

"—. Thanks!"

Kiba had evidently set aside his pride as a swordsman, and he moved into a joint attack with Xenovia.

"Me too!" Irina added.

That made it three against one!

With Xenovia grasping a blade in either hand, Kiba wielding a Holy

Demon Sword, and Irina armed with a sword of light, the trio leaped into a simultaneous attack!

The fight moved so fast that I was unable to see the tips of their swords... Siegfried was now fending off three opponents all on his own!

Kiba moved swiftly enough as he parried Siegfried's strikes that he appeared to be in several places at once. Xenovia lunged down from above, her Holy Swords wreathed in an incredible aura! Meanwhile, Irina glided through the air, thrusting her sword toward Siegfried from behind!

It was an expertly honed combination assault!

I felt certain of victory while I spectated. Yet with a flick of his hand, Siegfried managed to somehow block Irina's attack without needing to glance her way!

At the same time, he drew another blade from its sheath at his hip with his free hand.

Cling!

A sliver of argent light carved clean through one of Xenovia's blades as she brought it down!

That was the Holy Sword Kiba had given her! It shattered like glass!

Siegfried hadn't broken a sweat. "Balmung. A legendary Demon Sword of Norse legend. And that was just one strike."

Another Demon Sword! However, Kiba was thrusting straight for Siegfried's blind spot! He was trapped now! There could be no evading this! Both of that silver-haired guy's arms were already busy! With a horizontal slash, Kiba lashed out, and...

Cliiiing!

...a metallic noise cut through the air.

Kiba's Holy Demon Sword had been blocked by a fresh blade that Siegfried had just drawn from his waist!

"Nothung. Another legendary Demon Sword."

A third one?! What was most astonishing of all, however, was that Siegfried was already brandishing two other weapons. He shouldn't have been able to use another.

Inexplicably, a third arm had emerged from his back to grasp this new blade, parrying Kiba's attack!

Wh-what the heck is that limb?!

It looked like it was covered in silver scales! There was an eerie similarity to when my arm took on its dragon form.

And it was sticking out from Siegfried's back!

He grinned to see us taken aback. "This arm? It's a Twice Critical. A pretty standard Sacred Gear, but mine's a little special. A subtype, if you will. I can form a dragon's arm on my back."

A Twice Critical?! I'd heard that term somewhere before! It was a kind of Sacred Gear that ranked lower than my Boosted Gear. As I recalled, it should have taken the shape of a gauntlet, though. Was that whole "subtype" thing the reason it came out of his back?!

Siegfried readied himself with a Demon Sword in either hand and a third one gripped by his extra limb—a triple-wielding fighting style!

Kiba's expression tensed at this revelation. "...We're both Sacred Gear users, yet even putting his swords aside, I can't match the abilities of his Sacred Gear..."

"Just so you know, I haven't activated my Balance Breaker," Siegfried added.

What a brutal announcement!

I couldn't afford to forget that after all their experiments, these heroes had all undoubtedly unlocked their Balance Breakers.

But he'd fought Kiba, Xenovia, and Irina—the three of them fighting together, at that—to a standstill in his normal state?!

Fwoosh.

Azazel alighted nearby during the battle.

Cao Cao, meanwhile, rejoined his hero comrades.

Had they circled back to their starting point after a volley of attacks? I quickly glanced downstream, following the course of the river, and saw only destruction and smoldering earth!

Whhhhhoooooaaaaa! I had thought their contest must have been dramatic, given the explosive sounds I'd heard in the distance, but all of the Arashiyama scenery had been destroyed!

Knowing this was an artificial replica of the real thing, Azazel must have gone buck wild with his most powerful spears of light.

His armor was broken in a few places...and his black wings were clearly disheveled.

Cao Cao's uniform and robes were similarly torn here and there. I was beyond impressed. He'd held his own against the legendary fallen angel governor...?!

So this is the power of a hero... Or perhaps, of the True Longinus...

"...Don't worry, Issei. Neither of us went all out. It was just a little scuffle," Azazel stated.

That "scuffle" had left the whole downstream area utterly devastated!

"Your Familia makes a fine team," Cao Cao said as he cracked his neck. "Perhaps I should have expected as much from the servants of the famous demon youth Rias Gremory. I'd assumed this would be easy, but you've proven me wrong. If my assumptions are correct, it was your power, Issei Hyoudou, that brought all these unusually capable individuals together. You may lack natural talent and demonic potential, but your dragon qualities have attracted some of the best fighters. They do say that dragons excel at gathering strength, no? For better or for worse, *you* clearly excel in that respect. The continuous stream of famous beings seeking to battle you, your encounters with each of the Dragon Kings, and the support of all your *Breast Dragon* fans are proof enough. Even in the absence of your King, you have managed your Familia with exceptional calm. It might have been a naive and flawed strategy...but I shudder to think what you might accomplish with more experience."

"..."

I hadn't even considered those possibilities. Everything that had happened...was because of me?

Cao Cao narrowed his eyes in an amused expression. "That is why we do not intend to make the same mistakes as the old demon regime. I firmly believe you will one day be the most dangerous of all Red Dragon Emperors. The other members of your Familia pose similar threats. Thus, by engaging you now, we have hopefully attained valuable data for analysis."

W-was that how they saw me? Us? These heroes definitely regarded us as far more than the old demon regime did.

…We were in a bind. I wasn't used to dealing with opponents like this! Until now, my foes had always underestimated me, which led to them letting their guards down…

"I have a question for you," Azazel stated. "What is the Hero Faction after?"

Cao Cao didn't try to disguise the mirth in his eyes. "Lord Governor. This may come as a surprise, but our goals are simple—to know the limits of what it means to be human and to test them. It will be humans who overcome demons, dragons, fallen angels, and every other supernatural force. Yes, it will be humans who prevail."

"So you want to be heroes? I guess you *are* descended from them."

Cao Cao pointed up to the deep-blue sky. "This is but a small challenge from a band of frail mortals. We wish to discover the heights to which humans can aspire. That's all."

Humans…

They wished to learn what humans were truly capable of? That was their goal?

No, they had to have some other motive, too…

Azazel let out a tired sigh. "…Issei. Don't get careless. This guy is more formidable than Shalba, the former leader of the old demon regime. Remember that anyone who seeks you out is going to be pretty damn strong. This guy ranks up there with Vali in terms of the danger he poses."

Cao Cao was as formidable as Vali… If his attitude and bearing were any indication, he might have been even stronger…

And to think that he wielded the ultimate Sacred Gear, the Holy Spear, too. Talk about menacing…

Now that Azazel had returned, we adjusted our battle formation, and our enemies did the same. More anti-monsters rose from the shadows. There was no end in sight. Moreover, the enemy had, for the most part, been holding back.

Now, however, they were truly readying themselves. The second wave, it seemed, would be the genuine battle. By the look of it, they had more Sacred Gear users and Balance Breakers, too.

Lately, my life felt like one crisis after another. Would that goddess of salvation appear to me again this time? I didn't think I could rely on the blessings of some god of breasts for aid again...

My mind was racing, when...

Vrrrr-rrrrr...

...a magic circle, in a design I had never seen before, unfolded in the space between our group and that of the heroes...

"That's..."

Azazel seemed to recognize the pattern. Who was it? A fallen angel?

The figure who emerged from the light was that of a cute girl, a foreigner wearing what resembled a wizard's outfit.

A—a girl? I was taken aback.

She had a large wide-brimmed hat and a cape. She truly did look like a mage... Judging by her appearance, she may have been around middle school age? She was quite petite.

After turning to face us, she bowed deeply.

"Greetings," she said to us with a broad smile. "I'm Le Fay, Le Fay Pendragon, a mage on Team Vali. I'm so happy to meet you all."

Sh-sh-she belongs to Vali's team?! Why is someone from his group here?!

"...Pendragon?" Azazel said to Le Fay. "Are you related to Arthur?"

"Yes. He's my older brother. He's always looking out for me."

She was the cruel noble swordsman's sibling?! I would never have guessed he had a cute younger sister!

Azazel scratched at this chin. "Le Fay? I guess you're named after the legendary sorceress Morgan le Fay, then. I suppose the legend does say that Morgan was a blood relative of the hero Arthur Pendragon..."

Le Fay was staring at me, her eyes positively sparkling.

"U-um..." She stuck out her hand as she approached. "I'm a huge fan of the *Breast Dragon* TV show! I-if you don't mind, could I shake your hand?"

...

E-er...

I was so dumbfounded that I didn't know how to react. H-how could she request that in the middle of a battlefield?

In any event, I mumbled thanks for her support as I took her hand.

"Yippee!"

Le Fay was truly overjoyed... What was she doing here, exactly?

Cao Cao watched on, clearly as stunned as we were. After a moment, he rubbed the back of his head and let out a sigh. "You're with Vali? What are you doing here?"

Le Fay answered his question without hesitation, her smile still radiant. "I've brought a message from Vali! 'I thought I told you not to get in my way.' That's it! And you need to be punished for trying to spy on our team!"

Booooooooooom!

The earth shook violently as a tremendous roar erupted.

Wh-what now?! An earthquake?! It took all my strength to keep standing! Asia and Kunou had already tumbled to the ground.

Cr-crash!

That was the sound of something breaking! Desperately looking around, I saw that the land had split open, and a gigantic figure was emerging! Tearing through the dirt, flinging away huge masses of soil, was—

"Graauuuuuuuuuuuuu!"

A titanic creature!

Wh-wh-wh-whaaaaat is that thing?! Was it made of stone? Boulders? I couldn't tell, but it was definitely inorganic. Its arms and legs were enormous!

It had to be at least ten meters tall!

Azazel stared up at the creature. "A Gogmagog!"

Le Fay nodded. "That's right. Gokkun is our team's power specialist!"

Gokkun?! How could they have given it such a cute nickname?!

"Teach? What *is* that stone giant...?" I asked, frightened to hear the answer.

Sorry for asking all these questions today, Teach!

"A Gogmagog. It's a type of golem-like entity abandoned in the dimensional void in a state of suspended animation. They're mass-produced superweapons some ancient deities created. They should have all ceased functioning by now, though."

A golem! I—I see! So that was why it seemed so unnatural!

"There are things like that in the dimensional void?! But look at it! It's moving! That isn't suspended animation!" I said.

"Yeah, this is the first working one I've ever seen. Honestly, I've got tons of questions about this, too. I thought they were all abandoned in the void and nonfunctional. To see one in working condition... I'm bursting with excitement!"

Ah, Azazel's eyes were glimmering like those of a young child... He sure had a fondness for old artifacts and weapons created by the divine.

Still, he quickly regained his composure, muttering, "I see. So Vali wasn't just hanging around the dimensional void to spy on the Great Red..."

"That's right," Le Fay answered. "Vali was searching for Gokkun. Ophis mentioned finding a working giant in the dimensional void once, so we went hunting for it."

"H-hey, so who else exactly is on your team...?" I questioned.

They already had the descendant of Sun Wukong, Fenrir, and a golem, so I was feeling pretty nervous about eventually fighting them one day...

"Hmm. Well, there's Vali, Bikou, my brother Arthur, Kuroka, li'l Fenrir, Gokkun, and me. Seven in total."

Okay, so they had seven members. Still, this was too much! It was a band of one big name after another!

"Teach... I thought the Great Red occupied the dimensional void..."

"The dimensional void is the final destination for things that are a pain to dispose of any other way. The Great Red just likes swimming around in there, and they don't do him any harm. He's a special being. Basically, he's not among anyone's rankings or hit lists. All he wants to do is float through the void unhindered...," Azazel replied.

At that moment, the Gogmagog raised its fists over the assembled heroes before bringing them crashing down!

Booooooooooooooooooooooom!

With a tremendous *smash*, the golem crushed Togetsu-kyo Bridge in a single swing.

Whhhhhooooooaaaaa!

That was one of Arashiyama's famous sights! It was a good thing this was only a replica of the real thing!

The golem's strike eradicated a large number of the anti-monsters. The heroes, however, had all managed to leap to safety on the other side of the river.

"Ha-ha-ha! It looks like Vali's angry! He must have realized we were keeping tabs on him!" Cao Cao laughed, aiming his spear toward the golem.

"Take this!"

Swoosh!

The Longinus's tip extended, piercing the golem's shoulder.

Cr-cr-crash!

The huge golem recoiled from the blow, crashing to the ground! Whoa! The impact felt like another earthquake! That thing had to be impossibly heavy! The entire area was shaking back and forth!

Cao Cao's spear had knocked the golem down in a single hit! It certainly had a lot of functions, being able to generate blades of light and lengthen at will!

Now that the bridge was destroyed, the only way across the river was by flying, right?

I pondered our next move. And that was when another figure appeared, swaying uncertainly on the far shore.

It was a familiar silver-haired woman…Rossweisse!

"…Blurgh… Why are you all makin' so much…so much damn noise?! People are tryin' to sleep round here! Can't you just…? Can't you all just *shut up*?!"

She's still drunk?! And pissed, too!

The band of heroes glanced at one another, puzzled at the sight of this approaching drunkard. No sooner did they realize that she was a member of our Familia than they prepared to attack!

This was bad! In her present state, Rossweisse was in serious danger! We had to go help her!

But before we could race across the river...

"Huh? What's this? You want to go? You betcha. I wasn't that old codger Odin's bodyguard for nothin'. I'll give ya all a taste of this Valkyrie!" she cried, and far too many magic circles appeared around her. There must have been hundreds!

"Norse magic! This'll counter anythin'! Any attribute! Any spirit! Any damn divine being! Eat thiiiiisssss!"

Fwooooooooooosh!

A tremendous amount of energy erupted from Rossweisse's arrays, spiraling through the air and raining down on the band of heroes!

Wh-whhhhhoooooaaaaa! I marveled. It was incredible! Fire, light, water, electricity—magic of every type conceivable was ripping through all in its path as it bore down on the heroes!

Houses, shops, the road. Nothing was spared. Rossweisse laid all to devastation!

I had known she was an expert magic user, but I'd never imagined she could level an entire town!

Perhaps I should have expected as much after how well she had fought during our battle against Loki.

The prez sure knew how to pick good members... Rossweisse would undoubtedly do well in the Rating Game.

Mist began to enter my field of vision. Just when it looked like that magical assault was about to tear through the band of heroes, a youth wearing a robe over his uniform unleashed a fog from his hand, repelling the barrage.

—! *That mist technique!*

It was capable of defending against Norse magic attacks!

More vapor flooded from the mage's hand, shrouding all of the heroes.

"Perhaps this is getting a little *too* chaotic," Cao Cao said from within the fog. "But it was a splendid appetizer. Governor Azazel!"

Cao Cao paused for a moment before declaring brightly, "We'll be holding our experiment tonight at Nijo Castle, using Kyoto's unique force field and your nine-tailed fox madam! If you mean to stop us, please do attend!"

The mist thickened. Until a moment ago, it had only been wafting around our feet, but now it had risen to our chests and faces.

White vapor shrouded everything. I couldn't see more than a few centimeters ahead.

"We're back to normal reality, everyone! Put away your weapons!" Azazel called out.

Our group was returning to the real Arashiyama! It wouldn't do to be seen like this! I quickly dispelled my armor.

...

In the blink of an eye, the fog cleared, revealing Togetsu-kyo Bridge, busy with tourists like nothing was out of the ordinary.

The bridge wasn't destroyed. Meaning this *was* reality.

"Hey, Issei. You look like you're about to murder someone. What gives?" Matsuda asked, staring my way.

R-right, we'd only just crossed the Katsura River in the real world.

"...It's nothing," I answered evasively, letting out a deep exhale.

My fellow Familia members were wearing similarly grave expressions. Relaxing after all we'd been through wouldn't be easy...

Le Fay was gone, and the same went for that massive golem. Had they vanished at the same time as the mist?

Slam!

Azazel struck a nearby electricity pole. "Damn punks...! An experiment in Kyoto...? Who do they think they are, messing around with us?!"

Whoa... He was seriously ticked! I hadn't seen him get this angry in a long time.

"...Mother... My mother didn't do anything wrong... Why...?" Kunou was trembling.

All I could do to comfort her was stroke her head.

First Cao Cao's sudden attack, and now that experiment at Nijo Castle.

Prez, it looks like our school trip is hurtling toward an unexpected climax.

Life.4
Showdown in Kyoto! The Gremory Familia vs the Hero Faction!

"Ah, I'm stuffed! An all-you-can-eat buffet with Japanese, Western, and Chinese food! Yep, it's good to be a student of Kuou Academy!"

"You can say that again."

Matsuda and Motohama seemed fully satisfied, lounging in their room after a luxurious dinner and a soak in the public baths.

After the fight at Togetsu-kyo Bridge, we did some sightseeing around Nijo Castle before returning to the hotel.

I was visiting my two buddies in their room. Tomorrow was the final day of our trip. The plan was to explore the area around Kyoto Station and buy some souvenirs. We were currently using the flat-screen TV in Matsuda and Motohama's room to review the photographs we'd taken thus far.

"My pervert friends, feast your eyes on these four beauties fresh from a relaxing bath," Kiryuu announced as she entered the room, dressed in her pajamas. Asia and the others were following behind her.

"Whoa! I've always wanted to see Asia in her pajamas after a wash! All right, let's make this a viewing party!" Matsuda, in high spirits, started playing a slideshow of all the photographs he had taken.

The stream of images began on the bullet train, then moved to Kyoto Station, proceeded to the hotel, Fushimi Inari Shrine, Kiyomizu-dera, and then featured Kyoto scenery we had viewed over the past few days.

"This was when Motohama almost fell down the stairs."

"Matsuda, wasn't that when you stuffed your face with sweet rice dumplings at that restaurant and managed to get them all stuck in your throat?"

"You know, I wish you'd quit staring at girls from other schools with those perverted eyes of yours. You didn't have to bring those expressions all the way to Kyoto... It reflects poorly on the academy."

We all burst into laughter as Matsuda, Motohama, and Kiryuu shared their thoughts on our adventures thus far.

Our once-in-a-lifetime school trip.

As I enjoyed the little viewing party, I clenched my fist in determination.

No matter what happened, I would face tomorrow together with my friends.

And then we would all go home to Kuou Academy.

Once the viewing party had concluded, with bedtime approaching, the present members of the Gremory Familia, Irina, the Sitri Familia, Azazel, and Leviathan gathered for a meeting in my room.

We were using my quarters to discuss what was going to happen tonight—the experiment those no-good heroes intended to enact at Nijo Castle.

To be honest, though, my room wasn't large enough for a gathering like this. There was nowhere to sit. But that was what happened when you tried to fit more than ten people into a room only eight tatami mats in size.

Xenovia and Irina were taking part in the discussions from inside the closet... Did they like it in there or something?

Rossweisse still looked rather pale from her day drinking, but she was nevertheless attending the gathering. She had apparently taken some medicine to sober up, and she claimed to be back to normal, but she still didn't look well.

Azazel cast his gaze around at each of us before spreading a map of Kyoto in the center of the room. "Let's go over our strategy, then. Right now, the area around Nijo Castle and Kyoto Station is on high alert.

I've mobilized all those in Kyoto connected in one way or another to demons or fallen angels to keep an eye out for any suspicious individuals or activities. The spirits of Kyoto are helping, too. From what I can tell, the Hero Faction hasn't made a move yet, but we've detected several disturbing outflows of energy centered on Nijo Castle."

"Disturbing outflows of energy?" Kiba repeated.

"Yeah. Back when it was first built, Kyoto was laid out based on yin-yang and feng shui principles. Because of that, there's a lot of so-called power spots scattered all over the place. Think the pentacle at Seimei Shrine, the statue of the Jizou of Happiness at Suzumushi-dera Temple, or the *Hizamatsu* Pine at Fushimi Inari Shrine. There are more places here filled with mysterious powers than you can count. But now the outflows of energy are all out of whack and are concentrating on Nijo Castle."

"What's going to happen?" Saji asked, audibly swallowing.

"I don't have a clue, but it definitely ain't gonna be good seeing as they're using the nine-tailed fox matriarch who governs the mystical side of this city in their *experiment*. We're gonna have to base our plan around that point."

Once everyone nodded with Azazel's explanation, he continued. "First, the Sitri Familia. You'll be on guard around Kyoto Station. Your job is to defend the hotel. It's already protected by a strong barrier, so we should be able to avoid the worst if everything goes bottom up. Still, if any suspicious characters get near, your task is to deal with them."

"""""""Okay!""""""" the members of the Sitri Familia answered in unison.

"Next up, the Gremory Familia and Irina, too. Sorry about always throwing you in the deep end, but you're on the offense. Once we're done here, I want you to head to Nijo Castle. To be honest, your enemy is gonna be an unknown quantity. This could end up being a dangerous gamble, but your first priority is to rescue Princess Yasaka. Get her and escape ASAP. Hopefully, that will be enough to muck up their little plan. There's always a chance they were lying about that test, but given Cao Cao's attitude, it could be true. Then again, it could have all just been a ploy to get us involved."

"A-are we strong enough to face them?" I questioned.

It was all well and good to put us on the offense, but even with Irina, we were only five in total. Considering the strength and numbers of those heroes, there was no way that would be enough!

Azazel nodded. "Don't worry. I'm bringing in some professionals to assist. They've been our strongest reinforcements in a bunch of skirmishes with the Khaos Brigade. With them on your side, your odds of success should be a bit better."

"Reinforcements? Who, exactly?" Kiba pressed.

"Just think of them as a massive help. Seriously, this is good news," Azazel said, his lips curling in a pleased grin.

If he was willing to go that far in his praise, they *had* to be pretty skilled, right?

Still, who were they? He wasn't talking about the prez and Akeno, was he?

He couldn't possibly mean the Satan Rangers...right? I doubted it. Still, we could really do with their aid right now!

"Also, I've got some bad news. We only have three vials of Phoenix Tears to go around this time."

"O-only th-three?! Th-that won't be enough! We're going to be fighting terrorists!" Saji responded in an obvious panic.

"Yeah, I know, but demand has skyrocketed, what with the Khaos Brigade's attacks all over the world. None of the major powers have been able to secure adequate supply at their key bases. Phoenix Tears were never something that could be mass-produced. On top of that, the House of Phenex is having a bit of trouble, too. Phoenix Tears were always a luxury, but the price for vials has skyrocketed. There's even a rumor going around that the rules for Rating Games are gonna have to be changed when it comes to the tears. You'd better keep that in mind for your future matches."

Whoa... The situation's that serious? Honestly, it wasn't the most astonishing development. With Khaos Brigade attacks on the rise, there were more casualties and an increased need for recovery items. When you looked at it that way, this was an obvious outcome.

"This is still top secret, but each of the factions is searching frantically for more individuals with Twilight Healing Sacred Gears," Azazel confessed. "They're rare, but there *is* more than the one Asia possesses. Locating them would be a massive advantage, while also denying the Khaos Brigade a critical asset. Letting them get their hands on such a powerful healing skill would be trouble. Also, the current Beelzebub, Ajuka, has been conducting his independent research on healing abilities, but he hasn't yet— Ah, well, there's no need to discuss that now. I've got the Grigori experimenting with artificial healing-type Sacred Gears, too. In fact, Asia's been providing us with vital help on that front. The results look promising."

Asia's face turned red at this praise.

I'd had no idea! It sounded like super-classified stuff, so it made sense that no one had filled me in, but still... Asia was making herself useful behind the scenes in the underworld. She was such a generous and selfless individual! Seriously, I was overflowing with pride!

Although she didn't enjoy fighting, Asia kept up her training as well. If the chance presented itself, she might even unlock her Balance Breaker, right? I couldn't wait to see what effect it would have on her abilities.

"All right, that's the general situation. I'll give two vials of the tears to our offensive team, the Gremory Familia, and the other one to the supporting team, the Sitri Familia. Use them wisely."

""""""""""Yes, sir!"""""""""" we responded as one.

Azazel directed his attention to Saji. "I'm gonna need you to join the Gremory Familia during this operation."

Pointing to his own face, Saji said, "M-me?" Although an evidently unexpected order, Saji seemed to immediately recognize his role. "...Because of the Dragon King?"

"Yeah. We're gonna use Vritra—your Dragon King state. Those black flames can keep opponents contained and absorb their powers. You'll support the Gremory Familia like you did in that battle against Loki."

"S-sure, but I'll lose consciousness and go out of control."

"That doesn't matter. Issei will help bring you back like he did last time. Issei, we're counting on you to get through to him. You're a Heavenly Dragon, so you should be able to rein in a Dragon King."

"R-right!"

I *had* successfully done it before. When the time came, I would be there to help Saji.

Irina raised her hand. "Um, have each of the factions been informed about this?"

I was curious about that, too. *Had* they? I'd been explicitly instructed not to tell the prez about anything.

"Of course. A whole lot of demons, angels, fallen angels, and Japanese spirits are gathering on the outskirts of the city. They're maintaining a siege so those bastard heroes won't escape. If we've got a chance to bring them down here, we're gonna do our best to take it," Azazel responded.

"I'll be in charge of coordinating the outer forces!" Leviathan added. "If those naughty kids try to flee, we'll round them up!"

Leviathan's tone of voice was as buoyant and cheerful as ever, but I knew from experience that if the situation got out of control, she, too, was likely to start rampaging...

"I've also contacted Sona at Kuou Academy. It sounds like they're going to back us up however they can," Azazel stated.

Ah, so the chairwoman and the vice-chairwoman were ready for action, too!

That left only our Familia's Two Great Ladies and my underclassmen...

"Teach, what about the prez?" I inquired.

Azazel frowned at that. "Yeah, I tried to reach out... Chalk this up to bad timing, but they're visiting the underworld right now."

I cocked an eyebrow. "Did something happen?"

Azazel nodded in response. "Apparently, there was a riot or something in an urban region of the Gremory territory. They're busy responding to it, from what I hear."

A—a riot?! Don't tell me this is the Khaos Brigade's doing?! And the prez and the others are dealing with it alone?!

Azazel flashed me a forced grin, trying to calm my panic. "Some followers of the old demon regime are behind it. There doesn't seem to be any direct connection to the Khaos Brigade. Still, they're wreaking havoc, so Rias and the others had to get involved. It will be *her* territory someday, after all... Grayfia's assisting her as well. And with her in the fray, those rioters are as good as toast. It's hard to trust the veracity of this, yet, supposedly, Lady Gremory is out there, too. Whoever's responsible for the trouble in the underworld will be in for hell dealing with *three* Gremory women," Azazel said with a shudder.

Wow. Both Grayfia and the prez's mom had joined in.

Just thinking about the prez, Venelana, and Grayfia was reassuring. They were each an encouraging presence.

"The Flaxen-Haired Madame of Extinction, the Crimson-Haired Princess of Annihilation, and the Silver-Haired Queen of Extermination all fighting together... Heh-heh, those no-goodniks will be in for a treat!" Leviathan listed off those extremely ominous aliases with far too much joy...

Extinction, annihilation, and extermination... Those titles all but screamed *Don't touch me!*

Gremory women sure had formidable reputations. I got the impression that neither Rias's father nor her brother Sirzechs dared opposing their wives in private...

"...Sounds like you've got a rough future ahead of you, too." Azazel rested a hand on my shoulder, nodding.

Wh-what was that supposed to mean? I didn't really follow. However, I wasn't about to tick off the prez or anything. At least, I didn't intend to do so *intentionally.*

Azazel cleared his throat and turned back to the whole group. "That's it for my battle plan. I'm gonna take to the skies and try to scout things out. I want you all in position within the hour. If you spot anything unusual, check in immediately. And don't die, you hear me? Until we're back at Kuou, this is still your school trip... We'll protect Kyoto with our lives. Understand?"

"""""""""""Yes, sir!"""""""""""" we responded, and with that, our strategy meeting came to an end.

*   *   *

After completing my battle preparations, I went down to the hotel lobby, where I had arranged to meet Asia and the others.

It looked like I was the first of my group to arrive, but I spotted Azazel and Rossweisse sitting at a table on one side of the room.

No sooner did he notice me than Azazel raised a hand, calling out, "Issei? Good timing."

"Yes?"

What now? I approached uncertainly, when Azazel retrieved something from his pocket—an object resembling a shining red jewel.

"So there was another would-be molester outside the hotel earlier trying to fondle a woman's breasts. I made sure he didn't... And then this came flying from his body. It got me thinking..."

The molester had dropped a gemstone...? Why was Azazel giving it to me? And why had there been so many incidents like that since we had arrived here?

"That gemstone..." Ddraig's voice sounded aloud so that both Azazel and I could hear.

"What is it, Ddraig?" I asked.

"Yep, that's what escaped that box while you were on the bullet train."

...

Wh-wh-wh-whaaaaaaaaaat?! This?! This gemstone?!

"I thought as much. I detected your aura when I analyzed it." Azazel nodded, his suspicions, it seemed, confirmed.

Naturally, I'd told him what had happened when I'd tried delving into my Sacred Gear on the train. Azazel had attempted to use his resources to locate whatever I had lost, but he had been unsuccessful.

He handed me the crimson jewel.

Hmm... Doesn't seem to be any real change after taking it... What do you think, Ddraig?

"There's no mistaking it. It's pulsing with the same energy as me and you. No, wait..." All of a sudden, Ddraig sounded somehow dejected.

"Wh-what is it?" I asked.

"...I've started inspecting the data in that gem...," Ddraig explained,

his voice one of low dismay. *"Your possibilities, what was in that box... They've been passed around Kyoto from one person to the next...by touching people's breasts."*

Wh-what did he just say...? That didn't make any sense.

Azazel broke out into a chuckle, as though he had just solved some great puzzle. "Ah, I see. So all those groper incidents throughout Kyoto were caused by your possibilities—this jewel—moving around. Basically, anyone, man or woman, who came into contact with this thing would become obsessed with feeling up other people's chests."

"S-seriously...?! So you're saying all those groper incidents were because of my potential...?"

Had whatever been inside that box developed a love for boobs because I was the Breast Dragon...?

Matsuda had undoubtedly been the first affected. That would explain why, when he was sitting across from me on the bullet train, he had tried to touch Motohama's chest.

From there, it had spread around Kyoto, until arriving here...

I felt like I owed an apology to all the unwitting gropers and their victims. They were *all* innocents in this!

"So, Ddraig, what's the story with the jewel?" I asked.

Now that I had regained it, had anything changed? Did I gain a new power?

"...I can't say. Your power has definitely increased, and yet... T-to think that your abilities could develop by touching the breasts of so many people in this city... Is it really okay to unlock your potential like this...?"

There was no need to ask that! I had no idea what to do about this, either! I hadn't had the faintest clue that the situation would turn out like this!

"...You've caused a great deal of trouble to the people of Kyoto... You're going to have to find some way to aid those accused of being perverts, Issei," Rossweisse stated solemnly.

Obviously. It would be inexcusable to abandon all those who'd been arrested unduly. I would have to help them!

"I'll figure out how to handle that. But I wonder whether Issei's potential was trying to collect a certain type of power? Maybe something other than demon or dragon power. *Breast power*, perhaps...? Knowing him, I wouldn't be completely shocked if that was the case." Azazel tilted his head to one side in consideration.

Breast power... I-is there really such a thing?

"Trying to save some people while causing headaches for others... You're incomprehensible, Issei... I feel like throwing up..." Rossweisse continued to voice her disapproval as she raised a hand to cover her mouth.

Azazel let out a sigh. "Are you all right? You went a little wild, got drunk, and wreaked destruction earlier, you know. I heard you vomiting since we got back to the hotel, so it doesn't seem to me like you're one to be criticizing right now..."

"I—I don't want to hear that from you! If you hadn't gone drinking in the middle of the day... Ugh, I'm going to be sick..."

"I admit I was wrong," Azazel conceded. "But are you really going to be okay?"

"...I need to use the restroom."

Rossweisse went rushing off to the toilet! *W-was she still recovering?*

"...The Vomiting Valkyrie. Anyway, that gemstone belongs to you, so just hold on to it for now, Issei. I haven't got a clue what you're gonna have to do to release its power, though," Azazel said.

Right, that was the best thing to do here. I didn't want to cause any more trouble in Kyoto!

But what *would* I have to do to unlock this power? Ddraig evidently didn't know, either. I guess I would just have to hold on to it, then.

Welcome home, my potential.

I'd nearly forgotten that there was something I wanted to ask Azazel before the operation began.

"Um, Teach?"

"What now?"

"What kind of person was Cao Cao? I mean, the one from the Three Kingdoms period."

I didn't know much about the *Records of the Three Kingdoms*, but if our opponent was descended from that historical Cao Cao, it would be best to learn whatever I could.

"What *do* you know?" Azazel asked me right back.

I scratched my cheek. "...Er, he was Liu Bei's rival, right? A bad guy, I think."

Cao Cao was the enemy general constantly interfering with Liu Bei's plans.

At least, that was the impression I remembered from a manga I'd read as a kid and a puppet show I recalled watching.

Azazel broke out into a grin at this. "Well, you probably got that impression from the *Romance of the Three Kingdoms*. The real-life Cao Cao *was* responsible for a lot of death and destruction, but he also played a key role in a bunch of important political developments. However, if you ask me, his biggest strength was in gathering talented individuals around him."

"Gathering people?"

"Yeah. Cao Cao would make use of anyone who showed potential, no matter their background. That was why the state of Wei became so powerful, because of the people he recruited. Ironically, the Hero Faction's Cao Cao has also turned his attention to gathering useful followers. He seems to be interested in people with all kinds of talents. But there's an important difference between the two. The current Cao Cao is basically assembling useful resources by kidnapping them. And he isn't interested in angels or demons, only humans. That seems to be the Hero Faction's only principle, and their objective, when they seem to have one. To see that goal come to fruition, the current Cao Cao is more than happy to resort to terrorist methods, like brainwashing his forced recruits. If you ask me, staging terrorist attacks to increase your number of Balance Breaker users and develop the Annihilation Maker is crossing a red line."

I may have been a demon, but I was also a former human. Thus, I was surprised to realize that, in spite of our common heritage, I had no reservations about fighting Cao Cao.

It was a simple fact that I had been transformed into a demon.

Intrigued by this new way of life, it seemed I had dived headfirst into my new reality.

Demons had long life spans, and so painful though it was, I knew I would have to part with my human friends and family one day. Still, I wouldn't refuse to smack down a bad guy just because they were human.

Wait, do these hero guys fight out of some strong sense of justice or necessity to oppose evil? That is what heroes are supposed to do, right?

All this was too much for me to process...

Regardless, terrorism couldn't be permitted. Abducting people and conditioning them to join your cause was nothing short of inhumane.

Whatever their purpose, from where I was standing, *they* were the wicked ones.

Azazel craned his neck as he stared across at me. "What's the matter?"

"I was just thinking about what it means to be human or to be a demon... Or a hero, for that matter... I know that isn't really like me... The core members of the Hero Faction are all descended from famous real-life champions, and their abilities rank up there with those of angels and demons, right? But what does it really *mean* to be a hero? I'm not talking about the dictionary definition—I mean, like, to genuinely be one."

As ignorant as I was, even I knew that heroes were supposed to be saviors. I wanted to know what set these members of the so-called Hero Faction apart from ordinary humans.

"Heroes are people with special powers and abilities. In principle, they're supposed to use those talents to defeat evil and to carry out great deeds for the benefit of humanity. You could say that some people are born with the ability to become heroes. Honestly, it's really just because they have Sacred Gears. Those weapons are supposedly gifts bestowed by God to certain humans to help them save others, and yet... Suffice to say, not all Sacred Gear users become champions of the downtrodden. They don't always find happiness, either. Merely being born with the ability to become a hero doesn't necessarily mean someone *will*. There are plenty of folks out there who abuse their talents."

Born with the ability to become heroes... That was incredible. I was seriously jealous of them.

"Heroes... When I was still human, I always wanted to be one. I was as average as they come, and now I'm going to actually fight a hero... Heh. I'm a demon now and a dragon, so I guess I make a good bad guy, huh?"

"Are you worried about being a demon? About facing a hero—a human? Geez. Just what do *you* wanna be, Issei? What do *you* wanna do?" Azazel questioned.

"I want to be a high-class demon and a harem king!" I responded without hesitation. "But I still want to go all out for the prez and her Familia as well!"

"That's good enough, isn't it? Just keep working toward that. You can do it, right?" Azazel replied, breaking out into laughter.

At that moment, something clicked inside me. "Huh. I guess you're right. Oh, and one more thing. I'm going to save Kunou's mom!"

An innocent little girl was suffering because of those hero jerks. I had to help her!

Azazel ruffled my hair softly. "Good, good. I'm glad you've worked it out. But you'd better remember, you might be okay with it, but Asia and the others are gonna be facing humans as well, and they might hesitate. Take the lead, and they should stick with you. Just keep up what you've been doing. That'll help everyone else grow."

I guess the spirits of my other Familia members depended on my actions.

"Got it! I'll charge ahead with my friends at my side!" I declared.

Before long, my companions began to gather in the lobby.

As we left the hotel, we met the members of the Sitri Familia near the entrance.

"Don't overdo it, Gen."

"That's right, Gen. We promised to buy souvenirs for the chairwoman tomorrow, remember?"

"Right. Thanks, Hanakai, Kusaka."

"Genshirou, show those terrorists what the Sitri Familia is made of, all right?"

"You betcha, Yura."

"If you find yourself in danger, fall back to safety."

"I've been practicing, Meguri."

Saji's companions offered encouragement for him as we left. I'd heard that he'd grown closer to the other members of his Familia over summer break.

Unfortunately, he didn't appear to have made any progress with the chairwoman. The same could be said of me and the prez, though…

I let out a tired sigh, and Kiba placed a hand on my shoulder. "In the president's absence, you're our substitute King, Issei."

Wh-what?! I was taken aback by this sudden vote of confidence!

"—! S-seriously?! *I'm* our King?! Are you really okay with that?!" I asked, pointing to myself in bewilderment.

Kiba frowned doubtfully. "What are you saying? You've always said how much you want to become a King, independent of the president. That being the case, it's only natural for the rest of us to look to you for instruction, don't you think?"

"I—I guess that tracks… Still…"

Was I up to filling Rias's shoes? Doubt was building in my gut.

"During the battle earlier today at Togetsu-kyo Bridge, you were the one who told us what to do, even if we did have our backs to the wall," Kiba continued. "I can't say whether your strategy was the best one available to us, but we all came out of it in one piece. So I think you did a fair job, and I believe you should take charge again tonight."

Kiba…

He approved of the amateur orders I had issued out of desperation.

Xenovia, standing beside me, voiced her support, too. "That's right. Irina, Asia, and I work better when we're following someone else's commands. You might have taken the leader role on the spur of the moment, but it was thanks to you that we all managed to get back on track without the prez."

"Yep, yep. But don't act overly impulsive, all right, Issei?" Irina cautioned.

"Yes. You can't afford to overplay your hand," Asia added.

"I'm a newcomer to this team, so I'll leave this to you, Issei. You're my senior here, after all," Rossweisse said, looking as though she might throw up again... Would she really be okay?

Everyone was looking out for me and thought I had done a fair job... I was reminded just how great it was to be part of this Familia. A guy couldn't have asked for better companions.

Prez! I'll overcome any challenges as part of your team!

Huh? I couldn't help but notice what Xenovia was holding in her hands... It looked like some long object, wrapped in a cloth embroidered with magic symbols... Ah, I had a good idea what it might be.

Noticing my gaze, Xenovia lifted the weapon up. "Ah, this? It just arrived back from the Church—the new and improved Durendal."

So I was right! I'd suspected as much after hearing on the bullet train that Xenovia had sent the blade to the Church for some modifications.

"There won't be any time to test it before the fighting, but that's par for the course for Durendal and me."

I was curious to find out how much it had been strengthened. Even in its original state, it possessed enormous destructive force. If it was easier to control now, Xenovia could probably take a more proactive role on the battlefield.

"Sorry. I got a little carried away talking to everyone," Saji called as he rejoined us, waving his hand in apology.

The other members of the Sitri Familia cheered us on as we parted with them.

"Good luck taking the offense!"

"Let's catch up tomorrow!"

Now it was only us members of the Gremory Familia, Irina, and Saji.

"All right. Let's get moving."

And so we made for Cao Cao's designated battlefield—Nijo Castle.

After departing the hotel, we headed to the bus terminal at Kyoto Station.

From there, we'd take the bus to Nijo Castle. For appearance's sake, we were all wearing our winter uniforms. Xenovia and Irina were in their usual Church-issued combat outfits underneath. That way, if the fighting got intense, they could remove their uniforms for freer movement.

"Ugh…" Rossweisse covered her mouth with her hands.

She was still battling the occasional bout of nausea. Honestly, she still seemed in poor shape. Just how much had she drunk?

Over the course of this trip, I'd seen many sides to Rossweisse that I hadn't known existed. When we went home, I would have to try to make sure to keep her away from any alcoholic beverages.

At that moment, while waiting for the bus at the terminal, something suddenly leaped onto my back.

"Red Dragon Emperor! I'm going, too!"

It was a young blond-haired shrine maiden—Kunou. What was with this girl? Wasn't she supposed to be waiting in Kyoto's spirit realm?

"Kunou?! What are you doing here?"

Clinging to my back, hanging off my shoulder, she tapped me on the cheek as she responded, "I'm going to save my mother!"

—! H-hey!

"This is going to be dangerous. Didn't our Demon King girl and fallen angel governor tell you to leave this to us?" I said.

"Yeah, but still! I want to… I want to help save my mother! Please! Let me go with you! Please!"

Kunou was literally begging me. If I were to call Azazel, he would definitely send someone to pick her up and get her to safety… I understood how Kunou felt, though.

Maybe having her along would improve our odds of rescuing the nine-tailed fox matriarch?

All right. I would take responsibility for her. I would do my best to respect her feelings.

Before I knew it, a thin fog had begun to gather at our feet.

At the same moment, a warm, vaguely slippery sensation washed over my body.

It was the same feeling from before! Dimension Lost!

No sooner did we all realize what was occurring than the mist engulfed us.

When I came to my senses, I was staring at a subway station platform.

The sign hanging overhead read Kyoto, so we must have been on one of the underground subway platforms.

Had we been transported here?! We'd been doing a lot of teleporting recently!

A quick glance around revealed that my friends were gone. Initially, I thought I was alone, but...

"...I-is this a subway platform?" Kunou asked, still hanging from my shoulders.

Evidently, she'd been brought here with me.

"Looks like we got caught in the same thing that happened earlier," I remarked.

"S-so is this another copy of Kyoto in an alternate dimension? Those baddies have unbelievable powers..."

Kunou was right. It was one thing to catch us in that fog, but to re-create the entire Kyoto Station in an artificial battlefield was nothing short of incredible.

All of a sudden, my cell phone began to ring. It was Kiba. Had he been dropped nearby? Honestly, I was more stunned that my phone still worked than anything else!

"Hello? Kiba? Where are you? Have you been transported to this weird dimension, too?"

"Yeah. I'm at the Kyoto Imperial Palace. Rossweisse and Saji are with me. Where are you?"

"I'm with Kunou. We're on a subway platform in Kyoto Station. Hold on, let me check my map."

I set Kunou down from my shoulder and retrieved my map,

spreading it out on the ground. We'd all been provided with these before setting out.

Kyoto Imperial Palace is...here! Northeast of Nijo Castle... Wait, hold on.

"This battlefield is pretty big, isn't it? I mean, if it stretches out this far from Nijo Castle..."

"Indeed. They must have recreated the city of Kyoto, with the castle as the epicenter. Rating Game battlefields can be this vast, so that isn't particularly unusual, but whoever designed this place must have done a lot of research."

Maybe we could use this as a training opportunity before our next match? At least an area this size would offer us plenty of opportunities to move around.

"Kiba, how about we assemble at Nijo Castle?"

"Understood. Have you managed to contact Asia and the others? They must have been teleported here as well. I guess those heroes decided to give us a direct invitation."

"Right, I'll try calling them. See if you can get in touch with Teach and the others. Seriously, bringing us all here with no warning whatsoever..."

I ended the call with Kiba and reached out to Asia and the others. Our Church Maiden Trio were all together. It was a relief to know that Asia had Xenovia and Irina by her side. If she were alone, I would've been too worried to think of anything else.

I asked them to meet us at Nijo Castle as well.

After that, I checked in with Kiba once more. Apparently, he'd been unable to report to Azazel. Any attempt I made had the same result.

This was strange. We could contact one another from within this space, but communication with those outside was a no go. Rossweisse posited through Kiba's phone that our opponents might have placed a special barrier or some other magical technique over the artificial space.

Yet if they could do that, why were they all right with letting us talk to our teammates within? It really made no sense.

Whatever the case, thinking about it wasn't going to get me anywhere. I had to focus on reuniting with the others, and that meant getting to Nijo Castle.

We had taken the subway from Nijo Station to Kyoto Station on the way back to the hotel after checking the place out earlier in the day. That being the case, I could probably make my way there by following the subway line.

I started my gauntlet countdown so that I would be able to move quicker. Above all, we were in enemy territory. I had to be ready for anything.

"Welsh Dragon: Balance Breaker!"

A flash of red light enveloped my body, solidifying into a set of armor.

Kunou watched with admiration. "Hmm. I saw you do that earlier today, but your Heavenly Dragon armor really is beautiful. So *this* is a legendary dragon."

She tapped her hand against my Scale Mail here and there, positively brimming with interest. Her sense of curiosity was no different from the reactions of my other young fans. She may have spoken like a princess, but at heart, she was still just a child.

How could someone have robbed this girl of her mother? No matter their reasons or motivations, I couldn't forgive those heroes for abducting a woman who'd done no wrong.

"Kunou. I'll save your mom. Don't leave my side, all right? I'll protect you."

Kunou's face turned bright red at this declaration. "O-okay!"

She was blushing. It was so cute!

Unfortunately, I sensed a hostile presence approaching while we spoke.

I peered farther down the platform, and I spotted a man dressed in the uniform of those heroes walking toward us.

Malevolence emanated from him, and it was directed squarely at me. There could be no mistaking it—I was his target.

He came to a stop a short distance away, breaking out into a grin. "Good evening, Red Dragon Emperor. Do you remember me?"

...Nope. I didn't have the faintest clue who he was.

"I...don't have the best memory," I answered.

At this, the man's grin soured. "Fine. I suspected as much. I'm probably just a small fry to the likes of you. Why *would* you remember me? But thanks to the powers I gained during our last bout, I'm capable of going toe to toe with you."

The man's shadow began to move and swell, as though alive.

At that sight, I suddenly recalled a black-cloaked figure capable of controlling shades. He'd redirected attacks through them...

"Ohhh. You're the Sacred Gear guy who attacked my hometown, aren't you?"

The man chuckled. "Correct. You messed me up good back then. Things are going to be different this time, however. The regret, the fear, the anguish that you drummed into me has pushed me to the next level. So now I'm going to show you the skills of a *real* shadow wielder..."

A dull rumbling sounded as an indescribable sense of pressure bore down on me. The shadows projected by the pillars and vending machines around us began to twist uncannily.

His voice low, the man declared, "Balance Breaker."

The low-pitched sound grew more intense...

The sense of foreboding that the man was exuding continued to increase as the shadows gathered toward him, rising up and wrapping around his body. They enveloped him whole...and then they began to take shape, shifting into what looked like an armored figure.

A full-body suit of armor comprised entirely of darkness? It was just like *my* Balance Breaker.

"Kinda resembles yours, don't you think?" he whispered in evident amusement, as though having read my mind. "Yes, when you defeated me, all I could think about was building a stronger defense. I needed armor like yours. That's how much your terrible attack power left an impression on me, Red Dragon Emperor. This is the evolution of my Sacred Gear, the Night Reflection. In its Balance Breaker form, it becomes the Night Reflection Death Cross. How about I give you a taste of what you did to me last time?"

The man's dark suit writhed with eerie life. His face was heavily shrouded, enough so that only his gleaming eyes were visible. Appearance-wise, he looked like a monster…

Without Asia, I probably wouldn't be able to use a Promotion. Yep, my luck was running thin before the battle had even started…

Still, this would make for good practice. I would just have to do my best without a Promotion!

Heh, maybe my confidence had improved with my skills. I no longer felt anxious before a fight. Perhaps that was the result of being in so many heated conflicts. Admittedly, I wasn't *entirely* calm. I trembled slightly in uneasy anticipation.

That wouldn't stop me from fighting, however. With a few Rating Games and clashes with super-powered opponents like Vali and Loki under my belt, the sight of an enemy activating their Balance Breaker no longer filled me with fear or uncontrollable trepidation.

After all, my daily sparring partner, Kiba, had a bunch of Holy Demon Swords!

Vrrrrrrrrr!

I clenched my fists and fired up the booster on my back!

I lunged toward my opponent at tremendous speed, ready to strike with my left fist, and yet…

Fwoosh!

…my strike passed clean through him! His body seemed to scatter like smoke, and there was no impact whatsoever! My target was completely fine… It felt like I'd punched a cloud.

I immediately glanced over my shoulder before dashing toward my opponent again, this time loosing a strong kick.

Fwoosh!

Yep, as I'd half expected, this attack didn't connect, either! I returned to my original position, adjusting my battle posture.

My opponent hadn't moved at all.

"Attacks are useless against my shadow armor, physical ones especially so," he bragged.

Given the properties of the shadows enveloping his body, standard blows would be useless.

Good for him, I guess, but direct hits were what I excelled at!

I charged a volley of small Dragon Shots in my hands and hurled them his way!

However, the Dragon Shots disappeared inside his body. They hadn't made contact, instead getting sucked right in.

I could sense what would happen next, given the nature of this guy's abilities!

Sure enough, my Dragon Shots came flying back toward me from every corner of the station platform!

Boom! Boom! Boom!

"Dammit! So you can still do that redirecting trick?!"

During our last encounter, his shadows had been able to swallow all our attacks and then send them hurtling back at us from different locations! I took Kunou in my arms and leaped to safety as I parried my own energy blasts! I wouldn't be able to show my face in public again if I allowed myself to get taken out by my own attacks!

That dull rumbling sound intensified again…!

The shadows stretching along the platform all turned toward me!

They morphed, producing razor-sharp blades… Thankfully, my armor was pretty durable. Weapons like that wouldn't pose a threat. That was why it was all the more incredible that Sairaorg's punches were capable of damaging it!

I must have let myself get distracted, as a shadow appeared out of nowhere, wrapped around my left foot, and tied me to the ground. Not only that, but a barrage of other shadows formed into spears came flying my way!

"Not yet!"

I activated the Ascalon from my gauntlet and carved through my bindings before leaping to safety.

Talk about a nuisance. This guy was clearly a Technique-type fighter.

It was the kind of opponent I was most ill-suited against! Some would lash out with all kinds of incomprehensible attacks, and the defenses of others had a way of making conventional attacks ineffective. My opponent had both those qualities!

"Ha-ha-ha! That's it. Yes, well done, Red Dragon Emperor. But your attacks are useless against me. If this turns into a battle of endurance, I'll be the winner!"

Oh? He sounded pretty sure of himself. I suppose I couldn't fault him for it. If he stalled long enough, my armor would disappear once its time was up. What was I supposed to do? This was the worst type of matchup imaginable as far as I was concerned. Rossweisse and her magic would probably have been much more suitable.

"Hyah!"

Whoa!

Kunou, whom I was still carrying on one arm, stretched both her hands forward and unleashed a fireball technique at the shadow man. It was only a small projectile, and the man caught it in one hand, extinguishing it with a clench of his fist.

"And you must be the little fox princess? Was that fox fire? That level of flame won't do anything against me. You'll need far more," the man said with a laugh.

"Wh-why, you!" Kunou was beyond frustrated.

So we would need more powerful flames? Had he inadvertently revealed that he'd feel the heat even through his Balance Breaker?

Having hit upon an idea, I extended my dragon wings from my back and wrapped them around Kunou.

"Ddraig, shield Kunou with your wings."

"Sure. But what are you planning to do, partner?" he questioned.

I took a deep breath and filled my lungs with air. Then I lit a tiny spark deep inside me.

I'm going to win this, Ddraig!

I focused my Red Dragon Emperor power—and transferred it all into that spark!

"Boost! Boost! Boost! Boost! Boost! Boost! Boost! Boost! Boost! Boost!"

"Transfer!"

As I exhaled, I breathed out a huge plume of explosive fire!

Booooooooooom!

Roiling flames coursed across the platform, flooding the area.

"How's that feel?!"

My opponent could redirect oncoming attacks, but with the entire platform engulfed, there was no way out. On top of that, even if his shadow armor protected him from damage, it sounded like he'd still feel the heat.

"That fire breath comes straight from a former Dragon King. I guarantee it's more than hot enough for you!"

"Red Dragon Emperor! Daaaaammmmmmnnnnn yooooouuuuuu!"

The flames whirled around the man, forming a raging vortex. My enemy howled in agony as he tried to resist.

It seemed that he couldn't redirect the actual heat of the inferno. I, on the other hand, was protected by the armor of the Red Dragon Emperor, and dragons could withstand even the fires of a phoenix.

"Dragon flame...," Kunou muttered from within the safety of my wings.

Smoke filled the air, billowing all through the underground station platform. The whole area was scorched black. Evidently, whoever had created this dimension hadn't bothered to reproduce the emergency sprinklers.

Maybe I had overdone it a little? It was a good thing this wasn't the real Kyoto.

The man was lying flat on the ground, smoldering... His armor had vanished. Grievous burns dotted his body.

The sense of pressure and danger I felt earlier had abated. No longer was my opponent using his Balance Breaker. He seemed completely unable to keep on fighting.

"...You're strong. Even with my Balance Breaker...I couldn't stand up to a Heavenly Dragon..."

The man tried to stand, wobbling all the way.

"Do you want to keep on going? If we keep this up, you'll die!" I warned him.

Nonetheless, the man tried again and again to stand, and he fell each time back to the ground.

"...So be it. I-it would be an honor...to perish f-for Cao Cao..."

I could tell he was speaking from the bottom of his heart.

"Are you saying he didn't brainwash you?" I asked.

"That's right... I joined him of my own free will... You wanna know why, huh? Heh-heh-heh..." The man's breathing was heavy. His mouth and throat were obviously badly burned, but he continued nonetheless. "...You must know what kinds of tragedies befall those with Sacred Gears by now, right?"

I knew. Asia's life as a human had been ruined because of hers.

"...Not everyone born with a Sacred Gear has it easy. That power doesn't always bring happiness... What do you think would happen to a kid like me, capable of controlling shadows at will...? People feared and persecuted me," the man explained, sorrow plain in his tone. "These powers cheated me out of a decent existence... But there was one man who told me my abilities were wonderful."

Cao Cao?

"He said I was talented and unique. All because I had been gifted with a Sacred Gear... When he told me I could become a hero... What would *you* do if someone offered to blot out all your painful memories? I wanted to live for him, and if need be, die for him as well..." A rich, unmistakable sincerity hung on the man's words.

He's that devoted to Cao Cao? But the Khaos Brigade is a terrorist group!

They'd kidnapped Kunou's mother and were planning something horrible!

"Don't you think he might have just been using you?" I pressed.

The man laughed. "What's wrong with that? Cao Cao taught me how to live and use these powers...! That's enough for me... Thanks to him, I was able to make something of my worthless existence...! What's wrong with that?! Well, Red Dragon Emperor?!"

...

I listened on in silence as the man shed tears, laying bare his deepest thoughts.

"...To those treated like dirt just for having a Sacred Gear, he's a beacon of light...! My abilities existed to defeat demons, angels, *gods*, even...! Where else could I find anything like that...?! And...demons, and fallen angels, and dragons…they're the enemies of humankind…! That should be obvious! And you—you're both a demon *and* a dragon! You're a greater danger than most!"

A threat, huh? From the average human's perspective, I probably *was* something to be feared.

So Cao Cao had given this man, whose whole existence had been a journey from one tragedy to another, a purpose and a path to move forward. I couldn't imagine such a formative turning point.

And yet…

The man's legs were quaking as he staggered over. His hostility remained unabated.

"Don't you dare mock us humans, you demon scum…!" he screamed as he drew steadily nearer.

Right. I was a demon. Nothing would change that fact.

I clenched my fists, took a step forward, and sent a punch flying straight into his face.

"Yes, I'm a demon!"

Slam!

The man went flying back from the blow, crashing into a pillar and collapsing flat on the ground, unconscious.

"But *you're* the ones making a child cry with your selfish actions! I don't care what your reasons are. I'll do whatever I have to do to stop you."

After a final glance at the sprawled figure, I turned my attention to the subway tunnel stretching deep into the dark.

Ahead was the path to Nijo Castle. We had to go. Everyone else had likely defeated the heroes sent to intercept them and were undoubtedly en route to our destination.

"Let's go, Kunou."

"Mm-hmm!"

I lifted her up onto my back, spread my dragon wings wide, and took off.

Soaring above the subway rails, I blasted away one anti-monster after another until we reached the platform at Nijo Station.

There, I led Kunou up the stairs and outside, and we made our way to Nijo Castle's east gate. The rest of my team was already waiting for us.

"Sorry about the delay," I apologized.

"Bleurgh..." Rossweisse suddenly appeared, clad in her Valkyrie armor. She leaned against a pole and vomited!

Saji patted her back, asking, "Are you okay?"

She was a Hundred-Yen Valkyrie, a Drunkard Valkyrie, and a Vomiting Valkyrie all in one...

Rossweisse was truly incredible. She'd earned so many new aliases during our short time in Kyoto.

Kiba welcomed Kunou and me with a smile. "It's good to see you're both safe."

I was a little apprehensive about Rossweisse, but at least everyone else looked well.

The others' clothes were torn or charred a little here and there, but as far as I could see, no one was hurt.

Kiba and I were each carrying a vial of Phoenix Tears, just in case. Fortunately, neither of us had needed them.

"You're okay, Asia?"

"Yes. Xenovia and Irina protected me from those assassins!"

"You can count on us!" Xenovia declared, already clad in her combat outfit.

"Having a healer around is a huge relief," Irina added. She had cast off her school uniform as well.

Apparently, my worries about us being separated had been for nothing. Asia had been with the two other girls the whole time, so I should have had more faith.

Xenovia's Durendal was hanging from her waist in a decorated sheath! It really gave off a different impression now that she was carrying it openly. Its dangerous holy aura no longer overpowered all in its vicinity, so maybe she didn't need to store it in a hidden spatial fold anymore?

"…What about Rossweisse…?" I inquired.

"She helped fend off our opponents. However, she must have moved around too much, and now, well…" Kiba looked at a loss, just as unsure what to make of the Valkyrie's situation as I was.

Grrrrrroooaaaannnn…

No sooner had we all reunited than the huge gates leading into the castle swung open with a heavy noise.

Kiba flashed me an obviously bitter smile at the sight. "It looks like they've been waiting for us. The main performance is about to begin," he remarked.

I sighed in answer. "Seriously. Why do they have to toy with us?"

After exchanging nods of confirmation with one another, we all proceeded into the castle grounds.

"When I defeated my opponent, he revealed that Cao Cao was waiting for us at Honmaru Palace," Kiba said as we ran.

Honmaru Palace, huh?

We moved swiftly through the acreage, past the Ninomaru Garden, until we reached the moat. From there, we passed under the two-storied Yagura Gate that marked the way to Honmaru Palace.

At our destination was a row of orderly Japanese-style buildings and a beautifully maintained garden, all well lit even though it was now the middle of the night.

I glanced around for any sign of the party of heroes, when a voice called out to us.

"So you defeated the Balance Breaker–armed assailants we sent after you? They may have only had low- and mid-ranked Sacred Gears, but even so, a Balance Breaker is a Balance Breaker. I'm impressed you bested them so quickly."

Cao Cao appeared in the garden…and numerous other heroes lurked in the shadows of the buildings. Like our earlier encounter, they were all dressed in that distinctive uniform.

"Mother!" Kunou cried out.

I followed the girl's gaze—and spotted a beautiful kimono-clad woman up ahead. She had fox ears jutting up on her head and several tails peeking out from behind her. Man, the nine-tailed fox princess was seriously gorgeous!

"Mother! It's me, Kunou! Please wake up!"

But despite her daughter's appeals, Yasaka remained unresponsive. Her eyes were vacant, and her face lacked expression.

Kunou glared hatefully at Cao Cao and his followers. "You fiends! What have you done to my mother?!"

"I told you, didn't I? We need her for a brief experiment we're conducting, my little lady," Cao Cao replied, tapping the ground with the end of his spear.

Immediately after…

"Ugh… Augh, auuuuugggggghhhhh!"

…Yasaka began to scream, her appearance undergoing a massive transformation! Her body emitted radiant light as her features morphed. She continued to swell larger and larger, her nine tails expanding in size, too!

"Auuuuuggggghhhhh!"

A huge golden beast released a thundering howl into the night… We were faced with a massive fox monster!

It was enormous! It must have been at least ten meters in height, which made it practically the same size as Fenrir! But with those nine tails, it looked even larger than that hound!

This was a legendary nine-tailed fox spirit! I had thought that Fenrir's lean form lent him a certain elegance, but the true nature of this nine-tailed fox woman was just as incredible.

My dragon mentor Tannin carried a certain dignified poise, too. Were all legendary monsters this majestic and captivating?

Unfortunately, there was no awareness in Yasaka's eyes. It was clear she was being controlled. Words likely wouldn't be enough to get through to her. Did that mean we'd have to fight?

"Cao Cao!" I called out. "Just what are you trying to accomplish, making this fake Kyoto battlefield and manipulating Princess Yasaka like this?!"

Cao Cao rested his spear on his shoulder before responding. "Kyoto itself is a large-scale magical device, surrounding powerful conduits. The various famous power spots located in the city are rich in spiritual energy, in magic, and in demonic power. The ancient yin-yang masters who designed this city were trying to tap into that latent strength. Undoubtedly, that is why so many supernatural beings have found themselves drawn to Kyoto... The pseudo-space where we stand now is located in the dimensional void and is simultaneously both incredibly close and extremely removed from the real-life Kyoto. The power of those channels of energy moves through here. And the nine-tailed fox is among the highest class of Japanese spirits, rivaling a dragon. The fates of Kyoto and those nine-tailed foxes are inextricably linked. That's why our plan must be carried out here." Cao Cao paused there to exhale before letting slip an extraordinary revelation. "We plan to use the city of Kyoto and the power of this nine-tailed fox to summon the Great Red. A feat of this magnitude would typically require the presence of multiple Dragon Kings, but abducting that many dragons would be a challenge even for a god or Buddha. Thus, Kyoto and this nine-tailed fox will have to do instead."

—! ...Wh-what did he just...?!

"The Great Red? What will calling that massive dragon here get you? He's just floating in the void! What's the harm in that?" I demanded.

"Yes, the dragon is essentially harmless... And yet our benefactor sees him as a hindrance. His presence in the dimensional void makes returning home very difficult for her."

Ophis?

A vision of that small girlish figure flashed in the back of my mind. She was the leader of all these terrorists. From the perspective of the three great powers, she was basically the final boss.

The heroes were hoping to assist her in achieving her dream of returning to the void? But if they did, wouldn't it have potentially horrific consequences on every other realm? This was no joking matter!

Nervously, I asked, "...So you're going to summon the Great Red and then kill him?"

Cao Cao shook his head. "No, we might not need to go that far. For now, our plan is just to capture him. Depending on how the situation develops, we'll decide what to do from there. There's still much we don't know. For example, what kind of effect would the Dragon Eater exert on the Apocalypse Dragon? In any event, our experiment is merely an attempt to summon that mighty being, no more."

The Dragon Eater?

I frowned at the mention of this new term. Whatever that thing was, it didn't sound good.

"...I don't have a clue what you're going on about, but I don't care. If you catch that massive dragon, you'll be causing a huge problem for everyone. Give Princess Yasaka back."

As I spoke, Xenovia pointed her blade in Cao Cao's direction.

Durendal was still sheathed, but the pieces of its scabbard began to move.

Vrrrr-rrrrr!

With a violent noise, intense plumes of holy aura surged from the shifting parts of the sheath! Then that aura wrapped around the blade, solidifying into a massive sword!

This was the new and improved Durendal? No longer did its intense power overwhelm the surroundings. All that strength had been concentrated into the blade.

I could feel the energy within it even through my armor and standing a short distance away. Durendal must have completely fused with its scabbard, which now served to control the tremendous destructive potential.

"It's like Issei says. I can't really wrap my head around what your endgame is here, but what you're attempting threatens a lot of people. We're gonna have to stop it," Xenovia declared.

"I couldn't have said it better myself," Kiba agreed with a nod.

"Me too!" Irina added, conjuring a sword of light in her hand.

"It's always a life-or-death crisis with the Gremory Familia...," Saji lamented with a sigh.

Sorry, buddy. We're always getting caught up in problems like this...

"Well, this is for the academy and all my friends...," he muttered.

Black serpents suddenly appeared all over his arms, legs, and shoulders, wrapping around his body until it was completely covered in those dark snakes. Then a massive serpent rose up by his feet.

The huge creature positioned itself beside him, its whole body a mass of shadowy flame. Saji's right eye had turned deep red, just like those of the snake.

I was struck by an incredible sense of pressure!

Teach, haven't you gone a little overboard boosting Saji's abilities?!

Even in his regular fighting state, this power-up had turned him into a completely different person than the Saji I'd fought in the underworld!

"...Vritra, I'm sorry about this, but I need your strength. Hyoudou should help us cool off once it's all over, so let's let loose today, huh?" Saji whispered as yet more black fire erupted all around him.

The next moment, the serpent spoke back in a deep voice!

"My other self, which is our prey? The one with the Holy Lance? Or the fox? Either one is fine with me. Eons have passed since I last walked the waking world. How about I reduce them all to ash?"

Whoa, that flame snake was suggesting some frightening stuff. Evidently, it had recovered enough of its consciousness to speak, and this was just one piece of an ancient Dragon King... Its intimidating aura was completely different from Tannin's—more unsettling and terrifying.

Vritra was supposedly good at ensnaring its enemies. For the time being, I just wanted it to contain Princess Yasaka in her nine-tailed fox mode. But before I could relay that instruction...

Vrrrr-rrrrr!

...Xenovia raised the Durendal up into the air, which released a terrible sound!

The sword and its holy aura expanded to more than fifteen meters in length right in front of me, as though to pierce Heaven itself!

Dammit, that's long! Whhhhhooooooaaaaa! It's massive!

In our previous battles, Xenovia's dual-wielding combination of Durendal and Ascalon had produced a similarly enormous wave of holy power. At the time, I'd likened that energy to twin pillars of light, and yet this new Durendal easily dwarfed them!

Additionally, the weapon's aura was focused in the blade this time rather than dispersed.

Seriously, Xenovia?! The battle is only just beginning, and she's ready to let loose with an overpowered attack?!

"The first move is mine. Take this!"

As though in answer to my thoughts, Xenovia brought her fifteen-meter-long Durendal and its holy aura down on the band of heroes!

Like a huge uprooted tree, it crashed toward Cao Cao and his lackeys!

Booooooooooom!

The impact from Xenovia's strike blasted the entire Honmaru Palace into pieces! And the momentum of the holy aura didn't stop there. It tore on ahead through other structures, the public facilities, and even the distant scenery!

The ground itself wasn't spared, either, rent in two. Earth-shattering tremors knocked us from our feet and down to our knees.

When at last the attack subsided, everything before me had been reduced to ruin. The destruction passed beyond the castle moat, annihilating even the buildings outside without leaving so much as a trace!

That level of power was off the charts! Was it even fair to cause that much devastation?!

"Phew." Xenovia stopped to catch her breath as she wiped the sweat from her forehead, and she returned the Durendal to its sheath.

"Phew"? "Phew"?! This is no time for that!

She was acting as though the job was over and done with! Opening with massive overkill was plain uncouth! Actually…if it got us the win, maybe it wasn't too bad!

"Hey, Xenovia! That's a little excessive for an opening move!" I called.

The person in question, however, turned toward me, making a peace sign with her fingers. "Any good overture starts with a bang."

"What about our battle with Loki?! Hey, come on…!"

Truthfully, I knew arguing was a waste of breath. There was no getting through to that girl sometimes.

"Relax. I was just calibrating my strength. If I felt like it, I could've wiped this whole area off the map. My hope is to pull off something like your fully charged Dragon Shot, but it's kinda tough. Yep, I'm trying to reach the level of your Power-type fighting style!"

"Give me a break! That isn't anything like me! I'm not obsessed with destruction!"

Xenovia was a Knight, and yet she desired raw strength... It truly set her apart from Kiba. Perhaps she would have made a better Rook?

Xenovia tapped her new weapon's hilt. "This Durendal has been alchemically merged with Excaliburs."

My jaw fell open. *Excaliburs? Seriously?!*

"Let me explain," Irina began. "In broad terms, the multiple Excaliburs in the Church's possession have been used to create a sheath for Durendal. Their power is great enough to contain the Durendal's calamitous aura. On top of that, the Excalibur sheath lends its own attack strength to Durendal. The Holy Swords work to amplify each other in a way. The result is truly lethal!" As to provide evidence, Irina motioned to the leveled buildings.

"I see. So the Excaliburs hold in Durendal's aura while also boosting its potency. Which means all that strength has effectively been merged," I said.

"That about sums it up, Issei. Apparently, the Church started researching this idea when they realized the Durendal's aura could affect other Holy Swords."

"Ah. You mean when Xenovia kept Durendal in its spatial fold but fed its aura through Ascalon during our match over the summer? When we went to rescue Asia, and she used it to amplify Ascalon's power, right?"

Irina nodded. "Yep, yep! That's what got everyone thinking!"

So the Durendal and the Excaliburs had been fused into a single Holy Sword. Hold on, didn't the Church only have six of the seven Excaliburs? Had they been able to complete this sheath without a full set?

Xenovia lifted the weapon into the air. "The Ex-Durendal," she declared. "That's what I've named this Holy Sword."

The Ex-Durendal, huh? That seemed like a decent enough name—a good fit for a next-level power-up.

"It would've been nice if we'd taken them out in one hit," Xenovia remarked, her gaze shifting up ahead.

Unfortunately, that band of heroes wasn't weak enough to fall after a single attack.

Crack!

From the midst of the desolate rubble ahead of us, an arm suddenly shot out from the ground. Debris was cast aside as countless heroes emerged from the ground, enveloped in a thin fog.

Although they all looked a bit dirtied, none appeared injured. Had that mist protected them from the power of the Holy Sword?

The arm belonged to a huge figure who stood nearly two meters tall. An audible *crack* issued from his neck when he flexed it. Cao, behind the behemoth, was tapping his spear against his shoulder. They were both unaffected by Xenovia's attack. If they weren't ridiculously strong, they wouldn't have been such formidable terrorists, I guess...

Cao Cao rubbed his chin, bellowing in laughter. "Not bad at all!" He seemed to be enjoying himself. "You've already reached the level of mainstay—no, top-level high-class demons! You could stand shoulder to shoulder with the greatest of Familias! That demon girl, the sister of the Demon King, has certainly amassed a good team of servants. When you enter the Rating Game in earnest, you'll no doubt earn yourselves a double-digit ranking in no time at all. Maybe you'll even reach the top in a decade or so. Either way, you're a tough group. Shalba Beelzebub was a complete fool to underestimate you."

Siegfried broke into a grin. "He was so obsessed with his ancient pride that he couldn't see the newcomers were gaining on him. That's the reason Vali abandoned him, and it explains how the old Demon King regime collapsed. Anyway, what're we gonna do? I'm itching to go after taking that attack."

"Indeed. Let's begin with the experiment," Cao Cao said, and he knocked on the ground with his spear.

In evident reply, the nine-tailed fox—Princess Yasaka—began to glow! What was going on?!

"Georg, pour the energy from the power spots into the nine-tailed fox and prepare to summon the Great Red!" Cao Cao instructed.

"Understood," responded a youth wearing a mage robe over his uniform. Georg stretched out his hands, and multiple rows of magic circles appeared around him! The glyphs in the arrays began to spin at an incredible speed!

Not only that, the sheer number of them rivaled Rossweisse's capabilities!

"...It looks like he's making use of a deep wealth of magic techniques all at once... There's Norse magic, demon magic, fallen angel magic, black magic, white magic, spirit magic...," Rossweisse observed, watching with clear suspicion.

Is this mage that good? Wait, and he's the one controlling the fog, too, right? So he's got a Longinus and he's a pro magic user?!

A huge magic circle unfolded at the nine-tailed fox's feet. Its appearance was unfamiliar, but something about it struck a chord in my memory. This one bore a resemblance to the array Azazel had used when we'd summoned the consciousness of that enormous Dragon King Midgardsormr!

"Auuuugggghhhh!"

The nine-tailed fox let out a terrible scream. Her eyes opened wide, emanating a range of dangerous colors, while the golden fur covering her body stood up on end!

It was clear just by looking that she wasn't in her right state of mind! She would be in serious danger if this kept up!

"The magic circle and the sacrifice for summoning the Great Red are in place," the mist-controlling mage stated. "The next step is to see whether the Great Red will be drawn in by the power of the city. It's a stroke of unexpected good fortune that we have another Dragon King with us, as well as a Heavenly Dragon, to help catch his attention... That said, I can't leave the magic circle. Sorry, Cao Cao. It's taking all my effort just to maintain it."

Cao Cao waved his hand in acknowledgment. "Got it. All right, what shall we do now? Leonardo is busy using the Annihilation Maker with the others to engage the allied forces outside. I wonder how much time he'll be able to buy us? According to my reports, a number of seraphim have joined the Demon King Leviathan and the fallen angel Governor Azazel. Jeanne, Heracles?"

"Yes?"

"You called?"

An exotic blond woman wielding a slender sword and the giant from earlier both stepped forward.

"These two have inherited the determination, the souls, of Jeanne d'Arc and Heracles. Siegfried, who do you want to fight?" Cao Cao asked.

At this question, Siegfried drew his blade, leveling its tip at Kiba and Xenovia.

The woman, Jeanne, and the macho man, Heracles, broke out into laughter.

"In that case, I'll take the adorable little angel. She's so cute, after all."

"Guess that means the silver-haired lady is mine, then. Doesn't look like she's up for much of a fight, though!"

Our side exchanged glances... It was Kiba and Xenovia versus Siegfried, Irina against Jeanne, and Rossweisse facing Heracles...

"I suppose that leaves the Red Dragon Emperor for me. How about your Vritra?" Cao Cao cast Saji an inviting look.

Saji's flames roared intensely, but I raised a hand to hold him back. "...Saji, you need to deal with the nine-tailed fox. Try to find some way to pull her out of there."

"I get the monster showdown...? Fine. Don't die, Hyoudou."

"That goes for you, too. Good luck," I replied.

"I already Promoted to a Queen before coming here. I'm raring to go!"

After that brief exchange, black fire swept over Saji's body, expanding and climbing high into the air.

"*Vritra Promotion!*"

The jet-black flames roared up into the sky, gradually taking on the long and slender form of an Eastern dragon!

"Graaaaauuuuugggggghhhhh!"

The huge jet-colored dragon let out a tremendous roar before turning straight for the nine-tailed fox. Saji, it seemed, had completed shifting into his Dragon King form without issue. His black flames swept around the magic circle and began to give off a dull, dim aura. Vritra supposedly possessed a great many abilities, several of which he had used to considerable effect against Loki. His target was different this time, but hopefully, it would be equally effective against the nine-tailed fox spirit…

I turned to our healer. "Asia, look after Kunou."

"Okay."

"Kunou, can you watch Asia's back for me?"

"Leave it to me! But—"

"Don't worry," I interrupted, flashing the girl a thumbs-up. "We'll save your mom!"

My dragon wings spread wide as the propulsion unit on my back surged to life. My target was Cao Cao, the leader of the heroes and the owner of the ultimate Longinus.

When did it become the norm for me to be pitted against boss-level enemies? I felt like it'd been happening nonstop recently.

"Guess I just gotta see this through to the end," I muttered. "Hey! Are you stronger than Vali?"

Cao Cao grinned and chuckled at my inquiry. "Who's to say? I may be a fragile human, but I'm certainly not on the weak side."

"Quit messing around. Anyone who holds his own against Azazel has to be strong."

"Ha-ha-ha, that's true. But your Azazel is superpowerful, wouldn't you say? I haven't quite reached his level, Breast Dragon."

After that exchange, a brief silence blanketed the battlefield. Then…

"Auuuuugggggghhhhh!"

"Graaaaaauuuuugggggghhhhh!"

…Saji and the nine-tailed fox began to lay into each other like a pair of giant monsters from a movie!

Vritra's black flames whirled around the nine-tailed fox, encircling her. An intense burst radiated from the spirit a second after. Whatever was going on, it seemed to be causing Yasaka considerable pain.

Was this the same power-absorption technique Saji had used against Loki? If he kept this up, maybe we would be able to resolve this without injuring the princess! Yet just as I began to hope…

…the nine-tailed fox spirit spewed a fierce stream of fire from her mouth! It wasn't quite as powerful as that geezer Tannin's breath, but it still packed considerable heat! I could even feel it through my armor! Any subpar opponent would have been reduced to ashes in an instant.

Saji, in his Vritra form, similarly let loose with a column of black flame from his maw. The two attacks collided in midair over Honmaru Palace, triggering a massive explosion! The dark inferno surrounding the nine-tailed fox was extinguished. And so this contest between the two huge monsters continued!

"Dammit! I can't control my fire barriers as well as I did against Loki…!"

"Focus, my other self. My power requires concentration… But that alone won't be enough. This creature possesses great strength, even in her natural state, and she is now channeling the power of Kyoto. Moreover, that mage's circle is operating as some form of shield. The techniques are interwoven, a real nuisance… They're interfering with my powers, working to nullify my flames… When you drain the fox's powers, they're instantly replenished by the energy flowing through the city. At this rate, we may tire before she does."

I could hear Saji's conversation with Vritra through my Boosted Gear.

The nine-tailed fox, the strength from Kyoto's many power spots, that magic array—they were all obstacles. Facing them alone couldn't have been easy.

"Do you need me to transfer you extra power?" I asked through my Sacred Gear.

Maybe if I gave him a boost, Saji could use it to destroy the mage's circle…

"No. If you channel the Red Dragon Emperor's power to my other self before he masters his own abilities, it is possible he will lose control. The only way he will learn to handle these skills is through real battle," Vritra answered.

"Hang in there, Saji! If push comes to shove, I'll help you however I can!"

"...All right! Don't forget to kick that guy's ass, too!" Saji called back.

"Leave that to me!"

As we communicated through our Sacred Gears, Vritra and the nine-tailed fox both breathed more fiery attacks! Their high-energy flames met again, releasing a massive burst!

The confrontation between the pair of giant creatures sent explosions flying all around us, laying waste to the surroundings. We members of the Gremory Familia and our hero foes held firm, however, ready to do battle.

Now that Saji had claimed the opening move, it was our turn!

"Kiba! Xenovia! Fall back a little! We need to keep these guys at a distance from Princess Yasaka!" I called.

""Got it!"" the two of them replied in unison, taking off at a run with Siegfried in pursuit.

Ching! Clang!

Each clash of blades produced silver sparks!

Siegfried, fighting with three swords simultaneously, parried Kiba's and Xenovia's strikes using minimal movement, then he lunged forward with a sharp thrust!

It looked like the new sheath surrounding Xenovia's Ex-Durendal could be retracted, exposing the blade for regular combat.

"One blade isn't enough!" she cried, grabbing a part of the Ex-Durendal's sheath and pulling it back to reveal another grip, which she quickly separated from the main weapon.

As a fresh sword emerged, what I had thought was just an extended grip was actually an additional weapon! What kind of construction was that?!

Did Ex-Durendal house extra swords? Was it one of the Excaliburs? Seriously, that thing was full of fancy party tricks!

Xenovia, now dual wielding, readjusted her stance and increased the pace of her strikes.

Siegfried laughed, evidently amused at her increased effort. "This is getting interesting! Okay, I'll show *you* something special, too!"

Fwoosh!

Siegfried lashed out with one of his Demon Swords, forcing Kiba and Xenovia to fall back to evade.

I swallowed with trepidation.

Siegfried was emanating an indescribable sense of pressure and intimidation…! Just watching his murderous aura swell like that sent a cold sweat running down my back!

"Balance Breaker."

Three new silver-colored arms suddenly jutted out from the guy's back! I couldn't believe it! He was like an Asura! And those new limbs all drew fresh swords! He was employing a fighting style that used *six* swords simultaneously!

"The magic blades Tyrfing and Dainsleif. And a sword of light for fighting demons. I used to battle for the Church, after all."

With a fearsome weapon in each of his hands, he truly did resemble an Asura!

"This is my Chaos Edge: Asura Revenge—my Balance Breaker, and a special kind of Twice Critical. Its ability is simple—it gives me more arms to fight with. Pretty useful for a guy like me, who battles with only skill and a few good magic blades. Shall we see how long you can keep up?"

Kiba! Xenovia!

While I was worrying about them, Irina leaped into action against Jeanne.

"Light! Hyah!"

Irina spread her pure-white wings and hurled a barrage of luminous spears toward her opponent. It was a keen attack. Any human or average-level demon unfortunate enough to be on the receiving end of one of those projectiles would probably have been annihilated on the spot.

Jeanne avoided them all with little apparent effort, though. That lady sure was fast! She wasn't quite at Kiba's level, but her movements were swift enough that I had difficulty keeping up!

"Not bad! Your attacks are well honed, my little angel cutie! I'm moved!"

Wh-why does she sound so pleased?!

Jeanne pulled out a slender rapier and deflected Irina's next incoming attack!

"How about this, then?!"

Irina dived in close to Jeanne like a streak, her sword of light raised! Jeanne met the attack head-on, locking blades.

Claaang!

A screeching sound pierced the air as the two weapons pushed against each other! They were evenly matched!

A grin spread across Jeanne's face suddenly. She was planning something!

"Holy Sword!" she shouted, and another weapon abruptly emerged from her feet!

Irina was clearly startled, but thankfully, she managed to twist her body to dodge! Jeanne took advantage of that opening to push ahead with another thrust, and Irina extended her wings, taking to the air and falling back.

As she watched Irina hovering up above, Jeanne looked strangely amused. "Not bad at all! Heh. I underestimated you. You don't disappoint, my little angel cutie!"

"I—I'm Archangel Michael's Ace! Don't you belittle me!"

"Oh? You're with Michael? Got it. Since Siggy's showing off, I suppose I might as well do the same," Jeanne said with a wink.

...Siggy? Does she mean Siegfried? And "show off"? Don't tell me she's about to...

"What do you think of *my* ability, Blade Blacksmith? It's the Holy Sword equivalent of your friend's Holy Demon Sword forging power.

I can craft Holy Swords with practically any attribute. They don't *normally* hold up against the genuine article, but there are exceptions to every rule," Jeanne remarked, grinning.

A Holy Sword version of Kiba's technique. I'd always figured there were other skills like his out there. Kiba's ability was bolstered by his Balance Breaker, and after what Jeanne had stated about exceptions, an unpleasant thought came to mind.

"Balance Breaker!"

Grrrr-rrrrr!

An incredible number of swords erupted from below Jeanne's feet as she flashed Irina a cute smile. Holy Swords piled up, amassing into one enormous object!

Jeanne's creation was a huge dragon of Holy Swords!

Seriously?! A Holy Sword dragon?! What kind of mad scientist idea is this?!

"This is my Balance Breaker, Stake Victim Dragon. Like Siggy's, it's a special subtype Sacred Gear," Jeanne explained.

Irina's expression turned stern. "Saint Jeanne d'Arc… I'm conflicted about having to fight someone who has inherited the spirit of a sacred being. But this is for Michael and everyone else! Nothing is more valuable than peace!"

Irina lifted her Holy Sword up into the air with renewed determination!

Stand firm, Irina!

Boom! Boooooooooom!

Explosions rang out around us as Rossweisse and the huge muscleman Heracles leaped into battle.

"Gah! My spells aren't even affecting him!"

Rossweisse was casting techniques in every direction, yet even when they made direct contact with their target, Heracles merely plowed right through!

"Ha-ha-ha! Good, good! Your magic is seasoned just right!"

He was laughing, completely unfazed by Rossweisse's bombardment of Norse spells! On closer inspection, I realized he *was* injured. The wounds were minor, but they covered his body.

How could he withstand all that and enjoy himself? Just how sturdy was this guy?!

Booooooooooom!

With each of Heracles's punches, another one of Rossweisse's magic shots was destroyed. It was like he held bombs in his hands!

Rossweisse deftly avoided his strikes, yet Heracles's fist sent such terrible vibrations through the air that the swing shattered a distant tree to dust.

"My Sacred Gear, the Variant Detonation, detonates the targets of my attacks! We could have ourselves a good fireworks show if we keep this up, eh? However, everyone else is activating their Balance Breakers, so I'll never hear the end of it if I don't keep up with them! Sorry about this, but I'm gonna go full Balance Breaker and blow you away! Hraaaaaaaaah! Balance Breeeeeaaaaakeeeeerrrrr!"

As Heracles let out a tremendous bellow, a brilliant glow surged from his body. The light concentrated into clusters around his burly arms, legs, and torso!

When finally it subsided, the muscleman was covered with spikes! No, they weren't spikes, they were missiles...!

H-how could he...?

"Here's my Balance Breaker! Mighty Comet Detonation! Graauuuuu-gggggghhhhh!"

Rossweisse wasted no time pulling away from Heracles!

"At this rate, this place won't... Ugh!" With a grimace, she hurried away from Honmaru Palace. She was clearly trying to keep the rest of us out of the path of those missiles!

"Ha-ha-ha! You're a kind woman! Trying to distract me to keep your friends safe from the blast! Good, good! I'll play along!" Heracles bellowed with clear excitement.

Once she judged she was a safe distance from the rest of us, Rossweisse spun through the air and conjured more magic circles than I could count!

Heracles must have been really eager, because he was preparing to fire all his missiles at once!

Naturally, there was no way I would let that slide. I stretched my arm out toward him, readying a Dragon Shot! The moment Heracles launched his projectiles, I would shoot down as many of them as I could with an attack of my own!

Unfortunately, before my attack was fully prepared...

"Hey now, you're fighting *me*," Cao Cao said, appearing right in my line of fire!

Fine, then! I thought. *Eat this!*

Swoosh!

My Dragon Shot raced from my palm and exploded with a tremendous sound! Cao Cao had raised his spear, knocking my arm upward and sending my Dragon Shot veering up into the sky!

At the same time, Heracles's vast volley of missiles sped for Rossweisse!

Kra-booooooooooooooooooooom!

The projectiles erupted in an incredible burst that collided with Rossweisse's magic circles. The resulting blast engulfed the whole area!

I spotted a figure amid the smoke! It was Rossweisse! She'd landed safely on the ground, although she looked pretty banged up!

Even with the enhanced defensive attributes of her Rook piece and her protective spells, she'd still taken a nasty hit.

On top of that, her magic, which was strong enough to lay waste to an entire city, seemed largely ineffective against Heracles.

Did that mean Heracles was superior in both offensive and defensive capabilities? Perhaps his techniques were particularly honed against magical attacks?

Whatever the case, the priority was mending Rossweisse's injuries.

"Heal her, Asia!" I instructed.

Asia directed the warm green glow of her Sacred Gear at Rossweisse! Our battle mage responded with a thumbs-up.

All right. Looks like she's back to fighting condition. Way to go, Asia!

"Ha! Healing powers? All the better!"

Heracles looked nothing if not excited to see that Rossweisse was back on her feet. The guy was a total battle fanatic!

Kicking off the ground, Heracles rushed straight for our Valkyrie.

...Dammit. These cursed heroes all have Balance Breakers!

Cao Cao, having seemingly noticed my frustration, laughed and commented, "Isn't it great? More Balance Breakers than you could ever ask for. Fragile humans like us wouldn't be able to hold our own against the likes of you without a little help, after all." He spun the spear in his hands as he slowly descended to the ground.

A glance suggested he was full of openings, but I knew any attack I tried would be swiftly countered.

This was just a guess, but he struck me as a Technique-type fighter.

If I lashed out carelessly, he would deftly parry the maneuver as he'd just done, rendering my effort useless. It was an intimidating thought.

"Aren't you going to use your Balance Breaker, too?" I asked.

Cao Cao shook his head. "No. We can defeat you without having to go that far. Besides, I would prefer to fully savor your skills and abilities today, Red Dragon Emperor."

"...So you're treating me like a joke as well. Still, something tells me you aren't underestimating me. Not exactly."

"Indeed. I simply want to draw out your power and have us a satisfying little bout."

He was just like Vali—a more relaxed version of him, I guess. Cao Cao wished to gauge my strength by forcing me to fight him. Heck, he was observing my every move with undisguised curiosity.

Cao Cao raised a finger. "My companions have a theory. They suggested employing a Sacred Gear that can accelerate the flow of time against you to diminish how long you can maintain your Balance Breaker. If successful, it would eliminate your armor before you could battle to your full extent. Truthfully, we have a Sacred Gear user who can do that at our disposal, and they're very effective against time-limited techniques. I'm sure it'd prove effective, as that tactic requires no combat. There's no questioning that it would deal you a decisive blow... Yet I suspect it wouldn't be enough to defeat you."

What was Cao Cao saying? I didn't understand what he was trying to get at.

"You've been working to gain a deep understanding of your Sacred

Gear. If, for argument's sake, you were to release your Balance Breaker yourself and fight with your regular power-doubling abilities for, say, ten seconds while under the effects of time acceleration, what might be the result...? Your power could multiply to an incomprehensible level in the blink of an eye. Of course, it remains to be seen whether time acceleration would affect the regular workings of your Sacred Gear. Still, for one like you, who has been probing the depths of their talents, I believe it's possible."

Annoyed, I questioned, "What's the point of all this?"

Cao Cao shrugged. "This may come as a surprise to some, but I believe a direct, straightforward approach will be more likely to defeat you than any underhanded method... You are clearly wary of Technique-type attacks, and I suspect it will be hard to use them against you."

Fighting this guy was going to be challenging. We'd only interacted for a short time, and he'd already gained a deep understanding of me. It was truly off-putting.

"You carry two decisive weaknesses, Issei Hyoudou... You are vulnerable to Dragon Slayers and to light. The combined qualities of a dragon and a demon make you a truly formidable existence. Yet those twin traits increase your vulnerabilities, too. And I can see those weaknesses clearly. When I look at you, I want to prove to the world that there is no such thing as an invincible being. Well, that about sums it up. Shall we get started?" Cao Cao raised his spear and pointed it in my direction.

Our battle was about to commence.

First, I would need to use a Promotion... Should I become a Knight, perhaps? Or maybe becoming a Bishop would help me boost my Dragon Shots...? No, this was no time to consider practice. I had to go all out!

"Asia! I'm Promoting to a Queen!"

"Okay!"

With Asia's permission, I Promoted to a Queen and felt pure strength and power run through my body!

After our last major bout, I'd devoted some of my training to acclimating to each Evil Piece. That work had enabled me to reach a point where I could make good use of the unique traits of every piece! Now it was time to put that experience to use!

Burning with resolution, I unfurled my dragon wings and ignited my propulsion unit!

Boooooooooom!

"Jet!"

I extended my fist as I shot for Cao Cao at incredible speed! After considering my options, nothing seemed better than a direct attack!

I raced forward! Cao Cao dexterously spun his spear, lightly moving to one side to dodge my first strike!

He can respond to a rush this quick?! In that case...!

I changed my trajectory, launching for his new location! At the same time, I gathered a mass of demonic energy into my hands! When that bastard tried to avoid me this time, I would let loose with two separate Dragon Shots!

Smack!

Cao Cao kicked my right hand while using his spear to disrupt the aim of my left! My Dragon Shots veered off into the distance!

Dammit! He'd preempted my attacks so easily!

Thud!

Not a second later, something struck my stomach. When I glanced down, I found Cao Cao's spear jutting out from my gut.

"Gah!"

I coughed up blood as a raging heat gurgled up my throat.

H-he got me!

"You certainly aren't weak, but your overly direct fighting style leaves you with plenty of openings."

Squelch!

He slowly removed his weapon from my stomach.

At that moment, my gut—no, my entire body—was wracked with searing pain. Smoke rose from all over me, centered around my wound.

Trust me when I say it *really* hurt. This pain resembled that from a Holy Sword. The acrid smoke was similar as well!

R-right... It's the Holy Spear... I guess that means the effects are the same...

This wasn't good. I could feel my consciousness fading...

"Issei!"

Ah.

Asia's pale-green aura enveloped my body. The pain slowly abated.

She'd healed me. That had been a close one. Any longer, and I would've lost consciousness.

But my wound wasn't completely restored. Smoke continued to issue from around it. To my astonishment, the injury had reopened! Was that because long-distance healing was less effective? Asia's ability to cast her restorative aura from afar was certainly useful, but it wasn't the same as receiving it via direct touch. That said, it should have still been potent under regular conditions. The damage inflicted by that Holy Spear must have exceeded imagination...

I pulled the vial of Phoenix Tears from my pocket and poured its contents on my wound. Finally, the hole in my stomach closed. Thank goodness I had been holding on to these.

"I hope you realize you nearly died," Cao Cao stated with a casual grin. "You could have been annihilated, letting the Holy Spear pierce your flesh like that. Death comes surprisingly easy, wouldn't you say?"

I almost...died...? Seriously?

Yes, it had been a critical wound, but I had endured similar attacks in the past. Even after this one, I'd still been able to move somewhat, enough so that I'd considered punching Cao Cao in the face.

Had I truly been that close to annihilation?

Was that what occurred when a demon took holy damage? They ceased to exist? That's what had nearly happened to me? Smoke was coming off of me, so I guess it was true...

I shuddered at the sudden realization of how close I'd been to the end.

Th-that was dangerous. If I let myself get killed here, I'll never be able to show my face to the prez or Asia again!

Cao Cao rested his weapon on his shoulder. Was that a habit of his? Eh, I didn't care either way.

"Heed this. That was the Holy Spear. No matter you strong you become, you will never be able to overcome its attack because you're a demon. Not even Vali will survive its fatal holy power."

Yep, I understood that all too well now. I couldn't afford to touch the True Longinus. What was I supposed to do, then?

Cao Cao seemed taken aback by my reaction. "...Oh, so you aren't frightened? I expected you to be terrified. Maybe to cower in fear, even..."

"Huh? Of course I'm scared. But I'm not about to run away. I'll never hear the end of it from the others if I don't beat you. The Red Dragon Emperor is a serious opponent!"

"Ha-ha-ha!" Cao Cao burst into laughter.

What was with this guy? His facial expressions were all over the place.

"Good, good. I see why Vali has taken an interest in you. Very well. You've finally found a worthy adversary, Vali!" Cao Cao wiped amused tears from his eyes, then he prepared his spear, which extended a blade of light. "Let's do this."

Gulp...

The intensity of his already intimidating aura flared. Was he enjoying this? That only made the thought of fighting him even more alarming.

I stretched out my right hand, preparing to unleash a fully powered Dragon Shot!

"Boost! Boost! Boost! Boost! Boost! Boost! Boost! Boost! Boost! Boost!"

Fwoosh!

I fired a massive blast of energy straight for him!

"Getting hit by that would be quite troublesome," Cao Cao observed, preparing to deflect the incoming projectile with his spear.

I had expected as much, however. The moment I launched the Dragon Shot toward him, I ignited my booster pack and took off!

Whenever he dodged my Dragon Shots, he always moved to the side!

Cao Cao lunged out forcefully with his spear, carving the energy blast clean in two! But that didn't matter! Now was my chance to deliver a punch before he could regain his battle stance!

"Boost! Boost! Boost! Boost! Boost! Boost! Boost! Boost! Boost! Boost!"

I threw my full weight into my fist, pouring all my strength into it!

"I can sense your power!" Cao Cao cried out with evident joy, twisting his spear in an attempt to meet the blow.

Gotcha!

My attack was a feint! I stopped my fist before it could reach him, leaving his counter to carve through empty air.

Next, I struck with my left fist and, at the same time, transferred my boosted power into Ascalon, which was still stored in my gauntlet!

"Boost! Boost! Boost! Boost! Boost! Boost! Boost! Boost! Boost! Boost!"

"Transfer!"

Ascalon's blade shot from my gauntlet just as I leaped backward! A wave of energy pulsed from the Holy Sword!

Fwoosh!

Ascalon's aura coursed toward Cao Cao. It looked like I had finally taken him by surprise, but he didn't make the slightest attempt to get away!

Swoosh!

With a dull *thud*, Cao Cao's arm was sent flying through the air. Ascalon's power had severed it clean from his body!

All right! Feint after feint, and then the real attack!

Training with Kiba had paid off. I mentally relished the victory. Yep, that spear was definitely immensely powerful, and I had many weaknesses, but Cao Cao had shortcomings of his own.

His was the frail body of a human.

In terms of physical durability, I—being both a dragon and a demon—was superior. No matter how capable Cao Cao and his band of heroes were, they couldn't possibly have the sturdiness of people like Vali or Loki.

My plan had gone perfectly. I might not have won yet, but I'd proved I could fight Cao Cao.

The man thrust his spear into the ground and caught his severed left arm in his remaining hand. Completely expressionless, he stuffed the limb under his working one and reached into his pocket. It was then that I spied a suspicious-looking object.

That's...

Cao Cao popped open the vial, poured its contents onto the stub of his detached arm, and then reconnected it to his body. Smoke poured from him. A moment later, he looked good as new!

That vial...

There could be no doubting it... Phoenix Tears!

"Wh-what are you doing with that?!" I demanded.

Cao Cao grinned, obviously pleased with my question. "I picked it up through my black-market connections. When you know who to contact, all it takes is enough money. Although I'm sure the House of Phenex would prefer to keep these out of our hands."

How could this have happened? To us demons, Phoenix Tears were highly prized and precious healing tools... To think that they were falling into terrorist hands!

We could have prevented untold suffering caused by these people's attacks if only we had more of the invaluable items!

"...Your aura's flaring. Are you angry? You could bring ruin on everyone around you if you let your emotions get the better of you like that. You've already entered your Juggernaut Drive once."

That was none of his business! Dammit! Seriously, I wanted to teach these guys a lesson!

Crack!

At that moment, my armor broke into pieces...! What was going on?!

"I got a few strikes in as you jumped away. It looks like there was a bit of a time lag, but evidently, only a few quick hits with my spear are enough to shatter the Red Dragon Emperor's armor."

Cao Cao had inflicted damage without my noticing.

Sorry, Ddraig, but can you restore my armor?

"...Understood. But it will take some time. That's probably a side effect of damage from the Holy Spear."

Seriously? That damn spear is a real pain in the ass!

"A good attack. Strong, very strong. I may need to make more use of my own Sacred Gear..."

That bastard Cao Cao sure was having a lovely time... For all his strength, his body still didn't appear stronger than an ordinary human's. A single good blow would end this. Of course, that was true if I took another hit from the True Longinus as well...

Regardless, that was Cao Cao's weak point. Knowing this duel would be decided with one strike was scary, to say the least. Plus, he wasn't using his Balance Breaker. If he wished to, he could become much stronger.

While racking my brain about what to do against that Holy Spear...

"Irina!" Asia cried out.

"Huh? So you still haven't finished over there?"

That was a woman's voice.

I looked around and saw Jeanne holding a bloody figure in her arms. Irina.

"Well, he *is* the Red Dragon Emperor. It's not surprising that he'd last longer than his buddies," Siegfried said. The six-armed Asura was holding Kiba and Xenovia in the air. Both of them were battered and stained with crimson.

H-hey...

"You should have let me deal with him."

The muscleman Heracles threw something my way—Rossweisse. Her silver hair was coated in blood.

E-everyone...? This couldn't be... They'd all lost...?

"*Grrrr-rrrrr!*" came a loud roar.

That was Vritra. He was snared in the nine-tailed fox's many tails, moaning in pain...

Saji...!

Cao Cao tapped his spear against his shoulder. "I'm sorry, Red Dragon Emperor. It looks like we've reached the finale. You're strong. All of you are. For demons, you've reached exceptional levels. Sadly, it's not enough to defeat heroes. Demons, fallen angels, dragons, and spirits all forming an alliance against humanity. It's a frightening notion. Who could blame us for taking action? Our guiding principle is that humanity must defeat your dragons and Demon Kings. Well, it's *one* of our goals, anyway. Now then, Georg? How's the magic circle?"

The mist-controlling mage nodded. "It will be a little while longer. I wonder whether the Great Red will truly come?"

"Even if he doesn't, the data will still be useful. If need be, we'll just try another method."

"It took a lot of effort getting all this ready. I'd prefer if it worked *this* time."

"And do you think I don't? No one wants this to be a success more than me."

The heroes had seemingly forgotten us entirely, turning their attention back to their wicked experiment.

Jeanne, Siegfried, and Heracles left my beaten companions where they were and went to consult with Cao Cao.

"Everyone!" Asia ran our way, tears flowing down her cheeks as she began to heal us.

Our earlier promises to one another resounded in the back of my mind.

"We'll protect Kyoto with our lives."

Teach... I...I couldn't do anything...

My eyes went to Kiba, who was sprawled on the ground.

"In the president's absence, you're our substitute King, Issei."

Kiba, you put your faith in me...and I couldn't do anything...

"Mother! Open your eyes, please! It's me! It's me! Motheeeeerrrrr!" Kunou screamed for her parent, yet the nine-tailed fox didn't so much as glance in her direction.

"We'll save your mom!"

I hadn't been able to save anyone. We'd failed!

"Xenovia! Irina!" Asia continued tending to my friends, sobbing all the while.

What was I doing...? Why had I put in such a pathetic showing...? Even now that I had restored my Boosted Gear Scale Mail, Cao Cao paid me no mind...

Those damn heroes had acknowledged our strength, but they didn't think us capable of stopping things. We had done our best, and they saw us as no threat at all...

From the beginning, we were only an amusing distraction to pass the time during their so-called experiment.

I was supposed to be the Red Dragon Emperor. Some Breast Dragon I was.

I was pathetic.

My body shook from the frustration, and tears streamed from my eyes. Why was I so weak? This was the result whenever I needed to be strong.

Why wasn't it enough...? Victory was always out of reach. No matter how hard I tried, there were always opponents beyond...

Was this my limit...? Why couldn't I surpass it...?

I fell to my knees and punched the ground. My friends had been defeated, and there was no chance I'd beat Cao Cao. The odds of saving Kunou's mother...were practically zero.

The bare minimum for success, rescuing Princess Yasaka and fleeing, had been a pipe dream from the start...

No! I didn't want to give up! I couldn't let it end like this! I could still fight!

But I was no match for him... The truth stung more than anything else... I—I...

"Are you crying?"

Someone had called from within me.

...Elsha?

"Yes, it's me. Why are you crying?"

It was Elsha, a previous Red Dragon Emperor, reaching out to me from within my Sacred Gear.

I—I'm useless... Why am I still so weak...? I can't do anything when it truly counts...

"Yes, that must be frustrating. But have you forgotten what that fallen angel governor said about you being the living embodiment of possibility?"

At that moment, I recalled Azazel's words before my fight with Loki. *"Issei. I have faith in your potential. Every last Red Dragon Emperor was consumed by power and lost their lives because of it. You might be the most untalented Red Dragon Emperor in history, but you're the living embodiment of possibility. I mean, you unlocked your Balance*

Breaker by touching a woman's breasts and returned to your senses after going berserk thanks to them, too."

The living embodiment of possibility.

"You're a real-life Breast Dragon! And that's something. It's been a while since a dragon earned himself a new alias. Even if your physical strength and demonic powers are no match for Vali's or those of other legendary dragons, you can still take a different approach to using the Red Dragon Emperor's unique gifts to get stronger in your own way. All you need is effort, grit, and to forge an unlikely new path."

That was what Azazel had said back then.

I had to find my own way of employing the Red Dragon Emperor's abilities. That was why I was the Breast Dragon!

"Yes! You're the Red Dragon Emperor, and you're also the Breast Dragon. That's what Belzard saw in you! Unleash it all, right here, right now! Your possibilities!" Elsha declared.

With that, a brilliant light blasted from my pocket. I reached in to retrieve it, pulling out a glowing bright-red jewel.

Th-this is…

"Raise it up to the heavens! Let's call out to them!"

Call out? I didn't know what exactly to say, but Elsha took the lead.

"Yes, those breasts that belong to you alone!"

At that moment…

Flaaaaash!

…light exploded from the jewel, and an intense radiance bathed the entire battlefield!

"What's that?" Cao Cao, unable to ignore this development, finally turned his attention back to me!

Within the light pouring from the gem, a figure began to take shape. First one, then two, then more and more.

Wh-what's going on here…?

It was Elsha who answered my question. *"That gemstone has traveled from one person to the next, all throughout Kyoto. These figures are the products of their residual notions."*

In other words, they were the lingering thoughts of everyone who had been turned into gropers because of me...?

There had to be more than a thousand of them! What kind of pervert epidemic had I unleashed on this city?! This was way too many people to apologize to!

"Breasts..."

"B-breasts."

"Breeeeeaaaaaasts."

"Wow, those breasts..."

"What incredible breasts..."

The memories all began to intone the word breasts one after another! It was like a trade fair of sex fiends!

""""""Breasts, breasts, breasts, breasts...""""""

That horde of residual thoughts moved with a slow and uncertain gait; their whispered obsession sounded almost like a curse. Then they moved into a formation.

"""""""""""Breasts! Breasts! Breasts! Breasts! Breasts! Breasts! Breasts! Breasts! Breasts! Breasts! Breasts! Breasts! Breasts! Breasts! Breasts! Breasts! Breasts! Breasts! Breasts! Breasts!"""""""""""

This was awful!

I could only gawk at the strange spectacle. While muttering the word breasts, they were arranging themselves in the kind of circle that you might use for a ritual of some kind.

"...Breast zombies?" Cao Cao posited quietly.

My thoughts exactly! They looked just like zombies! Did all those people whose boobs had been mishandled as a result of that jewel end up like this? It was like a zombie apocalypse!

The tit-obsessed memories, having assembled into a huge circle, suddenly melted into the ground. Radiant light shone from the ring, carving a large pattern into the earth.

They'd created a massive magic circle!

I was flummoxed, unsure what was going on. Fortunately, Elsha filled me in.

"The preparations are complete. Now, let's reach for them."

R-reach for what? I thought back.

I had no idea what was happening anymore! My mind was paralyzed from shock!

"Those breasts that belong to you alone!"

Breasts that belonged to me… Naturally, the first person I thought of was my crimson-haired master.

"Now, call out for them! Summon them! Those breasts!"

I couldn't keep up with this overwhelming situation, so I did as instructed!

"I summon you! Breeeeeaaaaasts!"

Zzzzzhhhhh!

The magic circle released a huge surge of power! The letters engraved all throughout it spelled out the word *breasts*, and there were even what looked like hieroglyphics in the shape of those wondrous objects in there, too!

Could I really summon them?! C-could I really call the person whom I was visualizing…?

A figure emerged in the center of the magic circle. After a powerful flash, my crimson-haired prez was there!

P-Preeeeeeeeeez?!

Maybe she had been in the middle of getting changed, because she was garbed only in her underwear. She was clearly just as astonished by her sudden appearance as I was, and she looked all around. Who could blame her? This insane development would have astonished anyone!

"Wh-what's going on?! Where am I?! I-is that Honmaru Palace…? I—I'm in Kyoto? I-is that you, Issei? What are you doing here? What am *I* doing here?! D-did you summon me?! What's going on?!"

The prez looked like she was short-circuiting! For my part, I'd been left speechless, too. Even the heroes appeared unsure how to react.

I'm sorry, everyone! I never expected something like this to happen!

Elsha, evidently noticing my consternation, said to me in all seriousness, *"Touch them."*

"Huh…?"

I couldn't believe what I'd just heard.

However, Elsha gave the instruction again. *"Touch her breasts."*

"T-touch them?"

"Yes. Like you always do. You know, squish.*"*

"*Squish?!* Hold on, what's going to happen if I do that?!"

What on earth was she saying?! Was she truly a woman?! Was this really one of the greatest Red Dragon Emperors of all time?! This lady must have gone mad!

Elsha paid no heed to my disbelief. *"This is the final deciding factor to unlock your potential—Rias Gremory's breasts. They're the trigger. Use them to unlock the door to your possibilities."*

This was no good. Elsha was clearly insane. A predicament like this was beyond conception.

The prez's boobs aren't buttons to trigger my self-awakening!

"No, they are. *Please try to understand. I've been observing you for a while, so I'm sure of it."*

This was awful! *Too* awful! Yet I couldn't deny that Elsha's command felt powerfully persuasive!

The prez's body abruptly began to glow with a golden radiance!

"Wh-what's this?! I'm surrounded by light!" Poor Rias looked similarly baffled by this latest surprise.

Before me, a marvelous sight began to take shape.

Zzzzzhhhhh…

Sparkle! Glimmer! Twinkle!

The prez's breasts shone divinely.

Elsha? What's going on…?

"Rias Gremory's breasts have come into contact with your potential. They've been pushed to the next level."

Th-the next level…?

"Yes. Her chest has overcome the limitations of the Switch Princess… They've entered their second phase."

I'm sorry. I don't have a clue what any of that means. The second phase of what?

This was all so incomprehensible that I felt like breaking down into tears!

"Touch them, and you'll evolve, too. A dramatic transformation will become yours. All it will take is that one push to unleash the power of the Evil Piece within you..."

Those breasts... Switches...

Bah.

Blood gushed from my nose. I finally understood the situation.

I approached the prez, retracted the mask part of my helmet, and flashed her a smile.

She tilted her head to one side. "Issei?"

"Prez, please let me touch your breasts," I said with all sincerity.

"—!"

The prez was left speechless by this request.

Nonetheless, she only needed a quick moment to think. "...I don't know what's happening...but all right!"

My words had gotten through to her! What on earth was this situation?! This was incredible beyond belief! Part of me was trying to think of some smart follow-through to make what I'd said sound cooler, but there was no turning back now!

I would feel them! Yes, I would fondle them with my own two hands! Right here in Kyoto! The prez's breasts! Her glorious boobs!

It wouldn't do to let any of those cursed heroes lay eyes on this priceless sight, so the prez turned around so that only I could see as she removed her bra.

Click.

As the clasp was released, those magnificently voluptuous tits plopped down before my very eyes! I stiffened at the sight of small changes in those wondrous objects that I'd believed myself intimately familiar with!

Her nipples and pink areolae were emanating a pale, rosy glow. The prez's areolae were literally shining!

What on earth is this?! I-is it her "second phase"?! Awesome!

I could lose my mind trying to make sense of this crazy phenomenon! Now then, all I needed to do was caress them to receive divine grace!

A-ah, their glow was so magnificent.

I let the armor protecting my fingers dissipate, and I stretched out both hands, reaching toward those shining breasts.

Now that I thought about it, I had done something very similar when I had first awakened my Balance Breaker.

And now I was about to touch them again. Maybe I leveled up each time we did this. I was deeply moved!

Incredible. The sensation was amazing. With these boobs to help me, I felt able to solve any problem.

Switches! The Switch Princess! The prez was evolving alongside me! Maybe she was on track to becoming a real-life Switch Princess?!

Are you ready, Ddraig? I asked mentally.

"Baaaaah! Whyyyyy?! Oooooaaaaahhhhh!"

He was bawling. Such was the only course of action left for him.

Sorry! I'm sorry, partner! But I'm going to feel them! I have to! I need to!

"Here I go!" I declared, erupting into a massive nosebleed as I wrapped my hands around them.

Plop. Squeeze.

My fingers sank into that rich suppleness, that splendid, brilliant scene. Fresh sensations ran through my body, filling my brain with raw pleasure.

Ah, the prez's breasts were the best!

"…Oooohhhhh…"

And a sexy sigh! The killing blow!

Flash!

With that, the prez's breasts exploded with light!

"Th-this is…! A-aaaaahhhhh!" the prez cried out at the wholly unexpected development.

Her breasts still glowing, the prez ascended into the sky!

That luminous chest was bathing the entire battlefield in its rose-colored shine!

Incredible. She was climbing to the heavens, and her boobs continued to unleash that powerful light!

Moved to tears, I brought my hands together in joy.

Ah, breasts!

The prez continued to rise until, with a final, luminous burst, both she and the magic circle vanished.

U-um, Elsha? Where'd she go?

"Back to where she was before."

Seriously?! I had summoned her all the way to Kyoto for *that*?! This was crazy! When I got home, I would have to get down onto my knees and apologize!

"...What was all that?" Cao Cao asked.

He and the other members of his group were clearly left speechless by the display. They were trying to summon the Great Red, but they'd gotten Rias Gremory instead!

Thud.

All of a sudden, I felt a pounding in my chest.

Thump.

There it was again. The next thing I knew...

"You did it. Come on, let's go!" Elsha called.

In response to her cry, crimson light spilled from my body, overflowing from deep within me...! Some red-hot power was building!

I couldn't control it! Had this energy been lying dormant inside my Sacred Gear? Was this my Juggernaut Drive?

No, it couldn't be. The terror I recalled from last time was absent. This was a new wave of power, a sensation I had never felt. Yet it seemed nostalgic.

Ddraig, is this—?

"Yes, I feel it, too, partner... It fills me with memories. This...is my original aura. This isn't driven by extreme emotion, like your Juggernaut Drive. There's no curse here, no outflowing of passion. This... is the power I had back when I possessed my original body. When my only concern was to defeat the White One!" Ddraig's voice was filled with joy.

I had no idea what had just happened to him, but that red aura was now bursting from my entire body, filling the surroundings...

-O●O-

When I came to, I found myself in a vast white space.

Where was I? As far as I knew, I still should've been by Nijo Castle's Honmaru Palace.

Two figures were standing in front of me, further adding to my confusion.

The first was Elsha, and the second...was a fashionably dressed man.

Was I inside the Boosted Gear...? Was it only my consciousness that was here?

I still didn't quite understand how this had occurred, but Elsha gave me a warm smile.

"You've opened the door to a new path—one that doesn't involve your Juggernaut Drive."

"Elsha... Thank you for all your help. Whatever this is, it feels like I've accomplished something incredible by surrendering myself to one crazy event after another."

"That's fine. We let the momentum carry you to this point... After all, what you desired most was breasts."

There was no denying that I was always chasing after boobs.

"Now Belzard and I will be able to move on."

Move on...? She couldn't possibly mean...

"We exist here only as residual memories. It's time for us to be released from this Sacred Gear."

"...You mean you're going to die?"

"We're already dead. What you see now are only fragments of memories. Nothing more. You can't even call us souls. It's an unnatural state to be in, wouldn't you agree? Our departure is long overdue."

"B-but I still have so many things I want to ask you! I still need your advice!"

Elsha shook her head, despite my plea. *"You don't need us. Besides, I don't have much interest in breasts. Only you could have brought about all these irregular phenomena by chasing after women's chests."*

"I—I'm really sorry about being a Breast Dragon..."

"You'll be okay, so long as you have Ddraig and your friends. Go, Red Dragon Emperor. You haven't yet fully dispelled the curse of the Red Dragon Emperor, but you will one day. I'm sure you'll be able to release the other lingering memories, too, just as you have me and Belzard."

I... I was so touched, so filled with gratitude and excitement that I burst into tears. To think that my predecessors cared this much about me...

"Now, it's time for us to move on. Belzard, why don't you give him some final words?"

The man—Belzard, the strongest Red Dragon Emperor in all of history—smiled my way.

"Please, I'll treasure your gracious advice," I entreated.

Belzard nodded, stretched out his hand, and raised his index finger into the air. *"Poke 'em. Stroke 'em. Oooooh."*

—.

For what felt like a long time, I didn't comprehend his words.

"He seems satisfied. Now then, Belzard. Let's move on," Elsha stated with a gentle expression.

H-hold on! Are those supposed to be Belzard's final words?! What's with him beaming all satisfied?! "Poke 'em, stroke 'em, oooooh"? Come on! Those are the lyrics to "The Song of the Breast Dragon"!

It was too late for me to say anything, as the pair was vanishing into the whiteness of this weird place. I couldn't believe this! *That* was the final statement from the strongest of all my predecessors?!

They were already waving farewell!

Surely, they had to have something more practical to offer! I would've accepted anything!

Elsha and Belzard, both pleased by my breast fetish, faded away.

Once they were gone, I felt like I understood.

An awful lot of weird individuals had been Red Dragon Emperors. And I was no exception.

"After all, I'm a massive pervert!"

That cry was the first thing out of my mouth as I regained consciousness! I was way beyond help!

"Let's gooooo! Boosted Geeeeeaaaaarrrrr!"

Responding to my eager spirit, my aura wreathed my body in crimson and began pouring into my surroundings!

I was overflowing with energy!

It was coming from deep inside me, from my Sacred Gear. This was Ddraig's original power. If combined with all those negative emotions capable of triggering a berserk Juggernaut Drive, this really would be terrifying.

Fortunately, it was different now. I wasn't burdened by dark feelings. My consciousness remained!

"Ah yes. Now I remember. How could I have forgotten...? Yes, it was God. He was the one who sealed my original power away, and Albion's, too..." Judging from what he was saying, Ddraig had evidently recalled something critical.

However, it would have to wait, because we had to send these damn heroes flying!

"Let's show them what this long-sealed power is capable of!"

"Let's go! Red Dragon Emperor! All our power! The strength of the Gremory Familia! Let's draw on all of it and let loose!"

"Desire!"

"Diablos!"

"Determination!"

"Dragon!"

"Disaster!"

"Desecration!"

"Discharge!"

The jewels studding my armor recited a litany of dangerous-sounding words, all of which began with the letter *D*!

"DDDDDDDDDDDDDDDDDDDDDDDDDDDDD!"

A new way to put the power flowing through me to use entered my mind.

Heh-heh-heh. This will be awesome. Beelzebub, the adjustments you made to my Sacred Gear are being enhanced by these Red Dragon Emperor powers...

Possibilities. Mine. Ddraig's. Our potential!

With everything that had happened, my Queen Promotion had been nullified. I would have to Promote again! And this time, I didn't require Asia's permission!

At the top of my lungs, I declared, "Mode Change: Welsh Blaster Bishop!"

I Promoted to a Bishop! But as you might have expected, I was no ordinary one!

Bracing myself, I concentrated my red aura around my shoulders and began to give it form.

The result was a backpack, complete with a pair of massive, large-caliber cannons, one over each shoulder!

Bzzzzz...

That gathering hum was the sound of the weapons charging up.

My demonic power had increased to new levels thanks to my Bishop Promotion, which combined with my newly awakened powers, resulting in a ridiculous amount of energy accumulating in my backpack. I was readying an incredibly high-energy blast!

"...This is bad...," Cao Cao said.

It looked like he'd sensed the vast force accumulating in the cannons.

If I scored a direct hit, I could probably blow them all away, right? That was the plan, anyway!

Kiba, Xenovia, Irina, Rossweisse, Saji—my dear friends! You all fought well! And then these bastards chose to ignore us! I felt so pathetic, so powerless! I'm going to fire those emotions right back at them!

Once the energy was fully charged in my twin cannons—

"Boost! Boost! Boost! Boost! Boost! Boost! Boost! Boost! Boost!"

"Take thiiiiisssss! Dragon Blaaaasteeeeerrrrr!"

Boooooooooooooooooooooom!

My shoulder cannons let loose with an astronomical explosion! Try though I did to maintain my balance, the force threw my body backward…! It took all my strength just to keep from getting hurled away by the recoil!

And that concentrated surge of force was coursing straight for the band of heroes!

"Interesting! I'll see what you've got, Mr. Legendary Dragon!" Heracles declared, stepping up to take the blast head-on.

"Don't! Get out of the way!" Cao Cao bellowed, sending Heracles flying with a thrust of his spear!

The heroes quickly fell back. My blast passed them by, racing into the distance.

Booooooooooooooooooooooooooooooooooooooooooooom!

A tremendous explosion shook the artificial space, consuming the cityscape!

The power continued to spread wider and wider, until the entire city was engulfed in that brilliant light!

When finally it subsided, everything was gone! Even the game field itself seemed to be damaged, distorting all over the place!

"…He eradicated the entire city! Hey! If he keeps doing that, this whole space will be destroyed!" Heracles exclaimed. Apparently, he'd realized just how powerful my attack was.

"He's managed to warp the pseudo-dimension… Yet we built this place to be so durable… How can he wield that level of strength?" The grin had finally disappeared from Siegfried's face, leaving him frowning.

Heh. It was time for some payback. This wasn't over!

"Cao Caaaaaooooo!" I shouted, dismissing the cannons on my back! They dissipated into motes of light.

That had only been the beginning!

Next, I made some adjustments to the Evil Piece within my body! Right, what I needed now was speed! Incomparable quickness! I pictured myself as Kiba, a Knight!

"Mode Change: Welsh Sonic Boost Knight!"

I extended my dragon wings and took off for Cao Cao! The intensity of the boosters on my back multiplied, spewing a magnificent streak of demonic energy! I shot forward with such speed that the air trembled.

Not yet... I still wasn't fast enough! I needed to be quicker than he could follow! I required supersonic, godly swiftness!

"Armor Purge!" I called, releasing several portions of my Scale Mail!

The thick, heavy armor protecting my torso, my arms, my legs, and my head all vanished!

Casting aside all unnecessary weight, I rocketed ahead with the bare minimum in the way of protection! My Boosted Gear Scale Mail had been honed to a sleek suit. I had given up the majority of my defenses in favor of this streamlined form capable of moving rapidly.

I needed divine speed! To move beyond what anyone could track!

The intense g-forces left me nauseous, but I pushed though it, shooting through the sky!

It must have been how Kiba and Vali saw the world...

To be honest, my body wasn't used to this, but I had to see it through!

"I don't care if I slam straight into you! Cao Caaaaaooooo!"

"Boost! Boost! Boost! Boost! Boost! Boost! Boost! Boost! Boost! Boost!"

I caught him in my sights and threw my body at him!

"You're fast!" Cao Cao braced himself with his spear!

Good! We could decide this with a straight-up fight!

That was the kind of battle I best understood!

Wham!

I slammed into that bastard hero at breakneck speed!

"Gah!" Cao Cao coughed.

I grabbed him and kept on flying.

"You're mine now. Got anything to say?" I asked.

"I didn't expect you to rush in headfirst! But can that thin armor of yours withstand my spear? Sorry about this, but I've just finished powering it up! I can end you!"

Yes, with my Scale Mail as thin as it was right now, one hit from the True Longinus was enough to finish me. I would surely be annihilated the second it made contact.

But I knew that. I had known that all along!

Thus, I adjusted the Evil Piece inside me yet again!

"Mode Change: Welsh Dragonic Rook!"

The time for speed was gone. Now I required overwhelming strength and defense. My red aura wrapped around me, restoring my armor. And it didn't stop there. The suit continued to grow thicker and thicker.

Massive amounts of dragon aura accumulated around me. My arms must have been double, no, five or six times their original girth!

After that transformation, my insane speed abated, sending Cao Cao and me hurtling through the air. Cao Cao readied his spear, aiming its blade of light straight for me.

Slash!

I used the thick gauntlet protecting my right arm as a shield to guard. The Holy Spear pierced through the armor and stopped halfway before it could reach me!

A scowl formed on Cao Cao's face. "So I'll need to boost its power *again* to destroy your armor?! At this level, it should be able to slay a high-class demon in a split second!"

I raised my now-massive left fist into the air. My aim was perfect. I couldn't miss.

Let's do this, Ddraig, everyone!

"Don't you dare belittle the Breast Dragon, you bastaaaaarrrrrd!"

"Boost! Boost! Boost! Boost! Boost! Boost! Boost! Boost! Boost! Boost!"

My blow came crashing down on him!

Cao Cao hurriedly pulled back his spear and positioned it in front of him for protection.

"Damn yooooouuuuuu!"

Crash!

The moment my fist made contact, I pulled back a new firing hammer that had appeared on my gauntlet close to my elbow! My punch's momentum increased to untold levels as a huge power spewed out around me!

Then, from midair, I sent Cao Cao hurtling into the ground!

Booooooooooom…!

He'd taken the blow head-on! And yet, in the brief moment after my attack connected and before he fell, I saw that he was laughing.

The impact sent fissures through the earth and kicked up a humongous cloud of dirt!

With that bout of midair close combat finished, I landed with a heavy *thud*, clad in my oversized armor.

With a soft, fleeting noise, my armor vanished into mist, scattering to the wind.

"Hah... Hah..."

My breath was ragged, and I fell to my knees.

I was beyond exhausted...

I had just burned up an immense amount of energy...

At this rate, my Boosted Gear's time limit would soon run out.

I had gained a new technique—one that allowed me to freely Promote my Evil Piece even without the permission of my King. That, combined with the abilities of the Red Dragon Emperor, meant my demonic strength, speed, and offensive and defensive skills had all received an incredible power-up.

As a Bishop, I could bolster my demonic energy and fire supercharged Dragon Shots.

Promoting to a Knight allowed me to slim my armor and move at breakneck speed. Pouring my Red Dragon Emperor powers into my agility at the same time would grant me a vast range of movement.

And shifting to a Rook gave me the opposite qualities of a Knight—turbocharged defense and unbelievable strength, albeit at the expense of my agility.

By freely moving between the three pieces, I had access to all their unique qualities. Moreover, I could boost the skills of those Evil Pieces to their utmost limits, although doing so meant reducing my other statistics.

...That said, at my current level, I couldn't quite Promote to a Queen. If I tried, the excess strength could make me go berserk. There was even a risk of me overloading and burning out.

Beelzebub had given me the key. With that, I had reignited the original powers of the Red Dragon Emperor—of Ddraig himself.

Combined with the ingenuity of the Evil Pieces system, I had awakened a new strength within.

This was what happened when I was given the opportunity to unleash my possibilities... I had opened the door to a new path. All that remained was to walk it.

Unfortunately, the toll on my stamina was immense... If I tried this again too soon, I would probably collapse. And that was being optimistic.

"Partner. Releasing all that power has further reduced the time it takes for you to reach your Balance Breaker and extended the amount of time you'll be able to maintain it. However, it has also increased the amount of energy and fortitude your powers will consume, particularly when you keep changing modes. You should be able to lessen the effects of that with practice, however."

Right. Thanks, Ddraig.

Evidently, I still had room for improvement. Training and perseverance had brought me this far, so clearly, I was taking the right approach.

There was no way I'd be permitted to use this in a Rating Game, though. It was basically a brute-force Promotion done without the authorization of my King. Beelzebub had even mentioned something about refraining from using such powers in official matches.

Well, so long as I had it on hand for real-life battles, I would be able to rely on it.

As I slowly pulled myself up, I spotted Cao Cao rising to his feet as well.

That bastard. Was he still going to fight? He'd used his spear as a shield, so maybe he'd withstood my strike?

He pulled himself out from the crater that had formed when I had slammed him into the ground.

Blood was trickling from his nose and mouth. He wiped it away before cracking his neck and addressing me. "Well done, Red Dragon Emperor. I did you a disservice earlier. It seems that in your desperation, you've undergone a dramatic change. If I hadn't defended myself with my spear, you would have killed me."

That was the idea! Damn him! Damn that ultimate Longinus! He had the frail body of a regular human! I should have been the victor in a straight-up confrontation!

"That must be a new ability, one outside the normal rules of the Evil Pieces system... An illegal move, you could say."

I cocked my head to one side. I'd never heard that term before. "An illegal move?" I repeated.

"It's a chess term," Cao Cao explained. "It's what you call a maneuver that goes against the rules of the game. What you did is clearly against the methods of the Evil Pieces system."

An illegal move, huh?

Well, Cao Cao was right. I doubted that what I'd done would be allowed in a Rating Game.

"*I would have called it a triaina,*" Ddraig muttered.

A what? What's that supposed to mean?

"*A triaina is the weapon of choice for Poseidon, the Greek sea god. The word* trident *is probably more common. What you just did, that series of attacks that combined the qualities of three separate Evil Pieces, struck me as similarly keen and acute as a three-pronged trident.*"

An illegal move... A triaina. I liked the sound of that.

"Illegal Move Triaina. Sounds good. How about we call it that, then? The Red Dragon Emperor's Three-Pronged Promotion," I said.

That was a good enough name for now. However, I'd need to think of a new title once I managed to Promote to Queen this way.

"Terrifying indeed. In terms of direct offensive power, that technique might even rival Vali, so long as he doesn't use his Juggernaut Drive... Then again, Vali is improving by the day. There's no telling what his current level is...," Cao Cao remarked.

I harbored no hope that I'd caught up to Vali yet. He was a genuine fighting prodigy.

"That attack of yours looks like it has consumed more of your aura, more of your stamina, than you expected. You still have a long way to go before you can master it. No, even then, the drain will be significant... I'm guessing you have maybe ten minutes left in your Balance Breaker state at most."

Cao Cao wasn't far off. In fact, his analysis was almost spot-on. Of course, I wasn't about to admit that to him.

I would keep fighting right up to the last minute, if I had to. Regardless of any limit.

Sighing, I called out to Cao Cao. "You're a tough opponent, too. I thought you were making light of us, but it seems you're taking this seriously now."

"I was a fool to underestimate you, even if only slightly. I apologize. You, who have learned the secrets of the Red Dragon Emperor and do not lose yourself to them, are a formidable adversary. I'll have to reflect on all this." Cao Cao paused for a moment, tapping his spear against his shoulder. "How exhilarating. I haven't felt this good since I fought Vali one-on-one. Yes, there's no greater joy than battling a legendary dragon. And I suppose that's proof that I'm the descendant of a hero at heart."

Exhilarating? I was sick of all these combat maniacs. When would I finally be able to build my harem and live in peace?

"Are you planning on fighting an all-out war?" I demanded.

"Nah, nothing like that. Our current forces aren't suited to a prolonged conflict. We may be strong individually, but we can't win against the combined might of those backing you. I'd like to think we'd inflict some heavy losses, but we'd certainly lose. No, the better strategy would be to target your vulnerabilities with carefully planned strikes. To that end, we will continue working for our present organization."

He was willing to stick with Ophis for that? Cao Cao was an odd one, that was for sure. Maybe he had other reasons, too?

Vrrrrr-brrrrr!

A sound rang out as everything around us reverberated. I recognized the noise. It was the sound of something tearing through space!

I hesitantly looked upward, only to find a gaping hole forming in the air!

The image of that massive red dragon flashed in my mind.

"Looks like it's begun," Cao Cao said with a clearly joyful grin.

S-so the Great Red really has been summoned by the nine-tailed fox and that huge magic circle...?!

"Perhaps our magic circle combined with your enormous strength is what brought the True Dragon here," that bastard hero added, obviously mocking me.

My power-up did this?!

"Georg! Prepare to summon the Dragon Eater—" Cao Cao paused in mid-sentence, narrowing his eyes and staring suspiciously into the rift.

"...No. That isn't the Great Red... It's raring for battle...!"

"Roooooaaaaarrrrr!"

What emerged from the dimensional rift was an Eastern dragon, its long, slender body at least a dozen meters in length.

It certainly wasn't the Great Red!

A mesmerizing green aura radiated from its body as it glided gracefully through the night sky.

"It's the Mischievous Dragon, Yulong!" Cao Cao cried out.

Yulong?! H-he's one of the five Dragon Kings!

Cao Cao, though evidently startled by Yulong's sudden appearance, was directing his gaze not at the dragon but at the figure riding on its back.

I, too, focused my attention on it.

It was a tiny figure—and they soon fell from Yulong's back. Did they jump? From that height?

The person didn't seem bothered by the considerable plunge, landing safely.

"What a powerful current of spirit energy, and of a dragon's domination. All of Kyoto is reacting with strange undulations."

The small figure had the voice of an elderly man and was approaching us slowly one step at a time. He was so tiny—almost a child in stature...? Hold on, *was* he a child...? He couldn't have been any larger than a toddler.

His fur shone with a golden radiance, and his garments looked like a monk's robe... He looked just like a monkey, complete with a wrinkled face... Was he a spirit? A monkey one?

A staff was clutched in his hands, and prayer beads hung around his neck. Oddly enough, he was sporting a pair of almost cyberpunk glasses! His lips, which gripped a small pipe, were twisted in a dauntless grin!

"Ah, long time no see, you with the Holy Spear. You've grown," the elderly monkey said to Cao Cao.

Cao Cao's eyes narrowed in evident amusement. "Well now, if it isn't the Victorious Fighting Buddha. I wasn't expecting you to turn up here. Apparently, you've been upsetting our plans all throughout the world."

"You've taken your pranks too far this time, boy. It wasn't easy convincing the Heavenly Emperor to send me as his emissary for negotiations with the lady nine-tailed fox, and here I find you've kidnapped her. There are heroes who ascend to godhood, and then there are heroes whose descendants are little more than a poison unto the world. Conquest and tyranny last but one generation. Isn't that what they say, Cao Cao?"

"Poison? I'm honored that that's how you see us."

It was clear that Cao Cao regarded this old man with a certain reverence. Heck, all those so-called heroes were staring at him in awe. Actually, it may have been closer to strained tension.

Hold on, the Heavenly Emperor...? He meant Sakra, right? The Lord of the Devas? And this monkey was his emissary? So *he* was the one Princess Yasaka was supposed to hold talks with? He had to be one powerful old monkey to get a job like that.

"...Just who is that guy...?" I muttered under my breath.

"...It's probably Sun Wukong—the first-generation one," Kiba whispered. I guess he'd had his wounds mended, because he was walking toward me.

H-h-h-h-hold on! Seriouslyyyyy?! I was shocked beyond belief!

"S-s-s-s-so he's the *original* Sun Wukong?! That old monkey guy is the one from *Journey to the West*?!"

This was incredible! Was he the reinforcements Azazel had mentioned?!

The old monkey must have noticed me staring at him, because he grinned in my direction. "Red Dragon Emperor, you've done well, my boy. But you can ease up now. I'm here to give you all a helping hand. Leave this to Gramps. Yulong, take care of our spirit friend," the original Sun Wukong stated.

"*Hey, hey! Don't you go ordering me around, you old geezer!*" Yulong bellowed back. "*I'm worn out just from getting us here! Anyway, what's happening with the White Dragon Emperor's friend, that witch girl? Whoa! Is that Vritra?! Have you been fighting that fox spirit?! Man, how long has it been?*"

…Yulong seemed seriously psyched up!

"*He hasn't changed at all.*"

I-is that so, Ddraig…?

"I'll treat you to some fine Kyoto dining later," the original Sun Wukong said with a puff of his pipe. "How does that sound?"

"*You decrepit old fool! You'll treat* me?! *Me?! Me?! Me?! Don't act like I'm your errand boy! I'm a Dragon King! Hey, fox lady? See how strong I am?*" Yulong confronted Yasaka, complaining all the while.

Approaching Cao Cao, Sun Wukong called, "Sorry about this, Red, but I need to teach the boy here a few lessons."

At that moment, Siegfried unfurled his six arms, charging straight for the old monkey!

"Siegfried! Don't! You can't—," Cao Cao cautioned, but it looked like nothing in the world was going to hold that Asura guy back!

"Monkey boss man! If you're the genuine Sun Wukong, then I'll—"

"Stretch, Nyoibou," the old man said softly.

Thump!

With those calm words, the staff in Sun Wukong's hands elongated at a tremendous speed, sending Siegfried flying!

"—!"

Crash!

Siegfried was hurled into a pile of rubble with that one hit!

Wh-whhhhhooooooaaaaa!

That old monkey was superstrong! He took Siegfried down in a single blow! Even Kiba and Xenovia, who wielded the new Durendal, hadn't been able to beat him!

"You aren't ready to face me, boy. Nor are your Demon Swords, either. Let's go back to basics. You can start by learning how to run."

As the old Sun Wukong glanced back at Siegfried, Yulong exclaimed, *"Huuuuh?! Hey, Gramps! This fox gal is super buffed!"*

The Dragon King had been ensnared by the spirit's many tails!

It was a bitter struggle, yet Yulong still appeared so amped!

"Pull yourself together. You're a Dragon King," Sun Wukong chided with a sigh.

"Just so you know, I'm the youngest Dragon King! I'm still bursting with youth!"

"Sure you are. Weren't you the one who kept going on about retiring the second you won your last flashy battle? Put that youth of yours to use!"

"…Fine! Here goes!"

I guess the bizarre pair had reached an understanding. Judging by their interactions, they must have been good partners.

The mist-controlling mage released the magic circle holding the nine-tailed fox and aimed a hand at Sun Wukong. Apparently, he considered the old monkey more important than summoning the Great Red!

"Seize him, O mist!"

At the mage's command, the fog gathered around Sun Wukong.

"Submit yourself to the power of Heaven, the force of thunder that seals the dragon's jaw."

Thump.

Sun Wukong intoned an incantation, then tapped his staff against the ground. That was all it took to disperse the vapor!

"Your skills with that Sacred Gear still have a ways to go. Why don't you try asking that Red Dragon kid over there for help?"

He was praising me! I was touched!

"—! You cleared my fog…?! But I generated it with a Longinus!"

The mage was taken aback. Honestly, who wouldn't have been? He was using a top-class Longinus, and it had been useless!

"Take this!"

Whooooooooooosh!

Cao Cao, sensing an opening, extended the blade of his spear. Yet

Sun Wukong blocked it with just a single finger! Impossible! How could he stop that weapon so easily?!

"...A keen weapon. But that's it. You're still young. If I can stop that thing with a finger, you have no hope of destroying gods or Buddhas. Don't get cocky."

Cao Cao laughed in the face of this reprimanding. "...I see. So you still possess that monstrous strength you're famous for... I've heard all about how powerful you were when you were young. I wonder how well you hold up now?"

The first-generation Sun Wukong merely shrugged unconcernedly in response to this question.

Siegfried pulled himself up from the rubble, calling out to his leader, "Cao Cao, let's call it quits. The old Sun Wukong is practically a celebrity what with how many times he's foiled the Khaos Brigade's terrorist attacks. If we keep this up, we'll be putting valuable talent to waste. I underestimated him. He's too strong."

Hearing this, Cao Cao lowered his spear. "So it's time to withdraw? I suppose overextending ourselves here could prove fatal."

The band of heroes quickly assembled, just as the mist-wielding mage began to activate a gigantic magic circle beneath his feet. It was a transportation array! They were planning to flee!

"Let's call it a day," Cao Cao said. "Sun Wukong, members of the Gremory Familia, Red Dragon Emperor, we'll meet again."

Hold on, wait! Don't you even think about running!

They had thrown our school trip into chaos and hurt Kunou's mom!

I gathered my power, generated a cannon over my left gauntlet, and concentrated my remaining energy into it!

Vrrrrr-rrrrr...

As the force collected, it released a *buzz*. I didn't need to deal them a huge blow, only enough to make sure I hit them!

The first-generation Sun Wukong looked at me and grinned. "You trying to complete my errand for me, boy? Well, go ahead. He needs a good walloping. This won't last long, but how about I help boost your power?"

Sun Wukong tapped his staff against my armor.

Immediately, a tremendous strength surged from my body! Was this the power of his sage arts?!

Did I still have this much power left inside me? Had it been lying dormant?

Thanks, Gramps!

With this, I now had enough to let loose! I aimed the cannon right for Cao Cao!

"You think you can just go home after all that? Here's a little souvenir from Kyoto!"

Stzsssssssss!

A blast of concentrated demonic force erupted from the cannon on my gauntlet!

"You damn bastard!"

Heracles and Jeanne leaped in front of Cao Cao to shield him.

Now!

I visualized Sirzechs's unique style of magic attacks, an endless barrage from all possible directions!

No, I didn't even need to go that far! I just needed to adjust the trajectory of the bombardment!

"Twiiiiist!" I cried out.

In reply, the beam of energy warped, bending around Heracles and Jeanne!

Boooooooooom!

The blast caught Cao Cao by surprise, hitting him smack in the face!

"Guhhhhh…!"

Red smoke rose into the air as Cao Cao covered his face with his hands!

I had twisted it! I had altered my attack's trajectory mid-flight! There was still room for improvement, but this meant I could likely achieve the same result with my Dragon Shot. My battle with Sirzechs hadn't been for nothing!

Blood was dripping down from Cao Cao's right eye! His whole face was stained bright red! He brought a hand to his wound as his face twisted in clear frenzied rapture!

"…My eye… Red Dragon Emperoooooorrrrr!"

Cao Cao readied his spear and began reciting something! "O spear! The true Holy Lance that pierced God himself! Absorb the dynast ideal that lays dormant within me, grant me both blessing and destruction that I may—"

At that moment, Siegfried slammed his hands over Cao Cao's mouth, silencing him! "Cao Cao! Don't do it! It's too soon to use the True Longinus's Balance Breaker. You can't reveal Truth Idea yet!"

Those words seemed to calm Cao Cao, who paused to catch his breath.

"Let's retreat," Siegfried continued. "Leonardo is probably at his limit with the Annihilation Maker. The others have surely bought us all the time they can. We've collected enough information, so this wasn't a waste." His eyes were narrowed at Sun Wukong. It looked like he held a grudge for that earlier attack.

Cao Cao was staring at me through his left eye, his gaze stern and piercing. "I know. Sun Wukong. Red Dragon Emperor—no, Issei Hyoudou—we're withdrawing for now. I won't be able to make light of Vali now that I've been bested as he was. How is it that you always manage to steal the show at the last minute?"

Was he talking about my battle with Vali at Kuou Academy?

The magic circle shone brighter as the heroes teleported away, but not before Cao Cao could deliver a parting remark.

"Get stronger, Issei Hyoudou. Surpass Vali. Do that, and I'll show you the true power of this spear."

The moment they were gone, exhaustion washed over me. It took all my effort just to maintain my armor.

Those so-called heroes... Cao Cao... The strongest of all Longinuses... None of it made any sense.

Still, there was one thing that could be said for certain.

That group was disturbingly powerful, their leader most of all.

After the heroes had fled, only our group, along with Sun Wukong, Yulong, and Princess Yasaka, remained.

"Ah, that was rough. It would've been a real pain without Vritra..." Yulong landed on the ground, pausing to catch his breath.

Yulong and Saji, who had since returned to normal, had successfully quelled the rampaging nine-tailed fox.

Upon returning to his human form, Saji had passed out, and Asia was tending to him.

Good work there, buddy.

Princess Yasaka, however, was still a giant beast, and her eyes remained vacant. Whatever brainwashing techniques the heroes had used on her were likely still in effect.

"Mother! Mother!" Kunou shouted, but there was no response.

Sun Wukong puffed his pipe in apparent consideration. "Now then, what shall we do here? I should be able to use some sage arts to remove the negative qi from her, but it will take some time."

Suddenly, the old monkey seemed to hit on something, and he glanced my way. "You there, boy, Red. I hear you have some ability that allows you to listen to women's breasts?"

How did he know about that...? Was my technique that famous? If he'd watched a recording of my recent Rating Game, it would make sense that he knew about it.

"E-er, yeah, I do."

"Good. I'll help you, then. Can you use it on this young thing here and our nine-tailed fox princess?"

He wanted me to use my Boob-Lingual on them both? Did he want to probe their inner thoughts?

I didn't really understand his reasoning, but I used my remaining demonic energy to enter into that state where I could converse with breasts.

I concentrated my power in my brain, let my delusions take over, and triggered my ability!

"Gooooo! Boob-Lingual!"

I deployed the technique on both Kunou and Princess Yasaka! At the same time, I released my armor. This required all my remaining strength!

After confirming that my ability was working, Sun Wukong twirled his staff through the air and brought it back down. A new space unfolded around us, taking precedence over the field created by my Boob-Lingual.

The surroundings seemed to be undulating around me. Was my vision blurred?

"This is a special application of that technique of yours, my boy. I've changed it a little to let them connect directly."

Sun Wukong turned to Kunou. "Girl, try calling out to your mother with your heart."

Kunou nodded and closed her eyes. I heard her voice in my mind. "...Mother... Mother. Can you hear me, Mother...? Mother... Please come back... Please, Mother, please..."

Princess Yasaka gave no sign that she understood.

"...I won't be selfish anymore...," Kunou continued, weeping. "...I'll eat fish, even though I don't like it... I'll stop running around Kyoto at night... So please, please, please, Mother, come back... Forgive me, Mother... Please..."

It was a sorrowful appeal. Kunou apologized to Princess Yasaka repeatedly.

And then it happened.

"...Ku...nou..."

It was faint, but I definitely heard a reply!

Kunou lifted her head, crying out with her heart once more: "Mother! It's me, Kunou! Please sing me that song again! Teach me to dance again! I'll be good, I promise! I want to be with you...and learn all about Kyoto! I want to walk through the city with you...!"

A gentle light wrapped around Kunou and Princess Yasaka as the body of the nine-tailed fox gradually shrank.

When the glow subsided, Princess Yasaka had been returned to her humanlike form.

Kunou had done it! She'd restored her mother to normal! Before I knew it, I found myself adopting a victory pose!

"...Where am I?"

Princess Yasaka was trembling, and it looked like her mind was still rather fuzzy, but she was finally herself again!

Kunou rushed over, leaped into her parent's arms, and burst into tears. "Motheeeeerrrrrr! Motheeeeerrrrr!"

Princess Yasaka embraced her in turn, stroking her head. "…What's the matter, Kunou? You're always crying…"

Damn… I couldn't help but sob at this touching scene.

"*Sniff…* Kunou… Thank goodness…" Asia, having finished healing everyone, was bawling her eyes out.

Ah, what a wonderful scene. Congratulations, Kunou!

"Well, it looks like that's resolved," Sun Wukong announced with a tone of finality.

And so, after many twists and turns, our battle to save the nine-tailed fox Princess Yasaka had come to an end.

Maven

With the intense battle concluded, we had all returned to the real world and were gathered on the rooftop of the hotel where we were staying.

"Well done, Issei," Azazel complimented as he placed one hand on my shoulder. "Go get some rest. Relief team! Give the Gremory Familia, Irina, and Saji a good look over! They might not be badly injured, but they've severely drained their powers and physical stamina!" he added, giving directions to the staff.

I was more than happy to accept his praise. To be honest...I was plain exhausted. I definitely wouldn't be able to use my Balance Breaker again tonight...

The operation had ended with the heroes withdrawing. After doing heavy battle with several members of the Hero Faction, including the guy with the Annihilation Maker and his legions of anti-monsters, the joint forces of the allied factions were now taking care of all the cleanup duties.

To think that the heroes had managed to slip from the allied factions' siege of Kyoto... It was clear from that feat alone that they were a force to be reckoned with.

From what I heard, they had used the kid with the Annihilation Maker to create another army of anti-monsters as a diversion while they fled.

As for us, by the time we returned to the hotel, we were all on the brink of collapsing where we stood. My legs were quivering, and my head was spinning. I was plain worn out…

Asia was similarly exhausted after mending everyone's injuries and had fallen sound asleep leaning against me.

After we were treated by the relief team, we let them ferry us away.

"Sorry, Issei. As bad as it looks to be the one who leaves first, I think I'll go get some rest," Kiba said.

I waved back to him in response. He deserved time to recuperate, and I was grateful for all his efforts.

"Gen!"

"Genshirou!"

Saji was being carried off on a stretcher. The other members of the Sitri Familia were by his side. Worry showed plainly in their teary eyes.

Transforming into a Dragon King had completely depleted Saji, so once everything was over, he'd passed out. Ultimately, he hadn't needed me to talk to him to keep him from losing control, so he must have been putting considerable effort into controlling his powers. Did that mean he was growing? Well, in any event, it was clear that his friends adored him.

After all that, I received a phone call from the prez and explained what had happened. She would probably have a lot more questions once we got home, though.

…Was she going to kill me? Just as that dark thought surfaced in my mind, the first-generation Sun Wukong approached.

"Red, my boy."

"Y-yes?"

"You seem to have gotten your hands on a unique power, something other than your Juggernaut Drive. Good work. There's nothing special about that Juggernaut Drive of yours—it's merely power run amok. Pure destruction. After you use it, you die. However, you've got an important lady you want to look out for, no? They don't call you the Breast Dragon for nothing, eh?"

H-he was praising me! It was an honor to be complimented by the famed protagonist of *Journey to the West*! And he was talking about women, too! He motioned to Asia.

"Ha-ha-ha. Well, kind of," I answered bashfully.

"Then don't make her cry. You're the kind who gets stronger for the sake of dreams and women. Remember this: The Red and White Dragon Emperors are beings of extraordinary might. You can become inconceivably strong without your Juggernaut Drive, but that doesn't mean there's no danger in it." The wrinkled monkey stared deep into my eyes.

"...?"

I had no idea what he was getting at.

Sun Wukong puffed on his pipe and laughed. "I've heard that useless kid who bears my name has brought you a lot of trouble. I owe you an apology."

Was he talking about Bikou? Well, he *had* caused us a fair number of headaches. He was the joker who had started calling Rias Switch Princess.

"...Your emotions are what will activate your Juggernaut Drive. Remember that. You got in a good hit with your final attack against Cao Cao. Keep working on it. Don't neglect visualizing your goals, and make sure you put in the effort... Now then, I've finished what I came here to do for the Heavenly Emperor, so I guess I'll keep looking for that idiot grandson of mine. Messing around with the White Dragon Emperor... I'll teach the both of them a lesson or two. Yulong, let's go see Yasaka."

"Sure thing, old man. See ya, Ddraig!"

With those parting words, both Sun Wukong and Yulong left us.

Alone now, I clenched my trembling fists... They were all but numb. Was that proof of my exhaustion?

My new ability had come about by combining the qualities of my Evil Piece with the power dormant in my Sacred Gear.

There was still plenty of room for improvement, however. I would have to rededicate myself to my training.

...Sairaorg, Vali, and Cao Cao.

I wouldn't lose to any of them. I would get stronger. As mighty as I could be.

And then, one day, my dreams would come true.

Elsha, Belzard. We may have had an awkward parting, but please look out for me, wherever you are.

As the Red Dragon Emperor and as the Breast Dragon, I would do everything I could.

With eyes fixed on the sky during our final night in Kyoto, I made this vow to myself.

New Life

It was the final day of the school trip.

Given everything that had occurred last night, we members of the Gremory Familia were still exhausted, even after getting some rest. We had to drag ourselves out of bed to tour the souvenir stores before going home.

Although I was gasping all the while, I finally made it to the foot of Kyoto Tower.

Once our souvenir shopping was done, it was finally time to leave the old capital.

Kunou and Princess Yasaka came to see us off at the bullet train platform at Kyoto Station.

"Red Dragon Emperor." Kunou addressed me while standing hand in hand with her mother.

"Just call me Issei."

Kunou's face turned bright red, seemingly in response to my casual reply. "...Issei. W-will you come visit us in Kyoto again?"

"Of course."

The departure bell rang out over the platform.

"You *must* come back!" Kunou called out to me. "I'll be waiting!"

"I'll bring all the others with me next time. You can show us around the spirit side of Kyoto."

"Okay!"

Princess Yasaka, until now listening in silence, spoke up: "Azazel, Red Dragon Emperor, demons, angels, and fallen angels—thank you. I owe you my deepest gratitude. The Demon King Leviathan, the Victorious Fighting Buddha, and I are planning to resume our talks soon. I've always hoped we might be able to embark on a path of cooperation and friendship together. And I intend to ensure that our joint efforts prevent a cloud of terror from descending on Kyoto ever again."

"We're counting on you all," Azazel responded with a grin, shaking Princess Yasaka's hand.

All of a sudden, Leviathan placed her hand on top of theirs, too! "Heh-heh-heh. It's time for you all to go home now! Miss Yasaka, that cute monkey gentleman, and I are going to make the most of Kyoto!"

Evidently, she was really looking forward to it. It sounded as though she was planning to remain in Kyoto a while longer for discussions with the city's spirit population.

With our farewells out of the way, we boarded the bullet train.

Kunou waved to me from the platform. "Thank you, Issei! Everyone! I can't wait to see you all again!"

We waved back to her in turn, and the doors slid shut with soft *thud*.

Kunou continued to wave farewell until she passed out of sight.

We had been in Kyoto for four days and three nights.

Yet our time had been spent jumping from one thing to another. We'd visited Kiyomizu-dera, Ginkaku-ji, Kinkaku-ji, Arashiyama, and Nijo Castle, and we made countless new memories...

I would definitely return. I wanted to see Kunou and Princess Yasaka again—and I hoped to bring the prez and the others with me.

Ah...

Suddenly, I remembered something.

"I forgot to ask Princess Yasaka to show me her breasts as a reward! Nooooo!"

Part of the reason why I had fought so hard was because I'd sought that prize! With all the craziness, I'd totally forgotten! Dammit! The Kyoto air must have messed with my head!

"Nooooo! Foxy breasts! Whyyyyy?!" I wailed, clawing at the door.

-○●○-

No sooner had we arrived home from Kyoto than the prez immediately scolded us.

Asia, Xenovia, Kiba, and I were kneeling formally on the floor. For some reason, Irina had joined us, as well. Rossweisse, tired from all the traveling, had retired to her bedroom immediately after returning. It sounded like she had pushed herself too hard, and her health was suffering for it. Being a teacher was probably hard work, and there was that whole bout of drunken vomiting...

Her gaze radiating anger, the prez stated, "I'd like to know why you didn't tell me what was going on, but I suppose we *were* preoccupied with a little trouble in the Gremory territory... Did Sona know, at least?"

"Y-yes..."

We explained everything we could. Akeno and Koneko were still fuming, however.

"You could have talked to me about it when I called you...," Akeno chided.

"...Yes. You're so cold," added Koneko.

"B-but everyone got home safe...!"

Gaspeeeeerrrrr! At least you're standing up for us! My dependable underclassman!

"You know, Issei won himself the eyes of another lady over there," Azazel remarked from his seat, casually adding fuel to the fire.

Please don't stoke the flames for no reason.

"And a nine-tailed fox girl, at that."

Was he talking about Kunou?!

"I-it isn't like that! You're going to give everyone the wrong idea, Teach!"

"You saw Princess Yasaka. I'm sure you've realized Kunou is gonna grow into a real busty beauty like her mom one day, right?"

My imagination took over, and I found myself visualizing what Kunou might look like in the coming years. Y-yep, she *would* no doubt have an incredible bosom...

"...M-maybe. But I'm not into kids or underdeveloped girls!"

Thud!

Koneko hit me over the head!

"Gah! Why...?"

"...I just felt like it."

R-really...? I couldn't comprehend her thinking one bit...

"Oh well. Issei's managed to snatch a dramatic power-up, so cut him some slack, okay, Rias?" Azazel said in my defense.

The prez breathed a heavy sigh before nodding. "Yes, I'm happy to hear that... But summoning me to Kyoto with no warning a-and demanding to see my br-breasts..." She stopped there, face turning scarlet.

She was talking about *that*! I was still fraught with astonishment and wonder, too, over what had happened! The others couldn't bring themselves to believe it, but a sorrowful explanation from Ddraig had convinced them.

Really, it was an unbelievable development! The prez's breasts had since returned to normal and weren't radiating light anymore. However, that phenomenon, whatever it was, had been incredible... To think that boobs could give off such brilliant power...

By the way, I'd made sure to follow up with everyone whom I had turned into gropers and had set their lives back on track! I was genuinely sorry for causing them trouble!

"You picked a good power, Issei," Azazel commented. "Your rival, Vali, is trying to push his Juggernaut Drive to its limits, to become a Heavenly Dragon tyrant in the true sense of the word. If you go down the same path as him, you'll be consumed, just as you were during the old demon regime attack. You don't need that Juggernaut Drive for strength—create your own path. I think aiming to become a King is a smart move."

The road of a King? That made sense.

Honestly, I doubted I'd match Vali by copying his strategy. My only choice was to take a different approach altogether.

Akeno abruptly clapped her hands together, as though she'd suddenly recalled something important. "Ah, I hear that they've started broadcasting the *Breast Dragon* TV show in the spirit world. It looks like you're going to be even more famous, Issei."

"Seriously?! Whoa, I guess that's another extraordinary development... It's so surreal."

Honestly, that TV show was getting out of control. And now it was being introduced to Japanese spirits?

"You'll be a hero to kids the world over before long," Xenovia stated, nodding. "Yep, you'll likely be able to make your dream of reaching new heights a reality soon."

I tilted my head to one side in uncertainty. "Do you think so? I'm still not very popular with the girls at school, though... At this rate, I'll be surrounded by kids, not a harem..."

Evidently remembering something, Azazel said, "Right, right. That girl from the House of Phenex is supposed to be transferring into Kuou just before the Academy Festival."

All of us save the prez, Akeno, Koneko, and Gasper were surprised at this news.

"Ravel?!" I gaped. "Seriously?!"

"Yeah. Sounds like she decided to follow Rias and Sona's example, and she put in a request to come study here in Japan," Azazel explained. "She'll be a first-year. All the formalities have already been taken care of. She's been assigned to Koneko's class. Cats and birds don't usually mix well, eh...? It'll be fun to see how it unfolds, that's for sure."

"...Whatever."

Koneko sure didn't sound happy about all this. Did she dislike Ravel? Come to think of it, I had never seen them talk to each other. If they were going to be classmates, hopefully they'd be able to get along.

"But why is she changing schools all of a sudden?" I inquired.

Azazel stared back at me, his gaze meaningful and suggestive.

What was with that look...?

"Anyway, that's the situation. Looks like things are gonna get even tougher for you, Rias."

The prez wore a complicated expression—all the girls did.

"...Even after coming home, I still can't let down my guard," Asia said in a low tone.

"Be strong, Asia. I've learned you need to persevere to keep up with this guy," Xenovia encouraged.

Irina seemed to agree and added, "Hmm... I suppose I'll have to be tough, too, then..."

"I'll concentrate on attack rather than perseverance, thank you," Akeno stated with a provocative grin.

What was all this? Ravel wasn't such a bad person once you got to know her...

The prez let out another sigh before forcing a smile. "All right. Everyone is home safe now, so let's leave it at that. I'll have Grayfia ask my brother for more details later."

At last, the prez's mood was seemingly lightening...

She addressed us all, saying, "It's almost time for the Academy Festival. We've been busy preparing while the rest of you have been away, so all that's left is the main event. Additionally..." The prez paused there, her face turning grave. "We need to think about our match against Sairaorg. Rumor says it will be the last Rating Game between young upper-class demons. We can't afford to get careless. Let's focus on preparing for that, too."

""""""""""Okay!"""""""""" we responded in unison.

The Academy Festival was important, but so was our bout with Sairaorg.

"Issei. Will you help me with my training when we're up to it? After everything that happened in Kyoto, I've realized just how much I need to improve. I'll need your help."

"Sure, Kiba. We can keep sparring until the day of the match."

Our practice sessions were due to resume anyhow.

I was looking forward to testing my new powers against Sairaorg and seeing whether they would be able to break through his strength.

Undoubtedly, I'd have to awaken the skills of a Queen while in that new mode. There would be a great many challenges ahead. Plus, there was the problem of whether this new technique would even be allowed in Rating Games...

"We're definitely going to win!" I declared.

Sairaorg was going down!

Boss×Boss

"Sirzechs, I'll send you the data we collected on those heroes. In terms of their Sacred Gears, they seem to have three top-tier Longinuses, as well as a sizable collection of Balance Breakers. They've got plans beyond trying to summon the Great Red, too. Damn nuisances."

"I've heard gathering support under the promise of destroying the demon and spirit alliance. Their core members may have other goals, but there's no better pretext than justice when it comes to ensuring the loyalty of their rank and file. Because of them, the troops we sent to lay siege to Kyoto suffered heavy losses. The situation on the ground was dire. Not only can they create anti-monsters with the Annihilation Maker, it's also difficult to fight against that many Balance Breakers simultaneously."

"As far as humans are concerned, demons, angels, and spirits are natural enemies—nothing more than monsters. The truce between our three factions seems to be what set them off. If demons getting on with fallen angels isn't enough, an alliance between Heaven and the underworld must seem even more outlandish. It's not surprising that they feel threatened... Anyway, how are the talks with the spirits going?"

"Apparently, they want to open negotiations with the fallen angel side next."

"Heh. Looks like Shemhazai is going to get the meeting he wanted, then. Ah, right. Did you know Sakra has been sending Sun Wukong and Yulong to run his errands? They ended up being a great help this time."

"The Heavenly Emperor—Sakra. With the biblical God dead, he and Zeus are among the most powerful deities remaining. If he tried to act directly and wound up dying to the Holy Spear, the balance of power between our factions would be shattered all over again. Sending the original Sun Wukong to deal with things certainly seems like the safest option."

"But if those heroes, those humans, see us as their enemies, aren't we the final bosses they'd want to exterminate? Or the hidden bonus bosses, maybe?"

"Humans have always been fearsome, if transient, beings."

"I guess... By the way, Issei pulled off another comeback in Kyoto. There's no question about him getting his own title now, is there?"

"Hmm. He's done more than enough. I plan to recommend him depending on the outcome of his next Rating Game."

"Against Sairaorg, huh? He also took down a whole lot of terrorists, right?"

"Our youths from the Houses of Bael, Agares, Gremory, and Sitri are all capable of that, but only Sairaorg and Rias would be strong enough to challenge their leaders. We have great expectations for both of them."

"So they're already ready to brush up against high-class demon pros, huh?"

"Indeed. Once they start participating in more Rating Games, I would expect them both to quickly earn a great many titles. Obviously, numerous individuals affiliated with the House of Gremory are placing their hopes in Issei as well as Rias. They're eagerly looking forward to seeing how he performs. As his future brother-in-law, I am, too."

"You aren't wasting any time, huh? Geez. So as far as Issei's concerned, you'll be both a Demon King and a brother. Sure must be hard to be him."

"I'm very excited. I'm counting on Rias and Issei. I'm excited to watch them improve, and yet..."

"What now?"

"There's something I want to ask, Azazel... What on earth happened with Rias's breasts?"

"They've surpassed their limits this time around. You could say they've entered a second phase. I guess you could call her a Super Switch Princess now."

"I see... Perhaps we should move our merchandising plans to another level, then..."

"You're getting a good head for business. So will Issei be able to use that new power in his match? I only got to see a little of it, but it looks pretty damn interesting."

"The other decision makers don't mind him using it. It should be fun to watch. The question now is Sairaorg... In all likelihood, he..."

Vali Lucifer

"That's everything I have to report for now, Vali."

"That's fine, Le Fay. Thanks for showing Sun Wukong and Yulong into that artificial dimension. How did you find Issei Hyoudou?"

"I was so thrilled to finally meet the Breast Dragon!"

"...I see. Well, good for you."

"One more thing. The old Sun Wukong is out looking for you and Bikou."

"He may well find us soon. It won't be easy shaking off that monkey... And Issei Hyoudou has begun to delve into his Sacred Gear and reach out to his predecessors..."

"Vali?"

"Talking people into submission isn't my style. It'll be more challenging, and more interesting, to dominate the prior White Dragon Emperors with brute force. If you want to come after us, you'd better do so soon, Cao Cao. Issei Hyoudou and I will utterly surpass you before long."

Bael

"Did you hear, Sairaorg?"

"Hear what, Seekvaira Agares?"

"Rumor has it Rias Gremory's Red Dragon Emperor has awakened a new power."

"I'm pleased to hear it. Yes, so it's finally happened. I'm looking forward to our encounter, truly."

"But everyone's saying it's so overpowered it wouldn't be fair to use it in a Rating Game."

"That won't be a problem. I'll permit it."

"I also heard he's enjoying the favor of Ajuka Beelzebub."

"That doesn't matter, either."

"You're going to be squaring off against Sirzechs Lucifer's brother-in-law. You realize that, right?"

"A fitting opponent for my fists."

"And he survived a battle with the Hero Faction leader. That guy with the Holy Spear."

"Naturally. Issei Hyoudou wouldn't want to break our agreement."

Heroes

"The Kyoto plan ended in failure, but we're working on some changes for our next one. We should be ready to show it off soon, Cao Cao."

"Good, Siegfried. That's what matters."

"So as planned, I'll be taking one of these... What about you, Cao Cao?"

"My spear is enough."

"How's your eye since that attack from the Red Dragon Emperor?"

"...Useless. Heh. He really got me."

"You were carrying Phoenix Tears. Why didn't you use them...? We'd better find you a replacement. Are you planning to make him pay? An eye for an eye?"

"Of course not. I'm not some third-rate villain. This will serve as a valuable reminder, that's all. As far as I'm concerned, those two Heavenly Dragons, Issei Hyoudou and Vali, are the ultimate foes. Yes, I look forward to facing them again."

AFTERWORD

Ishibumi here. I turned thirty this month. I also noticed that I've been eating less recently. Maybe I'm getting old...

After a nine-month wait since our last full volume, number nine is finally here. Ah, there was a lot I wanted to include in this one, and it feels like I just kept throwing more in, and the result is a book that's thicker than usual. And at long last, we've had a face-to-face encounter with the Hero Faction! It was fun to write so many battle scenes!

I went to Kyoto for the first time around a year ago to gather reference material. I went on three school trips myself, one each during elementary, middle, and high school. Yet by some strange stroke of luck, they were all to Fukushima. Anyway, I really enjoyed the old capital. The food was great, and the scenery was unforgettable.

Volume 7, which served as the beginning to the third arc of the overall narrative, focused on Norse mythology, while this one was all about the spirits of Kyoto.

A nine-tailed fox made her entrance as the spirit boss! That said, she might only play a big role in the story this once... I went through a lot of changes while developing her. I originally planned for the mythical *oni* Shuten-douji to lead the spirits of Kyoto, but I changed it after receiving some friendly advice—something about inviting misfortune on myself if I featured an *oni* in the book...

Anyway, back when I was first outlining *DxD*, I had this idea of basing it around a diviner protagonist who marries a nine-tailed fox princess. In the end, I shifted my attention to demons, but I thought I'd reuse the idea in this story.

*   *   *

Volume 9 features a smorgasbord of Balance Breakers. When I was discussing my plans with my editor and Miyama-Zero, I let them know my concerns about introducing so many Balance Breakers all at once, but they were incredibly enthusiastic about it and told me to let myself run wild. It's thanks to them that I was able to pull this off.

Issei has finally powered up! He's begun to awaken a unique ability that belongs only to him, something different from his Juggernaut Drive. The prez, as his trigger, has undergone a huge transformation as well. Her breasts now radiate brilliant light! She's entered her second phase, complete with glowing boobs.

The cannons that come with the Bishop version of Issei's Illegal Move Triaina were Miyama-Zero's idea. Miyama-Zero was having a hard time picturing what Issei would look like as a Bishop and hit upon the idea of adding cannons to both of his shoulders. It kind of looks like the Satellite Cannon from *Gundam X*, don't you think?

Issei's Rook punch was modeled on the Sudden Impact move from *The Big O*. It's a massive increase in power activated by retracting a piston and then releasing it.

His Knight form was based on *Kamen Rider Kabuto*'s Cast Off and Clock Up abilities, and on the Wild Wurger's Raptor Wings technique.

What will happen when Issei becomes able to shift into a Queen? He may have won the approval of history's two strongest Red Dragon Emperors, but the other incarnations are still possessed by negative emotions. Will he be able to break their curse? It will be interesting to see what happens next!

We also spent some time in this volume delving into the Church Trio. Asia wasn't the only one who went after Issei. Xenovia and Irina did, too! These faithful maidens have all but fallen directly into the Breast Dragon's lap...

And Rossweisse got to show off as well...sort of. She went a bit wild, but she's supposed to be a mature, feminine influence who's different from Rias and Akeno. I hope you'll come to adore her as much as I do! She's a very hard worker, and she tends to go a little overboard when she unwinds. Rossweisse may be strict, but she's a good person at heart.

We've also been introduced to the sorceress Le Fay and the golem Gogmagog from Team Vali. I thought it was time to bring them into the narrative. Basically, Vali found Gogmagog in the dimensional void back in Volume 6.

The cast of characters is expanding, but I hope that you'll be able to follow the story so long as you're familiar with the members of the Gremory Familia, Irina, Ddraig, Azazel, Sirzechs, and Vali. The plot revolves around them. The others are there mostly to make cameo appearances and to act as villains.

Now then, it's time to talk about the Hero Faction. Its members are all human. When I started writing *DxD*, I found myself wondering who would feel most threatened if demons, angels, and fallen angels struck up an alliance. The answer, of course, was humans. Wouldn't *you* be terrified if you heard that demons and fallen angels had decided to team up without knowing why? Essentially, these heroes are following the path of many an RPG protagonist, destined to face off against dragons and Demon Kings. That said, Cao Cao and his friends have other plans… And Vali is involved as well.

The Hero Faction is pretty merciless and nasty, so they made a complete mess of our protagonists' school trip. Still, Issei scored a new power-up, and he seems to have enjoyed all that sightseeing around Kyoto, so maybe everything worked out?

The dragon we met is Yulong, the Mischievous Dragon. He's one of the Five Great Dragon Kings and a companion to the original Sun Wukong from *Journey to the West*. He's a true dragon, just as he is in the old tale.

I haven't yet decided whether we'll get to see all thirteen Longinuses. As Sacred Gears, the Red Dragon Emperor's Boosted Gear and the White Dragon Emperor's Divine Dividing are both excellently balanced in terms of offense and defense. And depending on the skill level of their users, the Dimension Lost and the Annihilation Maker are both extremely dangerous.

The Holy Spear, the True Longinus, still holds lots of secrets. Yet for as strong as it is, Cao Cao really let his guard down, didn't he?

Yes, this ninth volume was just filled with strange names and titles. It's one thing to come up with all these Sacred Gears, but it can be a real challenge thinking of names for them all. I've got to consider their Balance Breaker states as well.

As was mentioned in the story, there are variant Sacred Gears out there in the world, too.

Time for my acknowledgments. To my editor, H, thank you again.

My appreciation also goes out to all my readers for your continued support. I believe that the first volume of the manga adaptation will be released soon. My deepest thanks to Hiroji Mishima at Comicalize! I can't wait to see the finished work and to view those wondrous breasts for myself in illustrated form! Serialization has also shifted from *Dragon Magazine* to *Monthly Dragon Age*, which means you can read more each month!

This volume was about events occurring outside demon society, but in the next one, we'll delve into demon society once again as our protagonists face Sairaorg in a Rating Game. I hope you're looking forward to seeing Issei's stubborn contest against him!

And Ravel will be coming to Kuou Academy! She'll be a first-year student, meaning Issei will get another underclassman.

Volume 10 is when the Academy Festival will be held, too, so watch for how Issei and Rias's love develops!